An Unreliable
Guide to London

Influx Press, London

Published by Influx Press
Office 3A, Mill Co. Project, Unit 3, Gaunson House
Markfield Road, London, N15 4QQ
www.influxpress.com / @InfluxPress

First published 2016. Printed and bound in the UK by Clays Ltd., St Ives plc.
ISBN: 978-1910312223

Edited by Kit Caless, with assistance from Gary Budden
Editorial assistant: Sanya Semakula   Proofreader: Katherine Stephen
Cover art and design: Chris Smisson

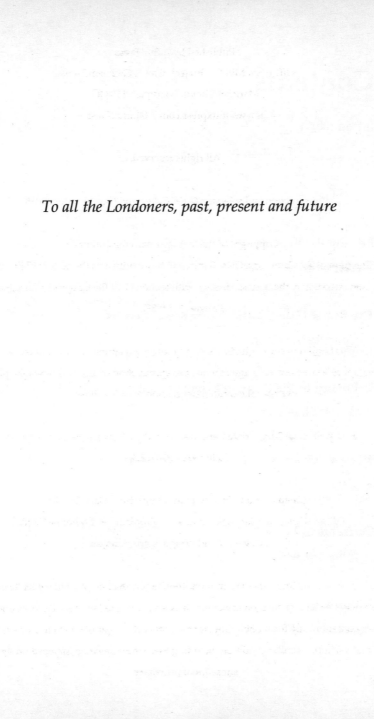

To all the Londoners, past, present and future

Contents

NORTH

SOUTH

EAST

Introduction

The idea germinated in Tottenham Hale Retail Park, five minutes from the Influx Press office. A walk through the park's rectangular brandscape of Aldi, Staples, Burger King, Poundland, Subway, Greggs and Argos is a walk through modern London.

It's a place where normal Londoners go about their day; passing through on their way to Tottenham Hale station or stopping off to get groceries for the evening. It's bland and functional. It is only used by people who know it is there. It feels out of date, yet part of the future. It is dull. And it is average. But it contains a wealth of stories just like any other part of the city.

It was here that the idea of *An Unreliable Guide to London* developed. Sitting in Subway we stuffed our mouths with meatball marinara and wondered why publishers weren't printing books set in the parts of London that we knew and interacted with on a daily basis. Why weren't writers writing about them? What novels had we read set in Hanwell, Cricklewood or Barking? These parts of the capital can feel like another world, another city that exists on the periphery of the imagination, lived in by millions.

London is an unreliable city, always changing. Spend a year

away from one patch you thought you knew well and when you return it will be unrecognisable. We try to tie it down but it slips from our grasp; it never was like it was. Money comes in, flows out. Demographics we thought were here to stay are forced to move, new waves of external and internal immigration alter its signage and its culture.

Whatever the reasons for this constant state of flux, it is a reality all those who live in the city must deal with. It is not simply the case that we can leave London for somewhere else — it is our home. But it's an unreliable home that exists in memory and imagination, in our stories and experiences, as much as in any physical reality. Each individual here lives in their own London, that no one else is privy to.

It is nigh on impossible to read all the stories of London. The city is saturated in fiction; from Defoe to Zadie Smith, Dickens to Kureishi, and has been in immortalised in print more times than we can count. But we have to tell our own stories as well as reading others, to keep adding to that pile. We know this city doesn't care for us as much as we care for it, but we write about our pockets of London because we know no one else will. After all, how could they?

This is a guide to a city you never knew existed, right on your doorstep. Blink and you'll miss it.

— Gary Budden & Kit Caless, April 2016

WEST

Beating the Bounds

Aki Schilz

I. Hanwell Unremembered

Hana (cockerel)
Weille (stream)

or;

Han-créd (a cock's crow, or the border between night and day)

Han-créd-welle (well upon the boundary; a wish caught like a dandelion seed in a mouth; the fading call of a rooster in crepuscular no-man's-land; a slipspace where dreams emerge from the subliminal) or;

Han (boundary stone, Saxon) next to a welle

There is a boundary stone near to the old Rectory in Hanwell, and near to the old well that springs from the River Brent which cuts through the township on its way from Dollis Brook in Hendon through to Brentford with its moored shipwrecks, then out into open water. The river brings gravel south and spits out great drifts of stones just beyond the bounds of Hanwell, as if to provide a physical demarcation to slice it from its neighbouring parishes. *It used to feel like the end of the world here.* Looking out from the backs of neatly terraced houses onto the rows of railway workmen's cottages, all you could see at one point was the river and endless green fields. It was certainly the end of London. Beyond that, who knew?

In 2014, the gravel deposits on the southern borders of the Brent increased in size, and flowerings of yellow broom on the banks also proliferated, which in turn inspired a spate of enthusiastic daytime couplings by younger Hanwell residents along the length of the canal; especially by the Flight of Locks. The police eventually stopped intervening and instead advised canal-ramblers to please not take photographs and post them on social media, but instead to walk at a brisk pace and ignore any grunts from the undergrowth. Neighbourhood teams printed alternative canal-path maps in a bid to avoid angry run-ins between young families or elderly residents and horny teens at key hot spots. The copulating couples, it seemed, considered two drowned girls — who went missing here in 1912 — their patron saints, and dutifully whitened the small cross carved into the canal path wall in their honour, before fucking wildly in the grass and flowers. Other small white crosses have since begun to appear along the canal, and a local jeweller has started to make white cross pendants which at last count were selling well from her eBay shop ('w7babe1968') and at the car boot up at Drayton playing fields. Hanwellites suspect this strange madness may have something to do with the imminent arrival of Crossrail; a short panic-induced swelling of local pride before the town is dragged into the bowels of the City via West Ealing, Hayes & Harlington, Greenford, Acton Mainline ... This is likely to be nonsense, but investigations into changes in river currents and water levels where the Brent pours into the Thames, mineral content in riverbed soil, and libido levels in the younger Hanwell population are ongoing.

Hanwell is small, and rumours are important. They tell us who we are, so we can echo this back whenever we find ourselves somewhere other than here. But somehow, it's never really where any one of us is from. We say 'Ealing'. Or, laughingly, 'West London', accompanied occasionally by a kiss of teeth or a half-hearted hand gesture we immediately regret making. Occasionally a boy from the White Flats gets a small 'W7' tattoo on his hand, on that triangle of skin between the thumb and forefinger, and slings it across the handlebars of his L-plated moped for a few weeks, but postcode pride is hardly a premium and there are no good tattoo artists here (unless you have a direct line to George Bone). Hendrix didn't even visit, though he owned a shop here. Bastard. We missed out on a chance for some crazy stories, parties that spilled onto Cuckoo Dene, rockstars stripping naked and running up and down the Greenford Avenue, the customary Christmas Day walk through the locale decorated with drunken celebrities waving at you from between pyracantha shrubs: like a live-action board game.

It was Ronnie Wood, with a cucumber, by the reptile enclosure.

That'd have put us on the map. Maybe then there'd be a few — more interesting — tattoos on display. If people felt real pride in being a Hanwellite. Of the Wharncliffe Viaduct, maybe, along a bicep, or a stylised rendering of Church Walk which no one calls Church Walk because it's just the entrance to the Bunny Park, once a repository for unwanted pets and now a place to get drunk on cheap beer and break up with your first life partner before pulling away on your roller skates. Maybe someone would go so far as to commission the once-maligned Clock Tower as an impressive thigh piece, the old windmill with blades fanning out across an expanse of shoulders, '89.6FM' along the wrist bone, Charlie Chaplin, old Jonas Hanway with an umbrella — someone could write a PhD thesis on Tattoo Culture as Aesthetic Body-Centric Commentary on Hanwell Through The Years, referencing the workhouse and the ophthalmia that smeared melancholy like blue smoke across our eyes for a time, the counterpoint of shelled ears vibrating with music pumping out of the Marshall amps sold to rockstars before they became famous. The town broadcasts its stories at a precise frequency; you just have to learn to tune in.

No one gives a shit that Deep Purple recorded here, that's old news. But there are other stories, and we turn them over like pennies on table-tops at The Cuckoo or at Café Gold with weak over-milky coffee and a thousand memories in our hands, some of them ours, most of them stolen. Did you know Jay Kay went Drayton Manor? Yeah, yeah, everyone knows that. So did Peter Crouch and Steve McQueen, and that vaguely famous novelist no one can ever remember the name of because it's difficult and foreign but she won a prize once. Then there was that guy or girl who lived in Hanwell who went on *Big Brother* a million years ago, blah blah.

But did you know that Elvis once came here? Swear to God. It was all hush-hush, he fell for a painter, some relation to that bloke who painted Ophelia drowning in an oil-spill of flowers, the model posed for that just up the road, in the Brent. Apparently he was a germophobe. No, not Millais; Elvis. He flew over in 1958. For a girl, an artist. It was supposed to be a secret one-day deal, but it didn't turn out that way. He'd met her at a grocery store in Philadelphia the year before; she was visiting America with her mother. She'd spilled milk on him and had been so charming about it he'd fallen for her instantly. Salt of the earth: she taught him that expression and it tickled him. He made just one successful trip to England to be with her, a blissful two-week period they spent together right here in Hanwell. They kept the paparazzi away but the neighbours knew. Neighbours always do. She's moved away since, must be an old lady by now, probably in the States — there's loads of us there — but she's still got a couple of cousins down Trumper's Way who tell the story to anyone who'll listen down The Fox. Pretty, she was. Wonder if anyone knows her full name; we could google her.

All these goings-on in Hanwell buzz around the Clock Tower. Walk past it and you'll hear the town giving up its secrets in a tumble that sounds like a rush of water. Careful, you know you can catch rumour like a cold.

The Clock's ugliness is impressive, its unashamed boxiness a source of comfort to those who drive through its shadow on their commute out of our little township. We can rely on its unchanging geometry, its wide white shoulders, the clusters of shops fanning out around it, whose faces change each time I return here (carpets permanently ON SALE on the corner; a Wickes down this road; a pub down that; two florists recreating the War of the Roses right here on Hanwell Broadway; a butcher; a Domino's; a tanning salon; a Lidl. Etc). Used to be a cinema just here on Cherington, you know. There's a mental health unit there now. And when did the Library close down? *I remember when ...*

I lived on Poets' Corner, which was destroyed in the Blitz. It's the only home I knew; we never moved. There are rumours there is still a German bomb beneath our house on Milton Road. *Split the house in half,* said someone, once. *No money, then, just built right over it.* It was, perhaps, a man who said this, one of the old men who seem to have lived here forever, and whom you spot from time to time when you return, snapshots of the Stages of Life, the riddle of the creature with first no legs, then two, then three. Snap, snap, snap. A grandchild comes to visit. The dog that has accompanied him everywhere disappears. His hair thins and he retreats like a turtle into his jumper and sun-worn tweed jacket. Smart, still, after all these years. Creases ironed into his slacks. At some point, the old men disappear, but their stories hang around at the cemetery on the way up to West Ealing, or snag in the wiring that holds the pigeons into the underbelly of the iron bridge by the upholsterer's, or catch in the feathers of the peacocks at the Bunny Park where children learn to say 'Hello? Hello?' to the birds that speak back from behind the bars of their huge cage, 'Marmoset!' when they spot the monkeys who stand wide-eyed shivering in sawdust, and 'Ice cream!' at the hut by the playground, warm with the smell of apple pie where there's always ice cream and everyone's favourite is mint choc chip.

Back on Milton Road, the last person to remember the day the fishmonger ran out of fish at Christmas, in the same week the butcher's was blasted to smithereens, goes to bed and thinks, well, that's it then, I've had a good run. Time to go. By his bedside, a snarl of wood he has used as a walking stick. Once, many years ago, he taught a young girl to count on the knots along the length of it. They spiralled upwards, and when he turned the stick, the number of knots seemed to change. She will remember this, years later, and will smile.

Nearby, Cowper's ghost shoulders a greater loss; a low-flying bomber emptied its contents at just the right angle to penetrate a bomb shelter, detonating deep underground and uprooting an entire row of houses. All those in the shelter perished, and above ground the blast threw off the faces of the houses so they stood naked and exposed, dripping wiring into the rain-glistened street. They were pulled out like rotten teeth, dragged away by lorries as people stood by to watch the slow demolition, then went about their business as usual. Tennyson and Nightingale, just over the road, still shake their heads sometimes, and the glass in the council estate windows shimmers. I was a pub once, says one of the windows. Shut up, says another, and shakes a cloud of pollen out of the trees.

II. Q&A with an ex-Hanwellite

How do I get to Hanwell?

Depends on what your plans are. If you are able to time-travel, I recommend a horse bus. If your intentions are nefarious or Crossrail-related, you can get here by tying a blindfold around your head and spinning really fast, then choosing the direction in which you feel least like falling. Keep walking. In fact, run. If you are trying to find your childhood, try walking the Bounds first, widdershins (May-time, join the crowd and imagine yourself a fox) then break away from the group and slowly make your way into the town, taking photographs of those things that take your fancy on a disposable camera (leave your smartphone at home). Click. No flash. St Mary's spire. The old violin factory. The sign for 'Hanwell and Elthorne'. A leaf by the canal path. The gateway to St Bernard's. An abandoned lollipop stick. You can look at them later, study their blurs and edges, and when you fall asleep you'll be better able to visit the Hanwell you remember, not the one you see. Much has changed. It may be a shock.

Otherwise, E1, E3, E8, E10, E11, 207, 83, 607, First Great Western (Brunel would be proud). Any of those are fine. Probably a few more. Check TfL.

How do I get out of Hanwell?

Soul-search till you realise your soul is happier being elsewhere. Feel nostalgic for about three years, before you've even left. Leave. Need transport? See above. Go the other way.

Best restaurant in Hanwell?

You've got the wrong book. If you'd asked me about the best view, however …

What has been lost in Hanwell?

That's better. If you want to know about everything that's been lost in Hanwell, just visit the old bandstand, you know the one, by the small stone in a too-large cage at the Bunny Park, the end by the viaduct just before the church where you responded to a woman who asked 'which town are we in?' with, 'Ealing,' and she nodded and said, 'Ely! Wonderful,' before looking doubtfully at the church over the rim of her fogged glasses. They were gold-rimmed. You thought she was the Queen. You saw the real Queen once, at the circus, but you can't remember if that was in Hanwell. It all seems a long time ago. You forget where those hills lead, the ones by the old tennis courts; is there another field at the bottom? Socks have been lost here, though they've been lost everywhere. Here, though, they are often stolen by rheas.

We used to kick footballs onto the roof of that bandstand, avoiding the condom wrappers and occasional syringe between the scrubby bits of grass — it was better when it rained, so the earth churned everything away and the sky was wet and clean and flat. You liked it best when the ground was heavy with water, leaving the between-space light enough for you to run through at full pelt and feel like you were slicing through the world. Someone told you that children used to make money retrieving golf balls, years ago, somewhere not far from here. Which makes you think of little Jake getting fed up of kicking footballs over from Hobbayne to Drayton, so one day he lobbed the sun warmed split-open body of an adder over the fence and it splattered its guts. There followed a chorus of angry secondary school yells that made you think you were at the zoo, or in a jungle. We are dreadfully trodden into restless paths, said Lord Dunsany, and H.G. Wells agreed, though he was only talking about the asylum, which is really a place for the restless. All the windows shattered there, once. No one ever did find out what happened to the two lamps that disappeared from the entrance. Some say overnight they turned into flowers. Others say one of the patients took them and buried them somewhere, to get rid of all the light. 'Men deny Hell, but not, as yet, Hanwell'. Who said that? There's one for the pub quiz. If you get the answer right, light a candle at St Mellitus and leave a small yellow ribbon at the base of the pulpit. They'll understand.

What has been found in Hanwell?

Oh, not much really. Hope, sometimes. Problems, mainly. A Saxon grave years ago that was written about in a couple of inches of column space in the *Gazette*, the decapitated body of a wallaby (twice), someone's keys hanging off a clematis by the viaduct with 'Connolly' etched into the fob, a single peach coloured vintage heeled shoe wedged into a pergola, a postcard from Brunel's structural engineer to his younger gay lover who never did make it into the history books, a photograph album of Hanwell and its environs from the war in a battered briefcase bought at a boot sale along with two chipped champagne flutes from a former Hanwell Carnival Queen to fundraise for her boob job, a trumpet belonging to a famous musician, a baby hedgehog rescued by a little girl moments before her dad lit the bonfire down the bottom of a garden on Half Acre Road (they kept him; they called him Cecil). A wedding ring. A knife the week after a murder that had nothing to do with the murder itself but had in fact been used to stab someone years before, in a case that remained unsolved. Etc. Etc. Etc.

Best place to fall in love in Hanwell?

Pass.*

Best place to find oneself in Hanwell?

Outside of it. But then, all the dangerous wastelands are those hidden within. Yeah, I remember Copley. Married a boy from there, once. He made me a ring out of plasticine.

And somewhere etched on this heart is a postcode just like those White Flats boys'. It's no different to their biro scrawls, no more grand and no less plain. And whenever I walk past the Hanwell Library on my way to the centre of the world so I can spin myself out of its orbit for a while, I can feel a scan brush through me like a lighthouse beam. *Going somewhere?* I pull my West Ealing coat tighter around me, look up at the sky opening out into the city, by the Viaduct where daffodils spring up like an army marching over the hill towards the hospital into the beyond, and I hear a faint beep.

*Actually on second thought, try your luck at the canal. If you don't go missing, you might just find love. Run fast. Run widdershins.

The Secret Life of Little Wormwood Scrubs

Courttia Newland

Here are the facts. Khalil Rahman is dressed in black from head to foot. T-shirt, thermals, trainers. His iPod is black, strapped to his bicep by a Velcro band; even his headphones are black. When he was younger, no more than six, he was told the colour black absorbs heat. He tallied that with what he remembered from summers inside his dad's car, when he'd climb onto the seats wearing knee length shorts and could barely sit due to the vindictive sting of hot leather, and knew it to be true. From that point on, whenever he needed warmth, Khalil wore black. Particularly in winter months, which last much longer than when he was a child, he rarely ventures out in anything else.

He runs beneath a pebble sky, oppressive and low. The lustre of grass is shimmering low tide in the breeze, bright in contrast with the clouds, although few are here to see either. A clatter of metal forced and slow, gained by intense struggle, comes from somewhere above and behind. It takes time to locate. There. A moss-green bridge, a squat goods train, grey with dirt and sharp angles, made all the more ugly by unfamiliar markings, words that make no sense. From elsewhere. Perhaps they do not belong. Far beyond, there are pealing cackles of high-pitched laughter. Abrupt, gone before fully registered. A child it can be presumed, although they are invisible, a myth, a mystery.

Khalil circuits the park. Trap music thumps in time with his heartbeat, footsteps shudder through his chest, jaws tremble as his soles connect. He pumps his arms, lifts his feet and lets them fall, focused on what's ahead. It's early, the way he likes it. The breeze makes sweat tingle on his cheeks. He doesn't hear the ripple of children's laughter, the old man's grumble of the goods train, it's all sniping lyrics, hollow bass and military snares beneath the rush of his own breath. Inside his skull, a catalogue of pleasurable images; a steaming pot of tawny curried chicken, the broad white teeth of his mother, the glint of Sabrina's hazel eyes and gleam of her thigh as his fingers slide upwards. He senses a body ahead; a woman dog-walking, terrier jerking its head back in momentary terror, aping its owner, luckily on a lead. The days of muggings and drug taking in this park have largely passed, retained only in muscle memory by those who were there. And of course, there is the clear and present terror. He reminds himself of this as he side-steps woman and beast, keeps running. Sees the t-shirt splayed across his tomb dark duvet; DON'T PANIC, I'M ISLAMIC. His sister bought it as a joke, black too of course, but Khalil knows he won't wear that t-shirt. He'll never wear that t-shirt. Fucking embarrassing, what does she think he is; it wasn't even funny.

This park belongs to him, Khalil's always felt. His forgotten space. His zone, his area. Dissected from its larger brother by the west London railway, once a depasturing waste ground, a 19th century rifle range, and in the northernmost section, a forest known as Wormholt Wood. In its centuries-old lifetime Little Wormwood Scrubs has been cleaved into sections like the long forgotten cattle that grazed it, from 26 acres, to 14, to nine. This ghost remainder, this emptiness. Apt its one short block from a road named after the North Pole. Winds are bitter, but often welcome, a respite. Good place to walk the dog, especially if you're from the yellow brick estate. There's a calm that's difficult to maintain once those low green gates are fresh memory, back in the grip of the oppressive city. The reality of the metropolis surrounds on all sides; Harlesden to the North, Ladbroke Grove to the west, Acton to the East, White City and Shepherd's Bush to the south.

He passes a clutch of older kids on an isolated bench, one young couple, arms pincered around each other. After them, a man in a red and black windcheater putting a solitary golf ball across grass, squinting concentration. Each has found their oasis of silence, their tranquil sea. Each knows there won't be another for miles. A sweet aroma of fish sauce, red chillies and coconut paste wafts from a Thai restaurant just beyond the gates. Years ago it was a greasy spoon with Pepsi Cola signage, egg and chips and bubble and squeak, glistening aluminium containers of Thai fare sold beneath the counter like class A. Now the only scrambled eggs are in the pad thai. Its owners expanded years ago, took over the next-door hairdresser's. These days, the interior looks more like Bangkok than Barlby Road. Nobody seems to mind.

They've broken his focus. He tries to out the voice like a burning match, but no matter how vigorously he shakes it stays alight. He inhales a deep intake of air through his nose, releases it from his mouth and looks up, towards the jagged green mist of bushes for just one moment, enough to see the interior shadow, to notice, before he's back on the path, eyes feasting on the darkness of tarmac beneath him. Enough to hear the voice say, what's? Sentence unfinished, impetus complete. It's coming towards him, or rather he's coming towards it, and while some part of him wants to keep his mind on what he's come to the park to do, what he comes to the park every morning to do, it's impetus that drives him to turn his head right, perhaps even a need to tell the story, be witness to the story, play some part in the story, known or unknown. So he looks. And sees.

It might be a rucksack. Shabby and forlorn as a tramp, slightly leant over. Not exactly hidden, still difficult to see if he hadn't caught it from the necessary angle. He turns his head, refusing to look back, thinking of that Bible story they learnt in R.S. He takes another circuit, sweat running down his temples, guts light and armpits sodden, a little cold. He steps away from the tarmac to reach the misty bushes and stops, jogs on the spot. It's a rucksack. Small and compact as a parcel, dark scuffed patches like scars. It's Friday the 22nd of July, 2005. This rucksack is now his story.

It's not the first secret owned by this flat, open land. He's read enough Wikipedia to know others lay hidden, even from those long familiar with its circular path, some of whom crawled its grass in nappies aeons ago, and now push creaking Zimmer frames, step by hesitant step. At a lazy glance, everything seems in plain sight. Nothing to view here. The appearance of the rucksack shunts his thoughts towards an original secret, one which permeates the city landscape, legendary as sewer rats the size of dogs, lost goldfish flushed down Armitage Shanks and grown to adult size, fantasy crocodiles believed to share the same fate. It follows that this earliest secret lies hidden, benevolent, the material of ancient folklore; few modern eyes have seen it to call it true. And yet he knows it as fact, tangible as the pebble sky, the grass, the dour bulk of the train and its iron bridge, the very park itself.

Like many others scattered across this city, the park's original secret is a stream. In existence since the Middle Ages, the stream became known as Counter's Creek in the 18th century, named after the bridge that crossed the water at the western end of Kensington High Street. Counter's Creek was mainly used for carrying sewage water to the Thames, until surface water drains fed the purpose built sewer constructed in 1868. It was a visible surface river on the west side of Little Wormwood Scrubs as late as 1930, where it was found on Ordinance Survey maps of the day. No one knows precisely when the creek disappeared. Ordinance maps dated 1935 show distinct ponds and weirs, but by 1955 they are gone. Like much of English history, Counter's Creek was forced underground. Today, on Little Wormwood Scrubs, the river is no more than vague patches of mud water and remnants of ornamental ponds long filled with earth. After cases of severe weather, flooding sometimes occurs.

He paces on the spot, muddy creek water sucking at his trainers, struck by the frenzied notion he's being watched.

He jogs towards the tarmac, faster, keeping to the path so he doesn't arouse suspicion. He exits through the side gates that lead into the estate and up the steady incline to his block, Ketton House. It's bad enough in this place. He's been called 'rag head', had lager cans thrown at him from a moving car. Khalil's a big guy, but the car drove fast, coughing smoke, and the person who said it was an old man outside the shops on North Pole, didn't even look at him, directing his blind stare at a passing 7, gears hissing as if London transport hated him too. As if he deserFved it. Khalil went home feeling like he'd missed an opportunity, to do what he wasn't sure. The same sensation churns through him as he bounds up stairs, rips off his headphones so he can hear if anyone's coming, tenses his shoulder and cranes his head to see the upper stairwell through turret-sized gaps between thin iron banisters. He's anxious until he's opened his front door and shut it behind him, until he turns his key in both locks.

Television, thick with occurrences. Khalil learns things he's trying to avoid, an impossibility he knows, but he's tried. Indoctrination is an infestation derived from many sources. He doesn't want that, so the screen is usually dark. Within seconds Khalil sees four faces. In days he'll know their names and murderous ideology, but for now there are only road dog expressions, unrelenting eyes. It's the second bomb attack on London in two weeks. Khalil stares at the faces like the old man did the bus. They look like people he grew up with. They look like him.

He gets up, walks to the kitchen, walks back to the television. He stares in that direction, but he's not listening. He goes back into the kitchen and makes himself a cheese sandwich with mayo and Branston's. He chews, stares at the screen.

Sabrina calls, a persistent ringtone, an accusing buzz. He ignores it. This is his first flat, a William Sutton Trust, and he lives alone as he's never had the chance before. Previously it was the hostel, before that his parents' flat. He told Sabrina he needed his own space. She understood, one of the reasons he cares about her, but she likes to check in, especially in the mornings, just in case he's been weak. Khalil follows her reasoning, he even finds it flattering. But today it's not conducive. Today he needs to be alone, so he can work this thing out. The four faces of the would-be bombers, which reoccur at regular intervals, say he needs to work this out.

Hours flee. He should be memorising scripts. One page of Shakespeare's *Macbeth*, one of Bennet's *Drummers*. His contemporary choice wasn't written for a Muslim actor, sure, but he likes the play, and can relate to it, so does it matter? It wasn't like *Macbeth* was written with Muslims in mind either, or any other character from the classics. It's how he auditions that counts. He doesn't want to play terrorists for his whole career. Besides, RADA, Guildhall and Central need more Muslim students. It's a plus, a USP.

He drinks tea, prays when the time comes. Waits. The news catches him short, almost when he's about to reach for his notes. The man was shot and killed by police inside a train carriage at Stockwell tube station. He was under suspicion as being one of the previous day's bombers; police say they've thwarted a potentially dangerous attack. In time, they will confirm he's not related to the bombing incidents and issue an apology. There will be flowers, protests, a grieving family in unfamiliar winter coats gathered beneath the metal shutters of the tube station. For now, the authorities are puffed with success, psyched with drama. Later, they will say the man is Brazilian. Khalil watches and learns.

He doesn't move from the television for the rest of the day. His drama notes lie in various places on his bedroom desk, untouched. The rooms grow dark, but he doesn't switch on the light. He imagines calling the number the newscaster repeats at 15-minute intervals. Leading the police to the rucksack, stiff arm outstretched, first finger isolated from the rest, stepping back, waiting for what needs to be done. Each time his thoughts are invaded by the eyes of the four suspects. Brittle, heavy lidded, black as his clothes. Or the eyes of the Brazilian whose photo is released to the public, filled with promise and perhaps trepidation? Wary of his unknown future? Khalil reheats the chicken his mother gave him on his last visit. He eats it for lunch and dinner. Sabrina calls 14 times; he doesn't answer once. On her fourteenth attempt she leaves a final, tearful message — if he doesn't want to be with her he should say, not act like a waste-man. She pauses for eight seconds. There is a series of audible sniffles. Speakers rustle like tracing paper. Her voice returns, soft, deep. She apologises. She's worried. She wants to know he's all right.

Khalil doesn't hear her messages until the next day, after the fifth suspect package is found on Little Wormwood Scrubs, detonated by controlled explosion. He calls back, apologising for almost an hour straight; he was concentrating on his drama studies. That night, they have dinner by the park, away from the windows. There are floodlights where he jogged on the spot the previous morning, a blue and white taped cordon, dark-clothed police leading dogs. Sabrina speaks in whispers, unaware she's caressing her headscarf. Khalil's hands tremble when he orders the pad thai.

In Pursuit of the Swan at Brentford Ait

Eley Williams

On purpl'd wing, with hiss long and obscene,
Gelgéis [bright swan] *glid twilit — twilit, twilit —*

— from 'The Basket-Weaver's Lament', Trad. (Anon.)

To research cryptids is to accept ambiguity. The Swan at Brentford Ait is the size of a house. The Swan at Brentford Ait is the size of a horse. Its wing-beats are entirely silent but have been heard four miles away, and the colour of its plumage is reported to be either a dim smoky purple or a vivid electric pink. I have dedicated a whole filing cabinet to my investigation — folders feathered with Post-It notes and photograph negatives, endless river-damp journal entries and tide table almanacs — and yet so much of the evidence is a tissue of contradictions.

If a monstrous swan ever existed on this overgrown island in West London, glowing beneath the yellow willow branches or squatting fat-haunched in the Thames' sucking muds, any verifiable facts have certainly become embellished over time. This is the nature of much folkloric discourse, especially that which concerns cryptids. Cryptids are animals whose existence is disputed or unsubstantiated by the official scientific community. I have had to explain this definition in a number of FOI requests. The United Kingdom is home to a number of such animals: there is Giglioli's twin-finned whale spotted blowing spray off Scottish coastlines, for example, and Cornwall's tooting Owlman. There's the froth-mouthed hound Black Shuck in East Anglia and the assorted cat- and boar-Beasts of Bodmin, Exmoor, Dartmoor and Dean. It would seem that fen, road and bay alike are territories for monsters both ancient and modern.

As with my cryptid swan, details of these animals' visual characteristics are scant and often seem inconsistent when one account is pitted against another. I admit that reports of their appearances are questionable at best and ludic at worst. This may be due to witnesses' faulty or mismatching recollections, warped by prior knowledge of the surrounding myths, or simply because circumstantial sketches can be conflated for the sake of a more exciting narrative.

Reports become swollen with hyperbole, embroidered with descriptive flourishes; with each retelling, the story gains lustre but any truth behind the tale grows harder to discern. Metaphors become mixed and fact segues into fiction. It is for this reason that cryptids are permitted to prowl a blurred line in the public imagination and exist simultaneously as phantoms and the site of anecdote and a speculative zoology. One listener will scoff, one will buy the stuffed toy, while another will keep an eye on a loch's taut surface for the merest hint of a ripple.

The Swan at Brentford Ait is one of the few London cryptids that still excites the local press with purported sightings. In recent years, it has been blamed with terrorising wildlife around Brentford and Kew as well as scuttling poorly moored boats. These stories are not always filed with the tongue-in-cheek register that one might expect, and are not merely the work of a cub reporter seeking to spice up a dull day in the newsroom. Although nowadays interest in the bird tends to be limited to the London boroughs closest to the Ait, I have discovered numerous accounts of the Swan in capital-wide and national newspapers' archives. Mostly it surfaces as a footnote regarding local superstitions, but sometimes there is factual reportage. In such instances, the Swan is invariably mooted as the culprit for damage that has been inflicted upon unattended boats or on riverside workshops. At its most extreme, however, and featuring a distressingly realistic pen and ink sketch to accompany the column, *The Morning Chronicle* quotes one Brentford resident who claimed to have seen a 'gargantuan, serene, rose-coloured bird' seizing the collar of a 'Miss Lettuce Sesselly — an errant girl from the nearby Trimmer's School' (report dated 12th March, 1832). Dragging her to the water's edge with its beak, the swan was seen 'drown[ing] the child in a stretch of water between Brentford and Lot's Aits, in full view of a wedding-party boat, whose cries of distress summoned a constable.' A reward is then offered by the *Chronicle* for the bird's capture, with all enquiries to be directed to the Keeper of the King's Swans and his swansherdmen.

The Swan's coverage in the press reveals an undeniable undercurrent of violence attached to its mythos. For every description of a peculiarly purple feather found amongst some reeds on the Thames or reports of massive webbed footmarks at low-tide, the emphasis of the article always falls on the cryptid swan's aggressive, predatory nature. Over the past 50 years a number of stray cats have been found bloodied, with weirdly broken limbs in or around Waterman's Park playground; at least in local anecdote, this has been tied with the stories surrounding the Swan. It is odd to think that this was the detail that sparked my initial inquiry; I am so fortunate to have caught wind of this 'superstition' and be able to turn my attention to a rigorous, prolonged investigation of the Swan's activity on the Ait. In many ways, it was lucky that I lost my job so that I could devote all my time to my research, and luckier still that I was able to commit a whole extra room to my studies and to the paperwork once my wife left me. It is from here that I can make my phone calls, and fax my evidence on to the appropriate authorities. The editor of *The Lancet* and the *British Journal of Criminology* both responded to my preliminary letters concerning the death of cats in TW8 postcode with the same line: upsetting as such a spate of pet-abuse might be, there is absolutely no evidence to suggest that any single perpetrator — let alone an avian one — came from the nearby river or its islands.

According to records of FOI requests that I have seen, at least one complaint per year is lodged with the London Boroughs of Richmond upon Thames, Ealing or Hounslow that is related specifically to the Swan. Reports of keening, screamed hisses are heard in that particular stretch of the Thames at night, and have been recorded as doing so since the 15th century, many of which are linked to sightings of the Swan. 'Heathrow's flight paths', 'engineering works on train lines at Kew Bridge station' and 'illegal use of fireworks' are all unconvincing reasons that have been provided whenever the cause for such regular disturbances is queried.

Bernard Heuvelmans' 1958 work *On the Track of Unknown Animals* is widely held to be the first book dedicated to cryptozoology and it is pleasing to see the Swan at Brentford Ait bobbing up amongst its pages, described as a huge purple wading-bird ('un échassier énorme et pourpre au milieu de roseaux'). One hundred and fifty years earlier, William Hickey's diary entry provides perhaps the most famous account of the Swan's appearance where he recalls seeing the Thames boil in a huge purple swan's wake. This account is central to my investigation, and it was worth all the bother at the British Library with the tinfoil, CCTV and nail-scissors in order to gain access to the original page and to have it here in my possession for my dossier, ready for publication.

Certainly the Swan at Brentford Ait exists in the area as a folkloric artefact. Not only does it feature as a plumed bogey-man, used to hush children that refuse to behave, but a huge, vaguely carnivorous bird also looms large in local skipping songs ('Don't be early, don't be late / or Swan'll drag you to the Ait! / Cob or pen, we do not know / but down among the mud you'll go!'). Mention of it also emerges in folksongs that derive from the area (where it is named variously as a huge bird 'at Brentford Ait', 'of Brentford Ait', 'in Brentford Ait' and with the Old Irish female name 'Gelgéis'). A variant of the 'Knock Knock Ginger' or 'Ding Dong Ditch' prank is known locally as 'Swan-pecking' (pronounced swannicking). 'Swan-pecking' is distinguishable from other versions by one extra factor in the ritual of the game: as one reaches out to bang on a victim's door, the prankster's knocking-hand is bent at the wrist in imitation of a swan's neck.

The Swan is also a locus for various superstitions which vary from the meteorological to the medical. If a purple swan is seen on the Kew side of the bank it foretells rain, but if the Swan is seen on the Brentford side a sunny, fair day is on its way. When the bird is spotted roosting in the centre of the island in the so-called 'Hog Hole' channel that is visible at low tide, it is believed that the river Thames will freeze over the following winter. In 1891, the weather was so cold that the river did just that; fans of the urban legend gleefully point out that the same week the Revd. Joseph Gallagher, visiting Kew Gardens on a jaunt from his parish near Lincoln, made the following off-hand note in his journal:

'On my return, a quite enormous swan the colour of periwinkles dogged my heels. Snake-necked and hissing but otherwise perfectly sweet tempered, I fed it some of my lunch and we walked a good quarter-mile in quiet companionship. I was put in mind of St. Hugh! We walked some way along the river, the bird and I, until he took to the river and made for a small stretch of water between two rather scrubby straits of land.'

There is another local belief that if the Swan is glimpsed during the day, it is a harbinger of doom. It was with some editorial satisfaction that a pink or purple swan was reported flying over the Ait in *The Brentford & Chiswick Times* the day before Brentford F.C. was relegated to the fourth division in 1962. In one fell swoop, Brentford became the first football team to play all of the other 91 clubs in league football, hence the wry chant that is often heard ricocheting around the terraces at Griffin Park when the score-line is not going the host's way: '91, AND IT'S BEEN FUN / NO BLOODY THANKS / YOU BLOODY SWAN'. More tragically, the third son of the famous neo-impressionist Camille Pissarro was said to have been struck by the sight of a 'huge, wine-dark swan preening in the water by Brentford' while sketching flowers on the riverbank. A week after communicating this event to his parents, caricaturist Felix contracted tuberculosis and died in a sanatorium in Kew. He was 23 years old.

Although it is a mere four minutes' drive from the busy the M4 motorway, the uninhabited Brentford Ait has a wild look to it; overgrown and bordered by rotting boats. It has appeared in texts under a number of names, including Makenshaw, Mattenshaw or Twigg Ait, and for a long time the island was notable only for its osier beds, used to supply London's basket-making trade. I hope my research will make it famous for a far more important reason. At one stage a 'notorious' public house was built on the Ait and its sign featured the purple swan flanked by two of its more traditional, pallid river-mates. The Three Swans and its associated eel-house had a reputation for raucous behaviour and salacious goings-on, described in March 1811 by 'Robert Hunter of Kew Green' to be 'a great Nuisance to this parish and the Neighbourhood on both sides of the River [...] the house of entertainment, under the aegis of the painted purple swan, has long been a harbour of the men and women of the worst description, where riotous and indecent scenes are often exhibited during the summer months and on Sundays.'

The Ait has gone through many transformations, from entirely bare to its current, busy-if-ruinous state. In the 1920s it was planted with a variety of trees in order to 'screen the unsightly Brentford gasworks from the genteel Kew bank' and the island features willows and alder, making it something of a haven for wildlife in the Thames. Certainly while searching for my lost cat some time last year, before my life became focused on finding the Swan, I remember walking up and down the riverbank dinging a tin of my cat's favourite food with a fork in the hope that it would recognise the sound and come miaowing and prrrping back. As I passed the Brentford Ait, a number of herons and cormorants watched my progress, sitting hunch-shouldered in the tree branches like sleek little gargoyles. I found my cat with its broken legs and neck an hour later, dragged under the swings of Waterman's Park and left for the crows. According to local guides, the Ait is also home to kingfishers and grebes as well as teal and wigeon.

As well as birds, the Ait's inter-tidal mudflats boast flatworms, freshwater shrimp, six species of leech and a number of rare snails including the two-lipped door snail and the German hairy snail. Populations of these latter gastropods are so small in the United Kingdom that naturalist Chris Packham and local conchologist Ada Flitchett are spearheading an ongoing campaign to halt recent proposed developments on the neighbouring Lot's Ait in order that the snails' safekeeping is assured during building works. A proposal to flatten Brentford Ait and use the land for an offshore nightclub fell through in 2008; just the week before, a bright pink swan was seen by some schoolchildren to be rummaging through a bin at the nearby 267/65 bus-stop. I have approached both Flitchett's and Packham's agents about the opportunity to promote awareness of my research, and I await their response with excitement.

A number of scientific explanations have been proffered to explain both the size of the Swan and its strangely coloured plumage. In an informal paper for *Dug and Dusted*, the European Archeobiology Society's monthly newsletter, scholars M. McLeith, C. Thornton and T. Lomas proposed that the swan must be the result of a genetic quirk, isolated and persevering on the unmolested waters near the Ait. Just as mudlarking and excavations of the leech-happy, snail-slick mud at Brentford Ait have revealed remains of Palaeolithic hyena, hippo and even straight-tusked elephants, this article argues that the Ait's 'huge' bird is a throwback to these prehistoric animals. A cousin of the moa, dodo or great auk, perhaps. Some students of the Swan in popular and folk culture claim that the colour could arise from self-plucking, a form of mutilation that many birds inflict when under stress. The theory here is that the swan's white feathers appear to be dyed pink by their own blood. A recent study highlighted the fact that white adult mute swans (*Cygnus olor*) occasionally display symmetrical 'salmon-pink colouration, evident on primary feather tips after moult (July–August), [which] spreads to secondary and tertiary remiges as the year progressed. 12–85% of surveyed swans were found to have this pink coloration'. A fungal infection of *C. sitophila* was listed as the most likely agent.

Others have posited that, just as flamingos turn various shades of pink according to the quantity and quality of specific shrimp and algae in their diet, so too a swan's ingestion of some specific strain of food might cause the unusual presentation. There has even been the suggestion that the Purple Swan at Brentford Ait *is* a flamingo, escaped from a local menagerie or collection; if not a flamingo, then a scarlet ibis (*Eudocimus ruber*) or a roseate spoonbill (*Platalea ajaja*). Some sequences of *The African Queen* (dir. John Huston, 1951), starring Humphrey Bogart and Katherine Hepburn, were filmed in the river by the Ait, and in a biography of its cinematographer, Jack Cardiff mentions that a large purple bird on the island kept disrupting shooting. Cardiff specifies that one scene had to be re-shot several times because a 'massive purple goose-thing' kept defecating directly in the camera's sightline during Bogart's famous 'Bold Fisherman' song. Cardiff had assumed that the bird was among the many imported for the film to make the rather unexotic wilds of 1950s Brentford seem rather more interesting.

The exact colour of the Swan at Brentford Ait changes according the source of the account. In the snippets of poetry and song that centre on the Swan, descriptions of the colour ranges from 'rosy' to 'puce' and 'fuchsia', from 'Turkish delight' to 'hot-pink' and 'blushful Hippocrene'. Farrow & Ball, the manufacturer of paints based upon historic palettes and archives whose names for colours famously include 'Elephant's Breath' and 'Churlish Green', lists one shade as 'Brentford Feather'. It is a charming, dusky lilac and can be seen in the tea-rooms at stately homes across South West

London, including Kew Palace, Boston Manor and Osterley. 'Brentford Feather' was a natural choice when redecorating my office; the second that all my wife's furniture had been moved out and burned in the garden, I got to work rolling three tins of it up the walls. With the blinds drawn against the sun, it really is the most handsome shade.

Another persistent, if fanciful, reason submitted for the recurring appearance of purple swans in the area has been supplied by a historian of synthetic dyes in a 1959 PhD thesis, found buried deep in Senate House library's archives. Unfortunately, the printed name of this academic has been irreparably obscured on the title page and so the author is unidentifiable (upon further enquiry, the head librarian informed me that the stain that concealed the name on the paper 'was probably mustard', and that there were no further records of the PhD's author in the building's holding records). According to this thesis, however, the dye mauveine was created in the late 1850s by chemist William Henry Perkin; in 1858, Perkin opened his colour factory in Greenford and became the first person to manufacture organic chemicals on a large scale. Here, he produced both mauveine and two other dyes, Britannia Violet and Perkin's Green. The water in the nearby Grand Union Canal was said to have turned a different colour every week, and it is thought a swan might have become stained by the dyes before making its way to Brentford Ait.

Even as the area surrounding its supposed habitat transforms and shifts, the spectre of the Swan at Brentford Ait remains alive and well; the Ait has weathered many battles, crises and mismanagements, but still celebrates its ancient monster. This is perhaps best demonstrated with the following microcosm. An old, decommissioned church is currently sitting empty on the riverside, swaddled in developers' hoarding and white plastic sheeting amongst the nodding purple buddleias. Across the road and overlooking Brentford Ait, St. George's church was built in 1887 and still, at time of writing, the design of a purple swan can still be made out in its remaining dirty stained glass windows. From 1963 until 2007, this church housed the world's foremost collections of self-playing musical instruments before the collection was moved to the purpose-built 'Musical Museum' along the river. On the occasion of this new structure's opening, Hounslow council commissioned local musicologist W. Rheedon to curate a commemorative recital. Thanks to a petition by local residents, he was mindful of the Swan's place in the local folklore and so part of this concert featured a brief arrangement of Tchaikovsky's *Swan Lake* theme fused with musical elements with Saint-Saens' *Le Cygne* and traditional folksongs from the area that cite or make reference to the Swan, all played on Wurlitzer organ, pyrophone and orchestrion. I used to listen to a recording of this arrangement over and over again every night by the river as I stood amongst the reeds with my jotting pad, binoculars and net. I have found a spot just beyond the glare of the developers' spotlights. Here I can no longer hear the traffic, and the breeze is always soft; I sit well into the early morning, with the Thames cool around my boots and my heart in my throat.

It was in my first week of my research that I saw a glint just out of the corner of my eye; I was not prepared then, and cried out, turning my head too fast. I stumbled and dropped my camera, losing it and my notepads to the water, and only just avoided falling in completely. My commotion must have disturbed the swan for when I managed to scramble back to my feet — soaked through, with silt in my teeth and my camera destroyed — the river was empty and all was quiet once more. I am certain, however. It was something violet and soft and huge in the moonlit water and it had trained its eye on me.

In the best tradition of Britain's cryptids, I know that the Swan will endure through art, song and custom. Evading detection but still courting intrigue, with accounts fuelled by hearsay and conjecture, the Swan at Brentford Ait will always tread the Thames' grey and even waters. Long may it roost there.

I will be waiting.

Select bibliography:

The New Penguin Book of English Folk Songs eds. Julia Bishop and Steve Roud (Penguin, 2012)

The Memoirs of William Hickey ed. Alfred Spencer (London: Hurst & Blackett, 1913-25)

An Index to the Journal Folklore, Volumes 79-103 (1968-1992) eds. Steve Roud and Jacqueline Simpson (Hisarlik Press, 1994)

Brewer's Dictionary of Modern Phrase and Fable eds. John Ayto and Ian Crofton (Chambers, 2009)

A History of the County of Middlesex eds. J. S. Cockburn, H. P. F. King, K. G. T. McDonnell (London Institute of Historical Research, 1969)

Bowyer, Justin: *Conversations with Jack Cardiff: Art, Light and Direction in Cinema* (Batsford, 2004)

Out, Damn Spot: Dye, Detergent, Industrialisation and the Tragedy of Affect (unpubl. PhD thesis: Royal Holloway, University of London, 1959)

Garfield, Simon: Mauve: *How One Man Invented a Colour That Changed the World* (Faber & Faber, 2000)

Heuvelmans, Bernard: *On the Track of Unknown Animals,* trans. Richard Garnett (Hart-Davis, 1958). First published in *Sur la Piste des Bêtes Ignorées* (Librairie Plon, 1955)

McLeith, M, Thornton, C and Lomas, T: 'The Curious Case of the Swan at Brentford Ait', *Dug and Dusted*, Vol. XII, Summer 1994 (European Archeobiology Society), pp. 23-24

O'Connell, Merita M. et al.: 'An investigation of a novel anomalous pink feather colouration in the mute swan Cygnus olor in Britain and Ireland', *Wildfowl* issue. 61 (2013), pp. 152-165

Staples Corner
(and how we can know it)

Gary Budden

I. On why you are at Staples Corner

Weak and watery November light. A Monday afternoon. You sit with your nose pressed against the cold glass of the 266 bus, breath fogging the surface and revealing the finger-traced declarations of a thousand other travellers. GAZ 4 LUCY, John B is a dickhead, a misshapen anarchic 'A'.

You think on what awful chain of events led you here, to the end of your known world, over your horizon. Dimly, you are aware you have lost something and that you must replace it. As the 266 chugs and rumbles, Nina checks emails on her phone and you try to remember. That's it. A robbery. You were pissed up, Highbury Corner, the Hen & Chickens. Meeting two old schoolmates. A few lagers turned into many. You never normally keep your laptop in your bag, but that day you'd come straight from the office in Tottenham. Then the bag was gone, and you were panicking in a toilet cubicle. Being informed by the bar staff that this kind of thing 'happened all the time.' That's it. That's why you are here.

As penance, perhaps, you travel to Staples Corner.

Cricklewood fades as you escape the Broadway, and concrete begins to colonise the landscape. You know you are headed to a divine meeting of arteries. Repeat their names. M1. A406. North Circular.

Aeons pass. Then Nina's elbow is nudging you to let you know it's time. We are at Staples Corner, she says. We are here.

You exit the 266, listening to the doors hiss like malicious laughter.

Look around you. This web of underpasses and roundabouts, of concrete walkways and steps to nowhere, how can it function? You are trapped in the fevered dying dream of a brutalist architect. You stand where logic has given up, and perhaps hope too. Perhaps this is what you see when you peer behind the veil.

You are here. Your destination stands temple-like over there. As the lorries force fumes into your lungs you panic and wonder how to cross. Slowly the Escher-like scene assumes some logic. A zebra crossing, an underpass. All is well. You feel a pleasant nostalgia for English novels from the 1970s as you cross, breathing in exhaust, clutching Nina's hand.

II. On how Staples Corner got its name

Not from the Staples stationery store that sits there now. There are no easy solutions here. You think how you could do with a new ruler, better pens, a notepad more befitting a proper writer.

Staples Corner, against all odds, has history. For sixty years Staples was a mattress factory, dealers in sleep and nightmare. Then an upstart, B&Q, took over. It couldn't last. Come 1992, the Provisional detonated a device below the A406 flyover. B&Q, damaged, was demolished, and replaced by another Staples; pens and pencils, not mattresses and their illusions of comfort, where fevered town planners laid and dreamed of Staples Corner.

III. Currys' car park, Staples Corner

You stand insignificant in front of the hangar-size stores. Here, you thought it would be simple. But your eyes dart nervously from PC World to Currys, Currys to PC World, heart racing. You are, once again, blinded by choice. You notice that here, in the car park outside Currys, Staples Corner, no people come in or out of the doors, no customers return to their parked cars. You and Nina stand in the car park, the only couple in existence, alone. A flock of diseased pigeons pepper the sky over the North Circular with an awful flutter of wings. It is cold, and you shiver. Panicking, you head into Currys, drops of sweat beading your brow, whispering to yourself: M1. A406. North Circular.

IV. Inside Currys, Staples Corner

Inside are many shoppers. Assistants lean on white counters and follow buggy-pushing families, imparting wisdom. They wear dark blue fleeces and smile without pause. Customers enter the store straight after you, but you know there were only the two of you in that car park. These other customers form on entry, visitors from a world you are not privy to. The carpet is womb-red. The air is artificial and warm. The atmosphere flickers.

After half an hour of talking, misunderstandings, boredom and a final decision, your elderly male sales assistant informs you that the model is not in stock. A leering impish face grins at you from the screen of every tablet and laptop. You hear a hissing and malevolent laugh leaking from a boombox speaker. All others seem oblivious.

You fight the bile that rises, try to ignore the spirit of this place, Staples Corner. You never considered the genius loci could be fucked-up, malicious, out to get you.

The sales assistant continues:

Go next door to PC World. We are the same company. They have five.

V. PC World, Staples Corner

You find your model quickly. You recognise it, even obscured amongst the other screens with the grinning faces.

You didn't see her arrive or remember instigating conversation, but the short woman who is now your sales assistant is in full flow. She has watery blue eyes, or perhaps they are contacts or perhaps something else entirely. This will be over soon, at least, you think.

Twenty minutes pass. You are still fending off add-ons and extras that she flings at you with the remorseless energy of an algorithm. Some stone-tape recording of a PC World, Staples Corner, sales assistant, stuck on loop. Nina, driven hysterical, starts to laugh and laugh and will not stop. You sadly realise the only way you can break this endless cycle, give this fretful ghost-assistant some peace, is through gritted teeth and complaint. It works but you have no satisfaction.

At Staples Corner there is no comfort in being right.

Sir, I regret to inform you we have no bags.

The watery blue eyes betray no emotion and the leering imp in the screens sneers. The checkout beeps and a man speaks into a walkie-talkie somewhere in the distance. Nina is holding her stomach, bent double by the iPads, spasms of hysterical mirth rippling through her.

VI. Staples Corner and how we can know it

Your replacement model, boxed up but not bagged, is tucked uncomfortably under your right arm. You stand shivering, waiting for the 266 and look at the monolithic mass of Staples rising high over the other side. You think of stationery and mattresses, bombs and watery blue eyes. Repeat your mantra. M1. A406. North Circular.

You think on what you have learned at Staples Corner as you head home, re-entering the world. You have been handed a question mark formed in concrete, and you know you must return.

Corridors of Power

Juliet Jacques

At the peak of the band's fame in 1985, Trevor Horn and Paul Morley of ZTT Records licensed a video game based on Frankie Goes to Hollywood. Several 8-bit renditions of their hits served as soundtracks for an oblique adventure, where you had to help 'Frankie' escape Mundanesville (a network of suburban houses) and enter the 'Pleasuredome'.

Whatever the Pleasuredome was, it could only be accessed once you had a personality score of 99%, completing challenges that raised your standing in Sex, War, Love and Religion. In one house in Mundanesville, you would find a dead body. Clues would appear, such as 'The killer is a socialist' and 'Joe Public has always voted Tory': eventually you could identify the culprit, providing some of the 87,000 Personality Points needed to complete the game.

You could play videos on the televisions, and sub-games would pop up. In one, you could be either Reagan or Gorbachev, and you had to win a spitting battle. (I always picked Gorbachev.) In another, you had to shoot celebrities — Reagan, Thatcher and others I didn't recognise. Elsewhere, you had to stop Merseyside being bombed, or collect flowers, with several vignettes accessible from the Terminal Room.

I loved the hermetic feel of playing games into the night, sealed from the prying eyes of small-minded suburbia. *Frankie* was my favourite, and the Terminal Room felt like its heart, insulated from the rest of its world, just the bleeps and dials of the mainframe and four smaller computers for company. Only one door in Mundanesville was locked: behind it were the Corridors of Power, a maze-like network with exits to every game. Once you found the key, you could navigate them: this was the game's *centre*, leading ultimately to the Pleasuredome.

*

Manja and I left Cinema 1 at the Institute of Contemporary Arts, not staying to applaud.

'That wasn't much, was it?' I said.

'He doesn't like the internet,' replied Manja, 'I *get* it.'

'The best advice I ever got was 'Beware the long synopsis.' It says: 'Witty and insightful films about how technology has warped our communications, old media melting into new ones in unpredictable, unprecedented ways.' We get 15 minutes of a bloke checking Facebook.'

'Drink?'

The artist, known only as Stevo, stood by the bar, lapping up the congratulations. Those too drunk or too tediously eccentric for his inner circle settled for talking to us. The usual questions:

Where are you from?

'Flitwick,' I said. 'Bedfordshire.'

'Ljubljana,' replied Manja. 'Slovenia.'

Are you artists?

'I work in digital video,' Manja replied. 'Frankie is an arts journalist.'

'And a courier,' I said.

Oh, that must be interesting.

'I go to all sorts of places. But I only see the facades.'

Where do you live, and how do you get by in London?

'We're in a warehouse in Seven Sisters,' said Manja, 'with five other people. It's not great, but we manage.'

Finally, inevitably: *Are you a couple?*

I gave Manja a beat, and then: 'No, we're just housemates. We lived together at Central St. Martins and now we're in the same place again.'

I saw a familiar face walk towards the bar. That face broke into a huge grin, and then its owner starting wagging both of her index fingers at us in happy recognition.

'Oh God, it's Claude.'

'Yes,' said Manja. 'And she's wasted.'

'Do you know those guys she's with?'

'Do I ever?'

'Did *you* invite her?' I whispered.

Manja shook her head, scowling.

'Hey guys, how are *youuuuuuu*?' Without waiting for our reply, she introduced us to Adam and Andrew. 'They're art dealers,' she declared, not looking at the middle-aged men in suits alongside her. Then she turned, telling them to, 'Meet Frankie and Manja, from my degree.'

'Oh, hi,' said Manja. 'Sorry, but we were just thinking of going.'

'Oh, come on!' begged Claude.

'I've got to get up early tomorrow …' I said.

'They promised to buy us drinks,' replied Claude, as Andrew and Adam looked at each other.

'Alright,' I said. 'If you insist.'

'Don't sound too enthusiastic.'

'I didn't.'

'What are you having?'

'White wine.'

'Get a bottle, yeah?' said Claude, waving her hand.

We sat down. Claude poured her glass first, more generous than ours. I looked at Manja but we knew this wasn't worth contesting; we exchanged several more glances as Claude talked loudly about selling two of her 'Intimate Self-Portraits', spending the money on champagne and taxis to parties, telling us which of the '90s artists that Manja and I hated had given her which drugs, and when.

Claude went to the toilet.

I whispered to Manja: 'What should we do?'

'Get the bus.'

I nodded. Adam and Andrew asked us about where we were from, if we were artists, where we lived in London and how we got by, before Claude returned with another bottle.

'Claude, *no*!' said Manja.

'Oh, you're so uptight … you Slovakians.'

'Slovenians.'

'I know, you keep telling me,' Claude replied, filling our glasses. Manja glared at her. 'If you *really* don't want it, I'll have it.'

Claude drank from Manja's glass. Manja took Claude's.

'Hey, that's mine!' said Claude.

'And that's mine.'

They stopped, laughed, clinked the glasses and carried

on drinking.

'Where are you going next?' said Claude.

'*Home*,' I replied.

'I was asking *them*,' Claude informed me, turning to Andrew and Adam.

'We're meeting our friends at a club.'

'Come on,' said Manja. 'We're leaving.'

'We should go too,' replied Andrew, getting up.

We went outside. Manja and I walked up The Mall towards Trafalgar Square, before turning to see Claude going in the other direction with the two men.

'Oh, for *fuck's sake* ...'

'We can't leave her,' said Manja, walking quickly after them.

'Where are we going?' asked Claude.

'Annabel's,' replied Adam.

'What's that?' said Claude.

'It's a private members' club,' Andrew told us, 'named after Annabel Goldsmith. Been there for 50 years □ everyone who's anyone is a member.'

'We're not,' Manja said.

'Don't worry, we'll get you in. Your friend might need to smarten up, though.'

'Is it far?'

'Ten minutes' walk.'

'We're *leaving*,' said Manja.

'Give it a chance,' implored Claude.

'Let's give it half an hour,' I suggested, curious to see inside such a famous club.

'*What*?' Manja replied.

'It'll be an experience.'

'Being surrounded by poshos?'

'You were happy to dress up for those art twats,' said Claude. 'Mr Curator, notice me!'

We reached Berkeley Square in silence. The first thing we noticed was how tall the trees were, their summer greens irresistibly beautiful. We walked past the railings around the park, locked at night, and stared up at the penthouses above the five or six-storey blocks of flats.

'If I was Damien Hirst, I'd buy one of these,' I told Manja, laughing.

'Have you ever delivered here?'

'I can't remember. These places all look the same.'

Adam and Andrew went down some steps, towards a basement. Claude grabbed my hand and dragged me after them. I raised my eyebrows at Manja, who grudgingly followed.

The doorman, dressed in a discreet black suit, sized us up.

'These your guests?' Adam and Andrew nodded. 'Your

friend really should wear a jacket,' he told them, looking at me.

'What if I tuck in my shirt and do up my top button?' I replied.

'You still need a jacket.'

As Adam and Andrew entered, Claude touched the doorman's arm.

'Come on,' she said. 'We've come all the way from Croydon for this.'

'We walked ten—'

Claude shot Manja her *shut up* look that we both knew so well.

'Croydon?' said the doorman. 'I *say*, we *can't* let the riffraff in.'

'It's alright, we're Londoners,' replied Claude, using a tone that left me unsure if she was playing along with his joke, or genuinely offended.

'Londoners or not, he still needs a jacket,' said the doorman. 'Ask at the cloakroom if they've got a spare. If anyone asks you about it, you'll have to leave.'

He waved us through. The cloakroom attendant greeted us with a smile.

'The doorman told me to borrow a jacket,' I said. 'Do you have any lying around?'

'Just this,' the attendant replied, handing me a black one,

I presumed from lost property. 'It's a medium. Leave your bags, coats, phones and cameras here, please.'

I thanked the attendant and put on the jacket, finding it a little tight. Claude threw her bags at us to check in and did her make-up in the huge mirror, opposite the toilets. We followed her past the bar to the lounge, where an elderly couple were drinking.

'They're staring at us,' said Manja.

'Then ignore them and get pissed, I'm paying.'

'You sure?' laughed Manja, but Claude had already gone.

I slumped into one of the red velvet chairs, by the fireplace, noticing how the dim lighting bounced off the mustard-yellow walls.

'Are you okay?'

'I think I have Stendhal syndrome.'

'He got that from looking at masterpieces in Florence,' Manja told me. 'Not from a few tacky paintings of dogs.'

Before I could answer, we heard a voice from the bar: '*How much*?'

'Our whites start at £25,' said the barman, 'with the Garnacha Blanco.'

'Fine, whatever,' Claude replied.

Before we could stop Claude, she had a bottle and three glasses. *Your money*, I thought as she handed over her debit card.

'It's dead down here,' she shouted. She marched towards the stairs, so we followed. On our left was a white door. Claude tried to enter, but it was locked. She knocked. No response.

'Leave it,' said Manja.

Claude knocked again, and then tried to pull the door open. The barman looked up at us.

'Excuse me, madam — that room is private.'

'Didn't want to go in anyway,' replied Claude, before stumbling upstairs.

At the top of the stairs, Manja and I gasped as we saw the indoor garden. The domed ceiling was decorated with fairy lights, a cheap imitation of the night sky; a few bulbs flickered and failed. I could hear water flowing but I couldn't tell where it was. The walls were covered in decking and green vines, with pot plants around the edges, all immaculately groomed, with patrons sat on purple and pink chairs around little tables with candles. By the bar, a group of men in brown or black dinner jackets stood smoking cigars.

'I feel like I'm in a bad Fellini film,' I said to Manja.

'Why do they all stand like that?' she asked, noting that they had their legs slightly apart.

'Assertiveness training, probably,' I replied.

One took a long draw and blew out the smoke, with a

contemptuous nod towards us. I glanced over at Claude, who had introduced herself to two men, tilting her head with laughter.

'Are you alright?' asked Manja.

'Yeah,' I replied. 'I just hate rich people.'

'What do you think these guys do for a living?'

'Estate agents, solicitors, bankers,' I replied.

'Arms dealers, maybe,' said Manja, half-laughing.

'I met someone recently who specialised in Asset of Community Value cases,' I said. 'She was one of the highest-paid lawyers in Britain, or so she kept saying. Anyway, landlords and property developers would hire her to challenge anyone who claimed that they were good for local people, to make it easier to kick them out. Honestly, how would you sleep at night?'

'You'd climb into bed, and when your husband asks, 'What did you do today?' you'd say, 'I closed down three arts organisations, two pubs and a children's playground.' Then you'd be out like a light.'

As we started laughing, Claude came over.

'Not talking to anyone, then?'

'No, we're alright,' I said.

'You two are so closed-minded!'

'These people run *everything*,' replied Manja. 'What could we possibly learn from them?'

'Nothing, with *that* attitude,' Claude insisted. 'Come and meet Martin, you'll like him.'

Claude grabbed my hand and yanked me across the room. 'What do you do?' I asked, to break the silence.

'I make programmes for assurance firms so they can check that people are paying the right tax,' declared Martin.

'They should check everyone here first,' I said to Manja, before Claude kicked me in the shin. Too late, as Martin had heard. He shook his head, picked up his bag and left.

'Proud of yourself, Frankie?' asked Claude. 'Coming into their club and bullying them?'

'*Bullying* them?' I replied. 'These bastards take over our galleries, turn our studios into luxury flats, wipe out all the jobs that we might take to sustain ourselves and charge us hundreds a month for a fucking shoebox in fucking Ilford, but joking about their taxes is bullying?'

Then I realised that everyone was staring at us.

'We'd better go,' whispered Manja.

I headed out, quietly. Claude pushed ahead of us, back down the stairs. She took a key from her purse, holding it up with a grin — I guessed that she'd swiped it from Martin's table — and opened the white door.

'Haha, nice one!' I said. Manja raised her eyebrows, impressed. And then we saw a large room, with 12 people sat around a long table. On the walls were several oil paintings, all dead white men, probably from the 19th century. The table was laid out for dinner, the finest china, but there was no food. At the far end was a computer screen, covering the entire wall. On it were some graphs, dropping across the X axis, below the heading PROFIT MARGINS 14-15.

As Claude pulled out a chair from under the table, I noticed that again, everyone was glaring at us — the men were in black tie, the women in ballgowns. As Manja whispered, 'This is it?' the man by the screen said: 'Excuse me — who invited you here?'

'Adam and Andrew,' replied Claude, smiling at them.

'Did you?' asked the chair.

'No,' they answered in unison.

'We met you at the ICA,' said Claude. 'You promised you'd get us in.

'Into the club,' stammered Andrew. 'Not in here ...'

Claude winked at me.

'What are you lot doing, anyway?' I asked. 'I thought you'd be having one of those parties where the Prime Minister has sex with a pig. Instead it's just spreadsheets.'

'Initiations do not happen here,' said an elderly man, before his companion elbowed him.

'We try not to combine business and pleasure in the dining room, but they're so hard to separate nowadays,' one of the few women told us.

'What's wrong with enjoying our work?' asked the chair. 'Now, please explain who you are.'

'We're artists,' said Manja.

The room went quiet. The diners looked at each other, nervously. Someone coughed. The chair of the meeting banged the table.

'Next on the agenda is the Arts Council, and how to abolish it,' he said, grinning at us.

'I wonder how Stendhal would have felt about *this*,' whispered Manja.

'We've explained who we are,' I said. 'What about you?'

'We're simply trying to get a good deal for taxpayers,' a woman said. Then there was a knock, and she opened the door, clearly expecting someone. In came Stevo in a purple crushed velvet suit. I watched Manja try to suppress a sneer as he sat next to us.

'Here is our artist,' said the chair. 'Can you tell us how you began your career?'

'I went to the Royal College of Art with a student loan and graduated in 2010. Since then I've worked and networked in my spare time. Once I started getting press coverage, I met some more curators and now it's going alright.'

'Did you ever need subsidies?'

'No, I used my programming skills to make the work and paid for the digital cameras myself.'

'Where did you get those skills?' yelled Manja. 'Who are your parents? Who did they know? How could you afford to live in London?'

'It's not fair to suggest that our friend hasn't worked extremely hard,' said the chair as Stevo fumed at Manja. 'You needn't get so angry, as the government, it turns out, agrees with you. We're just trying to persuade them that there are other options.'

'I agree,' said Claude.

'What?' replied Manja.

'I can make a living from selling things,' Claude declared, grabbing a bottle of wine.

'This is our point,' said one of the men.

'You started taking naked self-portraits because no-one bought your sculptures,' said Manja. 'And you're barely making anything from that.'

'At least I'm not living off hand-outs!' replied Claude.

'Perhaps not,' I said, 'but who funds the galleries where you exhibit or the magazines that cover you?'

'They could crowdfund, or be supported by patrons,' said the chair. 'The common man shouldn't have to pay for works that they don't like.'

'What the fuck do you know about the common man?' I shouted.

'Would you please leave,' said the chair.

The same woman got up to open the door. I heard footsteps.

'Quick,' she said, 'the waiter's coming!'

As the women hurried to put flowers in their hair, the chair went to the laptop beneath the projector, closed Excel and put on a backdrop of green hills and a blue sky. Several men applied lipstick and mascara, and music started, which I recognised as Wham's 'Club Tropicana'. They all sat, poured champagne and clinked their glasses as the food arrived.

Manja and I went to leave. She tapped Claude on the shoulder; Claude held up a glass of Bolly and we walked down the stairs without her. I returned the jacket to the cloakroom as we got our bags and wandered towards the bus stop.

'Did you see that Hugo Rifkind piece that was around after we found out about David Cameron putting his dick in that dead pig's head to get into that sex club at Oxford?' I asked.

'No,' replied Manja.

'He just says that whenever he read about how lavish the Piers Gaveston Society parties were, he just remembered seeing loads of toffs with mullets and women in taffeta from C&A.'

'What's C&A?' asked Manja, laughing.

'Cheap clothes shop,' I said as the bus pulled up.

We turned to see Claude coming out of the club.

'I thought you were staying?' asked Manja.

'As soon as the waiter left, they went back to talking about benefit cuts,' Claude replied.

'I'm sure they'll talk about their two minutes of decadence for years,' I said, with a smile.

As Manja and I walked back towards Piccadilly Circus to get the 38 bus, I told her how I'd spent years trying to suss out how to complete *Frankie Goes to Hollywood*. When I finally got through to the Pleasuredome, I just got a screen saying 'Welcome' with a bit of music. We changed at Dalston Junction, wondering how long it would be before the bars and clubs that we'd long loved here got replaced by ones that felt like Annabel's. Finally, we got home, unlocked the door and fell into bed together, not for a moment wishing we'd stayed for Stevo's afterparty.

The Arches

Stephen Thompson

Day he showed up here, more shuffling than walking, had more dirt on him than all of us put together, though we had the excuse of being on the job. Our line of work, gittin' dirty is what you might call an occupational hazard, but he didn't look like no mechanic I ever seen. Didn't look like much of anything 'cept beat down. Funky smelling too. Them other fellas wanted to run him off but I wasn't having it. If he were my child being disadvantaged, like to think somebody would stick up for him. 'Y'all should be ashamed of yo'selves. Leave the boy alone.' T made a face. 'Get ridda 'im, Joe. Di bwoy a stink out di bloodclaat place.' 'Is you giving me orders nigga?' 'Nuh call me dat, Joe.' 'Oh I'm sorry. My bad. Is you giving me orders *bitch*?' The others broke up laughing. T had it coming. Nappy-headed maw'fucker was always gittin' up in other people's business. He knew better than to prolong it with me and hauled his ass back under the Jeep he'd been trying to fix since creation, Clive, Wallace and the rest of them fools sniggering at him. Boy stuck to me like funny glue after that. Had me a ton a work to do but couldn't git to it for jawing with him. 'Got any spare change? Tryna get summing to eat.' Gave him what I had on me, about enough to git a burger and a soda. Flashed his yellow teeth. 'Big up fam! God is good.' 'Nigga please. God don't got nuthin' do with it. That's my money. I earned it. You know, like, working? You might wanna try it some time.' He laughed and slunk away.

That evening, as it was gittin' along for night, he wandered back into the garage. Smelt him 'fore I saw him. Didn't pay him no mind this time. Had my head under the hood of an oldsmobile, cutting up my fingers on a piece-o'-shit crankshaft, and I wasn't gon' let him or nobody interrupt me. I'm the same as every other grease monkey. You need something from me when I'm on the job you best git to waiting or git gone, and I don't give a damn whether you be John or Jesus. 'Where're the others?' He sounded scared, like he was worried about gittin' jumped. I straightened up, wiped my hands on my overalls, looked him over. Was about to tear him off a strip but he seemed all kindsa pitiful and I just didn't have the heart. 'Those lazy asses are always clocking off early. That's the problem with you Brits. Got no work ethic.' 'You're American, right?' I shook my head. 'Can see I ain't gon' git nuthin' past you.' He smiled and pulled a can of beer from his pocket. 'Hell boy, I thought you was gon' buy food!' He looked down at his feet, shuffled them some. 'I know, but it's proper cold out there. Beers keep the shivers off.' I snorted. 'Give it a while. They'll be bringing them on soon.' He spat on the ground, heeled it with his battered sneakers. 'What the hell … is you spoiling for an ass whuppin'? Show some respect for this place. Ain't much but I pay the rent on it and I don't take kindly to …' He suddenly walked off, swigging from his can, and started nosing around. Studied him a while, thinking who in their right mind would sell liquor to someone like him. Had a hunch it was that no good Ali from over there near the Silchester projects. Dude's got no principles. Wouldn't piss on his store now. Used to drop by every so often to buy fruit and veg and whatnot till I caught the son-of-a-bitch selling cigarettes to a bunch of school kids. Called him out and he barred me. Didn't bother me none. He don't want my money, fine. Polaks next door to him don't got a problem taking it. And they ain't never tried once to sell me out-of-date stuff.

Spend enough time in a place and after a while you can't see what's in it no more. Then a stranger comes calling and it feels like you seeing everything for the first time. Place was full of junk. Done wore out my voice trying to git them others to tidy up after theyselves. Couldn't git from A to B without tripping over something. Boy ran his eye over every wheel-rim and fender like he was some kinda government inspector, like he was fixing to write me up. 'Where's your Pirelli calendar?' 'Say what?' 'What kinda garage doesn't have a Pirelli calendar?' 'Oh please, ain't nobody up in here wanna look at pictures of skinny ass white women.' He laughed. 'So where in the States you from?' I'd had enough. Had to git back on it. The jobs were piling up. Faulty work and late work, two crimes no mechanic can ever commit. Not if he wants to eat that is. 'You best run along now, don't got time for idling. Done told you, I is a working man.' He pushed up his lips, thought he was gon' cry. 'Can't I kotch here for a while, fam? Just a little while. Won't bother you. Just wanna keep warm for a bit and finish my beer and then I'll be on my toes, swear dan.' He was obviously rolling the sympathy dice but I can't rightly say I blamed him. Made sense that he would. If you're him, in his fix, you do what you gotta do, say what you gotta say, to get by. Question of survial. 'What's yo' name boy?' 'Malik.' 'Malik? What kinda stoopid ass name is that? You one of them Nation of Islam niggas? Ain't got no truck with them. Bunch o' goddam fools, if you ask me.' He finished his beer, stuck his tongue out and drained the last drops on to it. 'I ain't a Muslim. Wouldn't be drinking if I was.' 'I guess not.' He crushed the can in his hand. 'How long you been on the streets?' His eyeballs shot up, rolled from side to side. 'That long huh?' 'It's been a while.' 'Where you normally sleep at? Store fronts and such?' He shook his head and reeled off a list of spots: Shepherd's Bush Green, Little Scrubs, at the side of the canal on Ladbroke Grove. 'I like it there. First thing in the morning, all the ducks and swans come flying in. That shit's nang fam, trus. One morning this peng yat was walking past and when she saw them coming out the sky she got shook for real, like she thought they were gonna attack her.' Like a kid describing his favourite toy, his voice was all up in his head but when he seen I wasn't really listening he put it back in his chest.

'You know what that canal's called?' 'Can't say I do, no.' 'The Grand Union. Don't know for sure how many miles it is, but it's gotta be a hundred and mash. Runs from London all the way to Birmingham.' 'Is that a fact?' 'Yeah. Look it up.' 'I'll get right on it.' He locked his eyes on me, waiting, but I had nothing more to say on the matter. What the hell did I care about canals and how long they were and where they ran to? I stood there studying him. Under his baseball cap and face fuzz, couldn't tell if he was good looking or ugly as hell. 'OK, here's the deal. I guess I don't got no objection to you taking a little shelter, but you sit yo' ass down and don't be touching nuthin.' He flopped down on an old office chair, one of those swivel things with wheels on it, and sat there looking at me with more contentment on his face than a cat warming a fire.

Crossed my mind to put him to work sweeping up the place, but it didn't seem fair. Never been one to ask for free labour. Man does a job he got a right to be paid cash money. Besides, he didn't seem up to working. I'd seen stronger-looking chickens. Put my head back under the hood but couldn't concentrate no how, so I straightened up again and turned to him and said, 'Let's go git us some food.' He didn't move. For the first time he seemed suspicious of me, frightened even. 'C'mon now, ain't nobody gon' hurt you.' 'I ain't hungry.' 'Boy, you gotta eat. Them bones o' yours need more than just skin.' 'Seriously, I'm good.' 'Bullshit. Now git yo' ass up.' He didn't move, just stared at me. 'Fine, suit yourself, it's your funeral, but I gotta eat and I ain't tryna leave you up in here by yo'self. Spell that anyway you like, still comes out as goodbye.'

He tried to stand up but immediately fell back on to the chair. 'What's wrong now?' 'It's my feet. They're killing me, blud. You know them ones, when you been on them all day.' He started flexing his feet, wincing like an old timer. 'Now ain't this is a bitch? Broke down cars I can deal with.

But broke down people …' I scratched my head. Couldn't think what to do with the boy. Train went by overhead, on its way to Hammersmith. Noise wasn't too bad but it caused enough rattling to raise Lazarus. Goddam arches were bound to collapse one day, old and crumbly as they was. Went to the office and dug out the little blow heater and came back and plugged it in and turned it on full blast. It couldn't heat a mouse hole but it was better than nuthin'. 'You can stay here tonight. Just tonight, mind. This ain't no flop house. Don't got no blankets so don't ask. John's back there if you need to take a leak. And I'mma have to lock you in.' 'What?' 'You heard. Be back first thing in the morning to let you out.' 'You make me sound like an animal.' 'Gotta do you like that I'm afraid. So make up yo' mind, young'un. Staying or stepping?' He rubbed his ankles. 'I'll stay.'

After I'd locked him in, I hopped in my ride and set out for Yum Yums on Ladbroke Grove. Was gittin' kind a tired of their food but it was close by and I was hungrier than a quarryman. Pulled out of the arches on to Bramley and got stuck behind a 295 bus heading for Clapham out of Harlesden. Goddam thing was crawling along, the driver trying to avoid the oncoming vehicles while making sure he didn't scrape the shit outta the ones parked on either side of him. Why the hell the roads gotta be so narrow in this country I ain't never figured out. As for driving on the left hand side ...

Sat waiting so long I started listening to my engine. That's the thing about being a mechanic. Put me in a vehicle and I soon get to studying it. Suppose you offer me a ride. I sit there nodding while you beat your gums about this and that. You think I'm listening, and for all you know I am, but really I got my ears cocked for what's happening under your hood. I hear things about a vehicle that regular folk can't. My old Toyota was ticking over like a dream. Rev counter was literally on point. That's what I loved about it. Reliable as hell. Design weren't much to look at, and you might as well be in a sardine can if you ever got hit, but you gotta hand it to those Japs, they sure know how to build an engine. Them others were always laughing at me, with their pimped out German models, until they broke down that is.

Gittin' impatient, I got out my cell and called Yum Yums and put in my usual order: brown-stewed fish, rice with black eye beans, side order of coleslaw and some fried plantains. It was ready and waiting when I got there. On my way back to my crib, listening to some Walter Jackson, I noticed I was gittin' low on gas and pulled in at the ugly little Jet garage on Church Road. It was times like these that I really missed the States. Hated self-service gas stations. Goddam pump was almost too cold to hold and it set me to thinking about Malik. Even with the heater on he was gon' freeze his ass off.

Been living in the Stonebridge projects since coming to London and even after all these years it still reminded me of where I came up. Buildings looked a whole lot different but the folk living in them were almost identical. Black mostly. Some good, some you wouldn't give the skin off of your chicken. Like always when I got back from work, found a lot of the young 'uns hanging around the entrance to my tower. Night before, there was a whole gang of 'em out front shooting some kinda video. Grime music they called it but it sounded a lot like rap to my ears. Stood there watching them for a spell, smiling to myself as they tried to look all thuggish and shit in front of the camera. Star of the video was a skinny light-skinned boy from around the way called Nines. You don't gotta guess where he got the name from.

Hadn't been gone but a couple of hours yet I came back to find Malik fast asleep, curled up on the floor in front of the heater, his raggedy jacket barely covering his bony frame. Had me an old mutt a while back. Named him King cause he acted like his shit didn't stink. Long dead now. Rescue dog. Rheumatic as hell. Poor thing could hardly walk and spent all his time sleeping. You couldn't find a worse guard dog. No bark and even less bite but he'd at least lift his head when someone came into the garage. Malik might have been dead for all the movement he made. Crept up and lay the blanket on him, arranged it some, but when I tried to ease the cushion under his head his eyes suddenly opened. They were bloodshot to hell and made him look half-crazed. For a moment he didn't seem to recognise me or where he was. Figured he'd been having a bad dream. Didn't like to think what he'd seen in it but the devil musta featured somewhere. He threw off his jacket and sat up. The smell coming off of him was so high I almost had to cover my nose. Heard a train go by overhead. The piece of track between Latimer Road and Wood Lane ain't exactly long, you can stand on the platform of one station and see the other, but it's plenty long when you gotta work under the goddam thing all day. Malik ran his hand over the blanket, slow like. Thing was coarser than a scrubbing brush but he stroked it like a man stroking a woman.

'Thought you could use it to keep the ice outta yo' blood.' 'You brought this back for me?' He snatched up the cushion. 'And this?' 'No, I got 'em for that other homeless dude lying next to you.' 'You went home and got them?' 'Might take 'em back if you don't stop asking stoopid questions.' That look again, as if he was gon' bust out crying. 'I don't know what to say.' 'Aw hell. It ain't no thing. Didn't wanna come back here and find you dead, is all. Imagine the fuss. Bad for business. Probably have to close up for the day. Longer, even.' He smiled. 'You sure you don't want something to eat. I got these …' I held up the paper bag. 'What's that?' Again the suspicious tone. 'Plantains. You like plantains?' I shoved the bag at him and a bottle of water. He drank a little of the water, smacked his chapped lips a few times, then opened the greasy bag and looked inside. Didn't seem sure to begin with, but eventually he took out a slice, popped it into his mouth and started chewing slowly. 'Been a while since I had these. Mum used to cook them all the time. Always served them on hard dough with loadsa butter.' He smiled at the memory. 'Imagine, with all the grease in these things, she'd still put butter on the bread.'

I pulled up the swivel chair and sat next to him, looking down on him while he worked his way through the bag of plantains. 'You from around these parts?' He shook his head. 'B, B and B.' 'Say what?' 'Brixton, born and bred.' He tilted his head back slightly and dropped a slice of plantain into his mouth. 'So how'd you end up over here?' 'I'll tell you that if you tell me what brought you here from the States.' 'That's a long story.' 'We got time.' 'You got time. I gotta get home and get some shuteye. Been up since six this morning.' 'Me, too.' 'Yeah but you ain't been busting your ass trying to earn a living. You been too busy begging.' He stopped chewing suddenly and his face fell. Felt guilty stomping on him like that. It was trifling and mean and I wanted to say sorry but the words wouldn't come out. Don't ask me why. 'A woman.' 'What?' 'You asked me what brought me here. A woman. Only thing ever makes a man do stoopid things.' He finished eating, stood up, stretched, then sat down again. The blow heater whirring. The low hum of traffic outside. 'You married?' he asked. 'Yeah but separated.' 'Oh. Sorry to hear that, fam.' 'I ain't.' 'She American too?' 'From Trinidad.' 'For real? My people are Trinny.' 'Lucky you.' He smiled but I knew he was fruntin', I knew I'd hurt him again. 'Listen here, I don't mean no offence but I'm what you might call a straight talker. No point shooting the breeze with me if you sensitive. Been that way all my life and don't much care for changing. Tried once, tried to be Mr. Tactful for my wife and kids but couldn't keep up the lie. End of the day, man's gotta be who he is, right?' He didn't answer, just sat there staring straight ahead, as if I'd put a spell on him.

The silence sat between us like a sleeping bear. Occurred to me that I hadn't talked about Faye in a while and I was surprised by how good it felt. Malik suddenly flipped over on to his side and propped himself up on his elbow and said, 'How'd you meet your wife?' 'C'mon on now, you don' gotta pretend to be interested in my life.' 'I am. Serious. Tell me.' I searched his eyes and saw nothing to suggest he was bullshitting. 'Did a bit of soldiering as a young man.' 'You were in the army?' 'Got called up. Did two tours in 'Nam, but trus' me, you don't wanna hear about it.' He was about to say something but I cut him off. 'Stationed in Germany for the final years of my service. Spent most of my leave in London. Met Faye in a little after-hours spot 'bout two blocks from here, a pokey little basement joint called The Globe, up there on Talbot Road. Been open since the sixties I heard tell. Can you imagine? Anyhow, about a month after we meet, Faye and me go get ourselves hitched. Quick, right? But we figured 'what the hell'. Biggest goddam mistake of my life.' 'What happened?' 'The plan was to settle in the States. We were all set. But then she has a change of heart. I didn't. Do I gotta stress the rest?' He worked that over in his brain for a while then said, 'And you never went back to America?' 'I meant to, but time went by and the place sorta grew on me and the kids were here and ...'

The arches shook, announcing another train. As it went by, Malik looked up, like he thought the ceiling was gon' cave in. Used to do the same thing myself till I got used to it. I was through talking about myself. 'So what about you?' He stretched out on his back, put the cushion under his head and pulled the blanket up to his chin. When he had himself set he said, 'What about me?' 'Ain't you kinda young to be sleeping rough? What the hell happened?' He waited a while then said, 'I don't like to talk about it.' 'Talk if you have a mind to, shut the hell up if you don't. Either way is fine by me.' 'Thanks for the sympathy.' 'Is that what you want, sympathy? 'Cause I'm fresh out.' He smiled and said, 'And yet you came back here tonight.' Heard another train approaching, last one to Hammersmith by my watch. The rumble always started under your feet, then spread to the walls and then finally to the roof. We waited, not looking at each other, till it passed. Suddenly feeling dog tired, I stood up and said, 'Well, reckon I'll be gittin' along now. You gon' be alright till morning?' He nodded and pulled the blanket tight around his body. On my way to the door, he said something which stopped me in my tracks. I turned and faced him. 'You did what?'

He'd been smoking. Fell asleep with the cigarette still smouldering in the ashtray. House went up. He and his two older brothers made it out but his folks got trapped. He could still hear his moms screaming. When he was through talking I said, 'That's one helluva weight to be carrying around.' 'What the fuck do you know about it?' 'Nuthin'. Nuthin' at all, except you can't go on blaming yourself.' He flipped on to his side, turned his back to me. I stood there watching him, not sure what else to do, what else to say, whether to leave or get the hell out. He didn't move or make a sound but he was crying sure enough. In the end I gave him what I felt he needed. 'You gotta find a way to move past that thing. But there ain't no sense trying to shift a stone that big all by yo'self. It'll kill you. Git some help with it.' Still no movement from him. I turned to leave, got as far as the door, but I couldn't go through it. I just couldn't.

Heard the key in the door and opened my eyes just as T came in, dressed in his overalls and carrying his lunch box. He saw Malik 'fore he saw me and said, 'Wha' di raas …' He was about to go over and start hassling the boy but I rushed out of the office, where I'd slept the night, and stopped him. 'Get away from him!' T froze and stared at me, bug-eyed and open-mouthed, like he'd just seen a ghost. 'Is wha' kin'a funny business a gwaan ya?' I ignored him and looked down at Malik. He hadn't stirred at all. Boy coulda slept through a hurricane. I turned to T and said, 'Ain't you got work to do?' 'Wait, wait, mek me try fi understan' dis. You mean fi tell me say you and him sleep ya last night?' 'You gotta problem with that?' He laughed and said, 'No. No problem at all.' He walked off, chuckling and shaking his head. I crouched down and poked Malik in the ribs. 'Time to git up.' He shifted his position slightly but didn't wake up. 'C'mon now. You gotta git up.' At last he opened his eyes. When he saw me he smiled and said, 'Tea, two sugars. Lotsa milk.' 'How 'bout a slap upside yo' head? Now git yo' ass up!' T came back, mug of coffee in his hand. 'But really, Joe. Wha di raas a gwaan ya?' Malik stood up, gathered the blanket around him, then went off to the bathroom, carefully side-stepping T as he went. 'I don't gotta explain shit to you T, but I will tell you this. Git used to that boy, cos you gon' be seeing a lot more of him round the place. I done hired him.' 'Fi do wha' exactly? Him can fix car?' 'No more than you can fix em.' That twisted his face nicely. 'He gon' be coming in every evening and tidying up the place. Look around. It sure needs it. And that ain't all. He'll be staying here at night, keeping an eye on things, till he can git himself fixed up. You don't like it, there's the door.'

I left him to go find Malik.

He was just coming out of the john when I got there. 'I heard what you said just now. We didn't talk about no job.' 'You don't want it?' He looked down at his feet. 'Depends on the pay.' I made my offer and he raised his head and smiled. 'What if I say I want more?' 'What if I kick you to the kerb?' He laughed and stuck out his hand. 'You got a deal.'

NORTH

N1, Centre of Illusion

Chloe Aridjis

London N1, particularly the district of Islington, is fast becoming a popular destination for film students and insomniacs. This is due, above all, to the preponderance of shadows, especially shadows of a particularly density, which provide inspiration to some and temporary refuge to others. Shadows, and optical illusions — for in N1 there is also optical illusion on a major and frequent scale, and visitors should head to its streets to witness the best collisions of light and shadow London has to offer.

Over the past few years it has been noted that certain local corners and junctions of Islington, above all those around where St Peter's meets the Essex Road, are the site of extraordinary optical illusions. It is still unclear why these illusions reside here, but researchers have concluded it must have to do with the way light particles interact with specific architectural features. Others reckon it's because this northern part of the borough was once an important medieval route from the City, a sleepy village where doomed cattle on their way to Smithfield would stop for the night.

Aware of this, and noting the recent surge in nocturnally restless locals, the famed German sleep clinic Sternhimmeltuch has opened its first UK branch in N1. Residents as well as travellers from abroad are welcome, indeed encouraged, to drop by for a trial night. Housed in a Victorian building near the corner of where Cross Street meets Florence, the sleep clinic aims to cure insomniacs while also addressing certain ailments that seem to arise from overexposure to optical illusion.

Two main categories of optical illusion have been established: those produced on land, and those produced on water. Thanks to the canal that runs through much of the borough, elements of this latter category have been seen to flourish. Some Islington residents for instance have proven more receptive to reflections on hard surfaces while others are specifically attuned to reflections on water.

As for the reflections spotted on the canal in N1, these include glitter patterns, wake patterns and cats' paws. Glitter patterns are ensembles of sun glints, instantaneous flashes of sunlight reflected for a moment on a sloping wave and then gone. The canal is especially abundant with cats' paws, which are dark regions of water where the wind touches down and tenses the surface.

On land, meanwhile, one of the most widely noted shadow appearances, for those in search of such things, has been that of the Brocken Spectre, looming three-dimensional shadows cast onto buildings, especially in times of fog. A golem silhouette, meanwhile, has been seen slinking across the old Carlton cinema in Essex Road, and smaller versions across the exterior of the Charles Lamb pub after closing time. Other buildings nearby have also boasted large unexpected shadows. Night, the great muralist.

Not far from the sleep clinic, and a five-minute walk from the Estorick Collection, lies another, even lesser known museum, with only five items: the Museum of Night. (Open Friday through Sunday, 6pm-11:45pm, entrance free as of 8pm). Its centrepiece is the Nocturnograph, a nuanced machine invented in the early '90s, which has since had many of its functions expanded. This elegant device, used to measure the various facets of night, has broadened its focus. According to shadow supervisor Mary Oliphant, the museum's head curator, Islington is the city district with the greatest concentration of shadows and hence it seems right that the Nocturnograph should reside here too. Some shadows are thicker, others more opaque, some denser, others more fluid, some smooth, others jagged. The Nocturnograph also registers localised urban glows, where the yellow from sodium illumination interacts with the blue-green mercury of streetlamps to create a steady visual magnet for night wanderers. Another item in the museum, equally alluring yet more variable, is a large terrarium full of black moths and nocturnal flowers.

After a visit to the museum one should head to the 24-hour café that recently opened in Camden Passage. Inspired by the now defunct Insomnia Café in Glasgow, it serves hot chocolate and homemade Victoria sponge cake with coffee icing as well as all manner of jacket potatoes. The place is frequented by locals in varying states of alertness; it is sometimes hard to find a table, even at four in the morning.

If no tables are free at the 24-hour café, head to one of Islington's best-kept secrets, a small elegant library in the lower ground floor of one of the houses in Cloudesley Square. This library is actually part of the private home of one of Islington's gentry, an elderly man who likes to have company at night when he reads. Free tea is served. Silence is imperative, otherwise visitors will be asked to leave.

Regardless of one's relationship with the night, Islington is unique in being able to provide nocturnal stimulation or solution. Sternhimmeltuch's arrival will now cement that reputation. In another location farther north towards

Holloway, a rival research institute has been busy setting up an embassy for insomniacs, a consulate for somnambulists, and a motel for the mildly sleep disordered.

Mother Black Cap's Revenge

George F.

'The coming communities are more likely to be found in those crucibles of human sociability and creativity out of which the radically new emerges: racialised and ethnicised identities, queer and youth subcultures, anarchists, feminists, hippies, indigenous peoples, back-to-the-landers, 'deviants' of all kinds in all kinds of spaces.'

— Richard J.F. Day, *Gramsci is Dead: Anarchist Currents in the Newest Social Movements* (2005)

'So, are you lot a bunch of anarchists then?'

A lost soul, abandoned by the Thursday night Camden carnival, meandered out of the desolate early morning wasteland that lies between Koko on Mornington Crescent and the Roundhouse at Chalk Farm. He wandered up to us in the hope of some after-hours entertainment, a disciple of the depressive hedonist coda that states that any and all persons must be available to amuse and bemuse at all hours. The six of us stand clutching a guilty bag of tools and locks at the junction of Kentish Town Road and Camden High Street, midway through our planning meeting, eyeing the target opposite us. As I stare through him, with his earnest, ovine eyes and blank hopeful expression, I feel a rising clot of disgust congeal within me. Here was one of the enemy, or at best one of those gradually trampling the identity and difference of the borough into the ground. A man-child of the millennium, a fecund and facile consumer-construct, choking the world with his insipidity, asphyxiating through mediocrity.

He stands directly between us and the gloomy husk of the Black Cap — boarded with black hoardings the night before — the gold lettering painted across the front glittering faintly in the sterile light of a double-decker night bus grumbling south. Its owners, Kicking Horse Limited, gave the staff 24 hours' notice and closed the venue, ambushing the shocked and indignant crowds with the announcement on her ultimate night. Their plan, as with all property developers, is to create new avenues for the affluent gentry, to penetrate the remnants of autonomous culture struggling on in London.

I look around our group of six: tight denim and ragged leather splattered with patches reading 'fuck the system', 'fashion is my philosophy', 'mutants'; belts of metal studs, Mercedes Benz trophies and bullets; faux animal skin prints of leopard, zebra, jaguar; ripped fishnet stockings pouring from cut-off jeans hotpants; hair in knotty tentacles of dreadlocks, sides shaved to the skin, painted emerald, azure, purple, black, strung with ornaments of severed dolls heads and mystic street totems; tattoos of rats and sea witches, Russian dolls with balaclavas and Virgin Marys holding crowbars; dramatic eye make-up and silver piercings through lips, septa, tongues; black boots and fingerless gloves. Most would assume we are part of the children's crusade that marches up and down Camden High Street every weekend — yet another crew of hopeless fashionistas concocting an identity through accessories, victims of manufactured desires and programmed insecurities. If anything, we are the antithesis of a black bloc — anonymous in our extreme individuation — at least, from an external point of view. Yet I'd bet almost none of the zombified participants in that weekly shopping trawl would have guessed the contents of the bag we'd stashed at our booted feet.

'Actually, I think we'd all identify more as nihilists. Now

fuck off.'

*

The alarm is deafening, and the fire door has swung shut behind us, imprisoning us inside without the vital tools to escape. For long seconds, my heart pounds in time to the searing klaxon as we race around the upstairs bar like rats in a trap.

'The window! We can jump back out the window!'

We try to lever it up, jamming it against the air conditioning unit. The drop down into the alley is an ankle-smashing ten metres, but somewhere in my fear-frazzled brain this seems logical.

'Call someone from outside!'

'They can't do the climb up to the window!'

'Fuck! Fuck! Fuck!'

'Are we trapped? Who closed the door?'

'Does it fucking matter? How do we get it open?'

'Where are the tools?'

'Just keep taping the fucking sensors!'

Even through my amphetamine-addled senses, the irony of becoming locked inside a building we had wished to open, and then secure, was not lost on me. It felt almost like a trap had been set, anticipating our arrival, a snare tightening and a set of metal jaws snapping shut.

Suddenly the fire door opens, and the empty looking face of our look-out from the street comes through it.

'Why's everyone shouting so much?'

'DON'T SHUT THAT DOOR!'

As the alarms quieten, we explore the darkness, locating fuse boxes and examining piles of debris. By the door is a glaring void where the painting depicting Mother Black Cap used to hang.

*

'MOTHER BLACK CAP IS BACK — AND SHE'S PISSED OFF!'

A day later, we dealt with the police, who were satisfied we had occupied the Black Cap legally, and that it was now a civil dispute between us and the owners. After a week of cleaning floors and locking doors, we threw them open to the crowds to celebrate her return for one final night of debauchery.

The girl on stage is re-enacting the stations of the cross — maybe she gets the Crass reference, maybe not — but it seems like it has never been interpreted quite like this. She has danced a furious pop-jazz ensemble to pounding hip-hop rhythms, stripping down to a giant pair of Y-fronts and tube socks. She squatted on the face of her disciples as they were prostrate across the back of one another, and then squirted water from her vagina into the faces of the braying audience. Now, she sits astride a chair, her fist inserted into her cunt, legs splayed in the air, pumping herself like some giant meat-puppet. Perhaps it's fitting. This is indeed a resurrection, and a crucifixion, but a queer, feminist one, that ultimately ends in sacrifice, and the death of a legend.

Behind her, a big-breasted DJ in a pink wig and the gigantic Polish sound engineer whoop and cheer as I watch from the wings with the other acts, feeling glorious in my Dutch milkmaid outfit of a gingham pinafore and ginger wig, complete with cap, pigtails and gimp mask.

Journalists mill through the crowds, taking quotes from flamboyantly decked out party-goers: 'It's not just about sexuality − it's about space. Where do the queers go, the punks, the marginalised and disenfranchised? These are the peoples that made Camden, created a zone where people could be what they wanted to be. There is no space left for us here. The bougies are squeezing us out like pus from a spot.'

'We're here, we're queer, we're anarchists, we'll fuck you up!'

The Black Cap is an embodiment of queer history, past, present and future, packed with a melange of old regulars and new faces from the squat collective. Tattoos and bare flesh, wild eye make-up and hair extensions, clean-cut twinks and hairy bears, butch femmes and mohawked crusties — a riot of sexualities and modifications and bizarre, wondrous in-betweens and ambiguities. Male and female collapse into one another and back out the other side. The dance-floor is packed, heaving with bodies grinding and bouncing against one another in a sweaty, amorphous confusion, or effortlessly whirling around like protons and electrons blasted free from the bonds of physics. Disco balls twirl in the gloom above and a row of plasma screens play porno featuring a man with penises for hands.

'I came here as a 20-year-old in the 80s and there were older gay people here, queer people. That gave me a sense of history, that I belong somewhere to a culture. I learnt a lot about my queer history from places like this. It's essential that we don't lose that.'

The first half of the night featured a smattering of anarchist poetry that prompted a passionate intervention by a short-haired woman called Abigail who decried the appropriation of queer culture by outsiders. I threw the microphone to her to allow her to voice her upset.

'This is a queer space for queer people, and we've got this cunt on-stage talking about men he admires!'

I couldn't deny it. My poetry had praised John Cooper Clarke, Alfredo Bonnano, and in my defence, Emma Goldman, but perhaps in such a fast-paced style that people could not catch every reference. It was simple enough to solve. Give the mike to the mikeless, a voice to voiceless.

Abigail shared her story with us. 'The last two years we've been regular and being a tranny, point is, you're so welcome. I swear to God we haven't been welcome anywhere like this have we? I swear. Nowhere. You don't have to be gay, you don't have to be lesbian. Everybody's welcome. And that's the Black Cap, that's what it's all about.'

Other acts smashed laptops on-stage to the tune of 'I Can't Live If Living Is Without You', sang Subhumans lyrics over cheesy pop backing tracks, or dressed in drag and performed Class War anthems with a trio of old crusties, flashing bulging genitalia through skimpy black panties and stockings.

'Camden used to be a land of punks, poor artists, squatters, sometimes all in one. Once upon a time a squat in Camden would not cause a headline nor an eyelid battering and now that's no longer the case. The squatters should be welcomed back to Camden — they were part of what made it what it is today.'

Oberon White opens the second half. He waits in the wings,

but there is something wrong. No matter how I introduce him, he refuses to enter the stage, and I am left floundering and laughing before a rolling rabble of reprobates. He is mummified, tissues and cloth wrapped around his head and arms. Maybe he is blind and cannot see me. I introduce him again, and then flee the stage to let him sort it out. Lurking by the dressing room, the murmurs of an expectant crowd are deafening in my ears. Slowly, he raises his arms, and staggers zombie-like on to the stage to peals of squealing violins. His assistant scampers on behind, and slowly unwinds the bandages from around him. Underneath, he is ethereal, ghostly face painted in a skull rictus, a Pierrot-clown with a black tear dripping from one kohl-rimmed eye. As he is unveiled, he begins to sing in a sweet operatic tenor, the crisp clear sonorous notes slicing through the sudden smoky silence of the bar.

'So what is wanted in Camden? A load of rich investors in sterile flats? I'm sick of amazing buildings and venues being taken over by "developers". And before you ask, I run a business here and have done for 20 years, I am totally opposed to the gentrification.'

As he sings, his assistant begins to unwind a clothesline hung with black-and-white portraits of victims of sexual violence: people persecuted for being queer in Russia, in the

Ukraine, in Africa, people beaten and jailed and murdered for their sexual orientation. Pictures of the fresh-faced Jody Dobrowski — murdered on Clapham Common in 2005 by thugs who suspected him to be gay; an image of the Admiral Duncan pub in Soho, bombed in April 1999, by a former British National Party member, killing three people and wounding at least 70; of Giovanna Del Nord, a 46-year-old trans woman, attacked minutes after entering The Market Tavern in Leicester, without warning punched in the head and knocked unconscious; of Steven Simpson, an autistic, openly gay 18-year-old, who had homophobic slurs written on his body and was set on fire at his birthday party. All the while, the only sound remaining is the sonorous tenor of the crying clown and the wailing lament of violins behind him.

'I'm a Camden resident and a few weeks ago while walking home, I witnessed something going on in the doorway of the Black Cap between a man and woman where the woman was screaming being pushed up against the door in the doorway. Others were intervening and I didn't want to get into a threatening situation, but I waved down a passing police car and asked them to go and investigate.'

All through the wild melee of the night, the police kept coming round, checking in on us, but with the in-house sound system having built-in limiters and a closed-door policy, they had more than enough drama dealing with the herds of thrill-seekers ploughing the trail up and down between Chalk Farm and Mornington Crescent. The queer scene has had a culture of resistance since the days of Stonewall and the Gay Liberation Front — we felt confident that tonight, we had reclaimed for ourselves a space in the heart of Camden.

'The area around the Black Cap is quiet and a perfect spot for far more serious and damaging crimes than squatters would commit. I urge Camden police to allow Camden Queer Punx 4Eva to stay in the Black Cap until they can agree what will be done going forward. As a member of the Queer community and a Camden local — I wish the Queer Punx well.'

One old-timer told us some history: 'When the Black Cap used to be split in two, there was a faux-wall between the front and back to hide the sodomites from the prying eyes of Babylon. Symbolically, the wall came down as the law and the culture changed. It is easy to forget that within living memory homosexuality was a crime. Times have liberalised, but also become less radical. Still this space — our space — is under attack, from the creeping tentacles of gentrification.'

A queer-punk painted up to look like a cat chipped in:

'The Black Cap used to be so fucking mainstream. I never used to go there. Just middle-class, bougie as fuck. Mug gay yuppies!'

*

We lose in court, the judge upholding the claimant's case that we were trespassers, and granting them possession of the building forthwith. At eight o'clock the next morning High Court enforcers crowbar the door and inform us that we have been evicted. A man in a zebra-print miniskirt with hoop earrings and an Alsatian on a string stands reading to the newly homeless crowd from a long scroll.

'And so, Mother Black Cap joins the ranks of the fallen across London, as yet more LGBT venues succumb to the curse of gentrification. RIP, dear Mother, in this incarnation born 1965, died 2015.'

A skinhead female next to him, two white rats climbing about her breasts, is furious, berating his every utterance.

'Queer liberation, not queer consumerism!

Out in the street, Camden is stirring, shoppers and commuters streaming towards the tube station across the road. As we sit on our collection of luggage, sleeping bags and feather boas, I look south towards the city. Sliding along the road towards us is a lumpen old lady, wrapped in diaphanous veils and cardigans of heavy-knit wool, pushing a trolley laden with treasures wrapped in plastic.

'She joins Madame Jojo, formerly of Soho, who opened her doors and her legs to many a punter and many a good time, from 1966 to 2014.'

Atop the crone's rolling pile, a mangy cat sits regally cleaning its genitals, a slender leg arched towards the clear blue skies. She approaches, the repetitive creak of one wheel growing louder and louder as she drags herself and her possessions towards us. Her face looks like rotting fruit left too long on the sun, the skin slack and riddled with spidery red veins, in shocking contrast to the thick electric blue arteries that stand like electrical cable between the delicate avian bones of her hands. She shuffles, seemingly held erect by her trolley, as if engaging in a slow motion collapse all the way down the length of the Camden High Street.

'The fire will not consume us! We take it and make it our own!'

'And let us not forget those stubborn bastions of mutual cock-sucking and feverish buggery: the Coleherne, 1955 to 2010, and the King Edward IV of Islington, 1966 to 2011.'

She pulls up alongside us, her breath wheezing, and turns a pair of eyes like pebbles in dish of red rice towards us, peering out at us from the folded skin of her face. Her trolley stands a scant inch from the shoe of a Metropolitan police

116

officer who has attended to ensure there is no breach of the peace. Her scarf, purple and black, is a fleshy wattle hanging from under her chin. She waits, timeless, patient as the ages, turning her gaze towards the uniformed man before her.

'Out of the way, copper!'

The officer leaps around, startled, and backs out of the way, nearly falling into the road in his surprise. A wry smile twists the blue lips, and she angles a gleeful glance towards us.

'Mugs, all of you.'

She departs, slipping between bailiffs and commuters and off towards Chalk Farm. She looks like she has been here since 1751 — a vision of Mother Black Cap herself, timeless, eternally wandering these streets, the Crone of Camden, as defiant and unstoppable as ever, rejected and reviled, yet as integral to these streets as the stones themselves. As she goes I turn my gaze skyward, looking up at the facade of the Black Cap.

'The Little Apple, Nelson's Head, Man Bar, Candy, Blush, the G-A-Y, all struck down in the flush of their youth and growing maturity. Whither next for the fags and the dykes? Where shall all the homos go? And what fate awaits the trannies and the benders? They are sexually cleansing the boroughs of London — first Soho, now Camden. Are we all to be forced to accept the high street's tepid and limp offerings

— like kittens licking skimmed milk from capitalism's turgid dugs? Are we forced to become vanilla — acceptable, so long as we cause no trouble — our sexuality and our lifestyle choices just another option within consumerism? We are here, we are queer, where can we have a beer?'

The rainbow flag is being dragged inside by a lumpen bailiff hanging out the window. The effigy of a banker in a suit slumps limply beside it. He is unceremoniously pulled within. The hand-painted cardboard sign falls from his limp plastic hands, and the words 'I $OLD CAMDEN' slap down on to a pavement at the booted feet of a High Court Enforcer. I sigh, and begin to gather up my possessions, wondering where there might be space for me now.

'WE DON'T WANT EQUAL RIGHTS — WE WANT REVENGE!'

The Camden Blood Thieves

Salena Godden

I have a meeting with my manager in the Camden pub, The Lock Tavern. The meeting is tense with that horrible sensation of having to fight my corner, of being a small coloured fish in vast ocean of great white sharks. There are worries about the record company and the release date being moved. During the meeting my heart sinks as I realise how much work I have to do, and how much more patient I have to be.

I also realise I haven't left the house or spoken to anyone for six days. My manager buys beers and it feels nice to be in Camden, sitting in the pub garden of the Lock Tavern. It is quite a lovely afternoon in August, I'd almost forgotten that it is summer and whilst he is at the bar ordering two more beers, I watch a butterfly and inhale a distant smell of beef burgers, the smoke and grease of a BBQ over the fence and somewhere else, somewhere in other people's lives.

He returns to the table with beer and two shots of gold tequila.

Salt. Shot. Lime.

And we laugh and begin to talk of other things, chasing the tequila with delicious ice-cold beer. I feel happy and relaxed now, and smoke my manager's cigarettes. He says he is quitting and gives me the whole pack. He asks me about my life, my love life, I tell him it's empty, and he laughs and starts telling me, 'You should get out more.'

'I know,' I laugh, 'I know.'

'You'll find it one day,' he assures me with a smile. My agent is handsome and tan. He wears all-white; a white linen suit and a white shirt. He makes me feel good, but too soon we finish two more beers and then he says he has go to meet another musician. We leave the pub at the same time, shake hands and say good evening. My head is buzzing and I realise I must be a little tipsy. The beers and tequila have made me feel hopeful and giddy. Above me the sunset is indigo and beautiful. There's a song on a loop in my heart, a melody, and I am humming it as I walk up towards the Kentish Town swimming baths and then hang a right onto Kentish Town Road.

Walking and humming I begin to realise how lonely I am. People pass me with their busy lives, engrossed in their mobiles phones or zooming past in cars filled with music and suddenly it dawns on me that my flat will be silent and dark, I dread it and feel afraid. Those beers and that tequila have made what was my romantic solitude now unbearable and a little depressing. There is a new bar in my Tufnell Park neighbourhood, it is themed like the Tarantino movie *From Dusk 'til Dawn*. I wander into the dark bar and buy a large rum and coke and sit alone. I feel a little strange, a woman drinking alone at a bar, sitting up on a bar stool. So I take out my notebook and remember the tune and begin writing some blues lyrics about the rum, the bar, the jars of olives and the patterns in the scratches in the surface of the wooden bar top. There is a beautiful Spanish girl behind the bar with bright green eyes and I write about her too, with her hair like oily black snakes cascading down her back, her white summer dress, her tiny waist and delicate wrists.

Before long a man in a white suit leans over to talk to me. He introduces himself and tells me he is from Algeria and soon I make him laugh. I feel boozy but witty. He rises to the bait and words reel out of me, rhetoric, irony, I think I am Dorothy Parker, or something, I am Mae West, this is a smooth script, rehearsed banter …

The Spanish girl behind the bar rolls her eyes at his clumsy attempts to pick me up, I laugh, she laughs, he laughs, his inept approach is endearing in a way. We all laugh and I feel like I am watching *Cheers*, I am hilarious, I am in a television sitcom. Soon it is midnight, I pay my bill and I find myself asking the Spanish girl for a nightcap.

'One for the road,' I grin and the Spanish girl says, 'On the house!'

She pours three shots of tequila.

Salt. Shot. Lime.

And we say cheers and thank you and lovely meeting you and thank you again and goodnight and … I'm a little better for the drinks and the laughter and I'm resigned to walk up the Dartmouth Park Hill to my home. I remember some black beans and rice I'd made for breakfast and I'm suddenly hungry.

The air is balmy, the moon is a Cheshire Cat smile, a perfect crescent, the stars are bright. Foxes are out a-strolling, cats a-leaping, the bushes and the undergrowth is a-lively with summer.

As I round the corner I hear something behind me, or rather a voice calling, *hey!* I turn to see it's the Algerian man from the bar. He trots to catch me up, I observe his suit is all-white, he is head to toe in white. He is shorter than me, I notice this now he is not on a bar-stool. I look down at him and ask him if he's following me, yes he says, and no, and then he says he wants to go for another drink with me. He tells me he liked our conversation and wants to continue it. I'm close to my house, but I don't want him to know where I live. I do not want to take him to my home. I hate people in my flat looking at my things, touching my books, making the place untidy with their looks.

We take a left and cut down the back of the Acland Burghley School and sit on the train bridge and watch the night trains. When the long freight trains come they feel like whales surfacing, I tell him, this is as close as you can get to the ocean in the city; sitting on train bridges, the vibrations of night trains are whales. We sit in the middle of the bridge, talking and listening to the trains. I tell him again about the ocean, that when I sit on train bridges the night trains become whales. He tells me he is a man with a broken heart. He tells me about his sadness. He tells me how he met his son for the first time, but he would not see his son ever again. He would see his son for this one visit only and forever. I thought it was very sad. He told me the story again and again, and no matter how many times he told it, the ending was the same, he would not see his son again.

I fish for my cigarettes and ask for a light. After he lit my cigarette, we tell each other some of the same things about our lives but he would not say what he did for work. He looked to me like a taxi driver. I mean, I did not think he was anything exciting or dangerous, I thought he was just an ordinary, albeit sad, man from Algeria who won't see his son again. With some new spirit he tells me he remembers he knows a secret members bar that is open all night. Suddenly this seems like a brilliant idea. We get back on our feet and head to the corner of Junction Road where he hails a black cab.

How strange, how bizarre, that we pull up outside The Lock Tavern.

'The pub is closed ...' I begin but he grins and bends to open a hatch on the pavement.

'Come! Quick!' he urges, and I'm so curious that I follow him down the stone stairs into what you'd expect to be the pub beer cellar. It's dark down there, but as my eyes adjust to the gloom, I see we are in a tunnel lit by candles, we are in a maze, a series of tunnels that appear to run under the road to The Stables Market and down to Camden Lock. A disused tube tunnel perhaps? There's a dank smell, damp and brackish, wet walls and moss. He leads me, left and right and down one more narrow tunnel to a heavy black door, we enter it to find a red room, a decadent room of dark red velvet and candles.

Pale girls shimmy and shimmer, dancing with handsome young men, also all wearing white. We stand at the bar as he orders himself a whiskey and me a rum. We take a big squashy sofa, it is like sinking in a puddle of leather red velvet chocolate cake. We drink, smoke cigarettes, and watch the beautiful people, writhing bodies, a smoky blur of white and flesh, the boom-boom of the bass-line and the chatter. We try to continue our conversation, but the music is too loud. Soon he becomes boring about the son story, yes, he is still telling the story about the son he will never see again. We have stopped making each other laugh and we have stopped hearing each other. With the loud music and the slinky bodies around us he leans too close and I smell the whiskey on his breath and he starts to tell me about a back room. We have to shout to be heard, this room is behind that red curtain, he gestures, but no matter how many times he tells me about the room, I don't want to go there, I don't know why, just that I don't. And soon he starts almost begging me to come to the back room. I can see the red curtain and again I shake my head at him, no. The more insistent he is the more resistant I become, I don't like his urgency. He flares up and tells me I have changed. He tells me I was nicer at the first bar and that I am different now. He curls his lip and spits, 'Why have you changed?'

His face hardens, his features suddenly have no warmth

and this room is so strange, so I tell him I have to go. I stand and go to leave, he goes to grab my arm and I shake it off and run, shoving through the crowd and out through the door. I retrace my steps, run down the wet tunnels to the stone stairs and push the trap door open to take me back up to the pavement, street level. I slam the trap door closed, I imagine I hear him running and calling me. I'm afraid he will follow me. Back on the streets I know so well, I begin to run, taking the back alleys, my head buzzing, heart racing, I shoot down the back of The Stags Head pub and then up towards The Fiddlers Elbow on Prince Of Wales Road, in a zig-zag, through the estates, just in case he is trying to follow me. I feel watched, I worry he may have jumped into a taxi and be following me.

Once on the Prince of Wales Road I stop and take a breath. I'm near the Kentish Town West Overground station, it is closed. I look up at the night sky, it is very late and dark and I feel alone, vulnerable. It is too quiet and so I start to sing to cheer my walk, I try to remember my new rum song from earlier and then I hear a harmonica. Faint at first, in the distance, but it catches me. There walking by the Kentish Town swimming baths, on the other side of the road, a shock of white hair, a crest like a Mohican and from underneath it, a man in a white suit plays harmonica. Sweet blues pours like molasses into the night air. I feel like I know the tune, I cross the road humming, I begin singing and we fall into step and a beat without speaking a word of introduction. I sing and the harmonica player blows into his cupped hands and we walk, playing together, up Anglers Lane and onto the Kentish Town Road.

Finally we stop and sit on a bench. We are at the top of Dartmouth Park Hill but like the Algerian, I don't want to lead him to my front door. He says he is locked out of his flat and didn't want to wake the neighbours with smashing glass and kicking in the doors, again, so he is walking until morning, just playing harmonica, and walking the streets of the neighbourhood. Then he looks at me and begins to sing. He tells me I am like this song, then he trickles it to me, eerily, a weak warbling voice. The words are French, he tells me it is about a girl who lives in a pile of books, a girl that is hidden in her tower of books and he says that I remind him of this song. And as he sings I find I remind myself of the song too. How does he know? I wonder, how does he know I live in a dusty pile of books and writing?

He is so thin and white that I can see how his jawbone works, I see his bones through his opal skin. His eyes are hollow and ink blue, deeply set, and pushed into his head as though his eyes were coal and face were made of snow.

He tells me he is psychic. He knows where people come from and where they are going to, he says the spirits of people exhaust him because he can feel them so acutely, empathically. He says he never eats or sleeps. Then he describes a time he was tortured in prison with electrodes and when he speaks he looks away, down at the pavement or at his roll-up. I imagine a cold police cell with a stone floor, I imagine electrodes pressed to the side of his hollow temples. I picture a basement, a chair by a bucket of water and one light bulb swinging from the ceiling and I shudder and continue to listen.

'Every girlfriend I have ever had has died,' he says, and he pauses as though recollecting each death, hardly once looking up or looking me in the eye. In profile his bottom lip protrudes, hang dog, it hangs flatly out over the ridge of his chin, and his accent, his voice is all French melodrama. He tells me about Marseille and the police picking him up to beat him up on purpose, just for sport, and he says he'll never go back to France again. I listen as he speaks seductively and slowly, taking time to draw breath and reveal each action and consequence. As I look up at the stars he tells me these stories, I watch the moon, the stars all a-glitter as I smoke and listen to this strange stranger.

He tells me:

'I used to squat you know ... I'd walk around like this, late at night and find houses that were empty and go have a nose about. You can tell when a house has been left for a long time and I'd find all sorts I tell you, rare and antique things, first edition books, candelabras, antiques and paintings. I could tell which houses others hadn't found yet, I had an eye for it. One time there was a house I had been checking out and then I decided I had waited long enough and I went to go in. The front door was jammed with old post, stacks of tin cans and glass jars, but I got in through the kitchen window. It smelled awful, there was washing-up all piled up and rotting. They'd been someone there quite recently, you could tell by the date on the milk. I could feel the presence of someone, I checked the other rooms and then I knew, I remember thinking, he's in there, that room, he's in there ... I stood outside the door and thought he's in there, that's the main bedroom, I just knew it. So I opened the door and there was a stink and a hot wind, like an almighty hot gush of wind, I saw the electric fire was on full and then I looked and I saw there was a body, someone there, he suddenly sat up in the bed, whoosh, with a gasp and this hot wind with his hands out stretched, bags of blood attached to his arms, I saw his yellow dead face, dead pale, drained he was, and I tell you, I ran and got out of there as quick as I could. Did

I go back ever? Well, once I got over the shock. There was a painting on the kitchen wall, a Gustav Klimt print, I went back and took it. I think the door opening must've caused some sort of vacuum, what with the heater being on full and that must have been what made the dead body sit up, it was drained of blood though ...'

Then he says:

'I tried to sell my blood in Camden. There are men in the market trying to buy blood all the time. I was approached by one man who said, come with me, and so I followed him down some stairs, along a dark tunnel under the Camden market to a dark basement. There were red velvet curtains and a bed and all the equipment and stuff. Before I knew it, I was in a heavy sleep, I didn't see him put a needle in my arm, he just touched me there, here, in between my eyes with his thumb, like this ... I went totally under ... Then what happened was ... well ... when I came around I saw he was fitting up a second bag, then filling up a third bag from my arm and I couldn't lift my head or move, I was paralysed as my blood was being drained from me and then I went to sit up and the man did it again, he put his thumb between my eyes and I was under a spell, in this paralysed state. I thought, *he's going to take all of my blood, he's going to drain me, he is going to kill me right here and now*. I saw him fitting up

130

a fourth bag to fill with my blood and I thought it's now or never and I just about managed to sit up and pull the needle from my arm and that broke the spell and I said, 'You are a dirty blood thief, dirty filthy blood thief, now give me my money!' Did he pay me? Too right he did, he knew I knew something was up, he knew, and I tell you I ran out of there as fast as I could ...'

I shiver, remembering the Algerian, I am trying to say something, but I cannot get a word in edgeways, this man in white, he is full of horror. Momentarily, I imagine I am imagining him, so I reach out to touch his sleeve to check he is really there, he is, and he says I am not the first person to think he is a ghost, lots of people have said that. I look up at the night sky and listen as he continues. He tells me about breaking into an empty house and finding a cot with the skeleton of a dead baby in it. The cot was in a cupboard under the stairs. Such darkness, such sadness under the stars.

'... I am being poisoned.' He blurts to me, 'I hardly eat now in case she has been in. Who? This woman. She breaks into my room and has been feeding me her schizophrenia pills, tampering with my food, I know she has. How can I tell? I can tell alright. You know when she's been in. She's trying to poison me and these pills, right, they make your blood thick, you can hardly swallow, they make your blood like syrup and thick and once one morning I woke up and opened my eyes but I couldn't see, my eyes were still in the back of my head, but my eyelids were open and I started screaming. My blood was so thick and I could feel my eyes, they were dry and rolled in the back of my head and I couldn't turn them to look forwards. Imagine that! Imagine!'

I do, and I leap up and say, 'Stop now, that's just horrible, horrible ...' but he continues, 'Imagine opening your eyes and they are still in the back of your head and you can't see!'

'I can imagine it, now stop, stop, stop!'

I scrunch up my eyelids and blink and blink again to make sure my eyes still look forwards.

The harmonica man, he has so much bleak and black about him, so much darkness in a white suit, and I ask him to try a smile. He tries a weak smile and it fails and falls off his face. There is a chill in the air and he shivers and we decide to walk some more. We head down the hill to the an all-night off license on Fortess Road, opposite the Thai Blue Moon Restaurant and we buy a bottle of vodka and then walk back past the Acland Burghley school and cross the bridge.

'This is a good spot and we can hear the night trains ...' I begin to tell him, 'the trains are the whales of the city night.'

And I think how strange to come here with two different people to talk on the same bridge in the same night, I realise I have been in a loop all night, running in circles. It is good to stop running in circles.

He takes out his harmonica and plays, improvising with the long slow mail trains clattering and groaning below us. He plays and I begin to sing with the trains as our percussion, the ocean is all train tracks. The night trains are whales beneath us, moaning, disappearing slowly into the blackness of the tunnel, they light up the discarded shopping trolleys and plastic litter. There are feral cats and foxes skulking, the moon is sinking in the distance, the purring of a summer's night, animals glowering from the shadows. We are watched by the first blackbird and Aurora begins to paint the sky all fuchsia and violet.

Dawn is rose and the bottle is done. The dew makes us damp and we shiver, our teeth chatter a little. I make a decision to invite him back to my home for a warming cup of tea. Back at my place I play him some records. His eyes are wide as a child's looking at my things, his eyes eat everything, the photographs on the walls, the shrines and precarious piles, papers and books left open everywhere, he looks at it all.

I think I must begin to fall asleep, all I remember next is his thumb stroking between my eyebrows. He tells me that very day he met his father for the first time, but he would not see his father ever again. He would see his father for this one visit only and forever. He tells me this story again and again, and no matter how many ways he tells it, the ending was the same, he would not see his father ever again. Not after tonight, he repeated.

I was somewhere between sleep and dreams but still listening to the words of the sad story, it reminded me of … something … bzzzzzzz … the air is thick … smoky … I smell something … his hand over my mouth and nose … I am heavy.

I hear a voice in the dark, it is seductive, then I hear two voices, he is the Algerian, they are one voice, they are one, and then they are two voices, I feel hands, many hands, hot smoke and breath, I do not know these words or the language. I feel as though I'm falling but I'm tied down, I am under, and I am falling into black space. I hear the breathing, it is close to my neck and hot.

I am hot when I wake up. My head is hurting and weighed down. I try to sit up, I try to look around the room to see where I am but I am blind. My eyes are open, I can feel it, my eyes are wide open, but my eyeballs are rolled back and glued to the back of my skull. I blink and blink and no matter how many times I squeeze my eyelids, open, shut, open, shut, the irises are rolled back into the back of my head. I panic. I want to rub my eyes and claw and slap at my face, but my arms are tied down, I cannot move my arms, I cannot move my head, my heart banging in my chest, horrible, panic, black and red, the bloody velvet of the back of my head, the inside of my eye sockets, my veins, my brains, my thick, slow blood. I try to move, I want to scream, but my voice has gone, no sound, I am gaping mouthed, silent as a fish, I am tied down, wires suck hungrily from my arms, needles with mouths are attached to blood bags, I am in a red velvet room, I am underground, I am being drained …

I am hot when I wake up, I am sweating, and I am alone on my sofa. I blink and I can see, I am home. I can see! I try to make sense of it all and sit up and shake my head as if this will shake the nightmare. I look in the bathroom, the bedroom, but I am totally alone in my flat. The heating is on full, it is stifling. I open all the curtains and windows, I need air, as I begin to recall and process fragments of it all, deciphering the dream from the memory and the fiction. I remember the bar, the Algerian with his white suit. Then the loner, dressed in white, playing harmonica in the road under the moon. I remembered the bridge and the percussion of freight trains, whales in the night ...

I walk about my tiny flat, thirsty and paranoid. I look in the wardrobe and under the bed but nobody is hiding there, no God or Devil. I begin to tidy up. Everything is where I left it before I left for my meeting yesterday, nothing is stolen or lost, nothing out of place — except for one thing — with dishwater bubbles dripping off my hands, I glance up and hanging on my kitchen wall, a huge beautiful framed painting. It is a golden picture of a girl in gold leaf by Gustav Klimt, the figure, she lies naked, she is sleeping and surrounded by colours, dreams and patterns, it's like that story and it is like the song about the girl who lives in a pile of books. I sit alone at my kitchen table staring up at the Klimt painting, shining gold, for a very long time.

Notes on London's Housing Crisis

Will Wiles

Day to day, it's easy to forget that London is in the grip of a profound housing crisis. This extraordinary city remains one of the best places in the world to live, work and have fun. On the surface, the capital is prosperous, busy and happy. But gather Londoners around a dinner table and the talk will often turn to house prices. Many people have friends and family members in grim conditions that at times seem inescapable. For some of us, paying for the roof over our heads has become a treadmill. Our ability to choose where we live is retreating. Many people feel that they have been short-changed by the city.

These problems can at times appear insurmountable and inevitable: just part of the condition of London in 2016, a condition that arose in the natural course of the city's development and that we all have to accept. But the failures of London's housing supply were not inevitable. The city could have turned out very differently. It's sometimes hard to remember that: the city is an aggregation of human intentions and decisions, all of which could have gone another way.

London is always changing, but also remains very much the same place. At present I live in Camden, and from the 30th level I'm able to look out over a city that would be recognisable to a Victorian: the green expanse of Regent's Park, the silver band of the Thames, that grey-brown-yellow patchwork of brick and stucco. Even the contributions of the last century have mellowed into timeless familiarity: the Post Office tower, the cathedrals of culture on the South Bank, the great metalled hulk of Midlands East Coast Station down at King's Cross, Cedric Price's space frame over the Great Court of the British Museum, the tree strucs of Soho, Fitzrovia and Finsbury, and the far gleam of the CLR James Linear struc, winding its way through Brixton and Peckham. In the east, the sun rises behind the towers of the electronics giants — Pye, EKCO, Marconi Systems, Beer Cybernetics — at Wapping, and glints off the wings of a wide-bodied BOAC Comet 20 as it begins its final descent into Stafford Cripps International at Cliffe.

I'm presently plugged in the Walter Sickert Housing Structure, a tree overlooking the Dickens Linear. As I write, seated at the dining table in my kitchen pod, I can see some of my neighbours in Dickens are upgrading what looks like a living room. A service crane has attached itself to the old pod and, with an eruption of escaping pigeons, out it comes. Everything is automated, pushbutton; right now in the struc's control centre, or at County Hall, an operator from the GLC's housing authority might be watching blocks moving on a screen, but they don't need to do or approve anything. The crane extends, removing the pod from the ziggurat side of the struc, dangling it over the canal; then it turns sharply, transferring the pod to an access rail. The replacement pod is waiting there, clean and shiny, yet to be baptised by the London rain and pollution. Through the binoculars I can make out the brand: Conran, very chic and minimal, but a triple-width pod has a lot of room for minimalism. It's exactly the kind of conspicuous, expensive good taste I've come to expect from Dickens Linear. Already the crane has it clamped, and repeats its just-completed actions in reverse, swinging out over Camden, then retracting to move the pod into its dock.

In a few short years we'll be celebrating the 50th anniversary of the first strucs — half a century in which we have been able to take this kind of endless flexibility for granted. Or rather, half a century of being promised total flexibility and finding that the reality doesn't quite live up to the pledge. Still, it's a system with remarkable strengths. Plug and live is only a couple of grand for a starter set, easy terms, manageable even if you're on nothing more than the UBI. Upgrade your rooms as you please, as plainly or as expensively as you please. Nothing to pay but the rent on your docks. And, if you tire of your neighbourhood, move house. Every pod you own can be moved to any SLOC in Greater London within 12 hours. Pushbutton arrangements. Wake up in Camden, get on the Bennet, book your new docks, go to the pub, and go to bed in Blackheath. Think! Don't drink and reSLOC. Remember where you docked your home.

But those neighbours of mine, down there in Dickens Linear — when did they last reSLOC? That living room of theirs is triple-width — their whole SLOC must be ten docks, double-width kitchen, double-width bedrooms, who knows what other extra bolt-ons. A top-level view out over the city, but it's a linear, so they can be on the train, Tube or Ringway in no time. If I had a SLOC like that I might never move. But I probably won't — because people like them might never move. And it's nice to be able to afford a Conran living-room set every three years. On the UBI plus a writer's pay I'm stuck with a basic Ikea 'Konstant' living room pod I bought in 2010. Its growing shabbiness would be bad enough, but I'm way behind on the operating software upgrades. It's prone to glitching in the lights and hifi, and more embarrassing afflictions. Imagine having girlfriends over to 'Ceefax & chill', only for their new Pyephone to pick up something nasty from the defective Bennet firewall. Meanwhile, dock rents continue to rise — some people have to pay more than £200 a month just for a three-bed home in central London. This is the present reality. For a few, housing costs are nudging towards an intolerable 20% of their household budget. It's worth taking a step back and understanding how we ended up in this state.

After the Second World War, housing was in huge demand across the developed world, and was accordingly built in vast quantities. To begin with, this new housing was designed exclusively along pre-War lines, as individual surface houses and apartment blocks. Some of these were constructed using novel techniques, and along modernist aesthetic lines, but typologically there was not a great deal of advance. But come the late 1950s and early 1960s, architects and designers were thinking more radically, and proposing continuous serviced frames into which mass-produced home units could be plugged and unplugged. The home could thus be liberated from the vagaries of the building site — it would no longer have to be 'built' at all, but instead could be mass-produced in factories, completely standardised. Cars and consumer goods were being made that way, said the pioneers, why not homes? The giant structures into which these consumer-friendly homes could be inserted would be very expensive to build, at first, but this was balanced out by the tumbling cost of the residential pods.

'Struc' housing of this kind was proposed by myriad architects including Archigram in the UK, Paul Rudolph in the USA and the Metabolists in Japan, and many others in Europe and the Communist bloc. On four continents, famous designers were clamouring for the same (or at least highly similar) technology. In retrospect, that gives the struc an air of inevitability. If it hadn't been tried in New York, surely it would have been tried in Tokyo; if not in Tokyo, then in London, surely.

No, not surely. Very little is truly inevitable — least of all an extraordinary breakthrough like the struc. The first experiments in the form were vastly expensive and desperately open to failure. Success had numerous preconditions: manufacturers taking up the idea, consumers adapting to a new way of thinking about their home, the law accommodating new forms of tenancy. My parents were surprisingly reluctant to part with their two-bedroom, trad house in Ladbroke Grove, even against the option of living twenty levels above the same neighbourhood in Alan Turing

Linear.

It's also arguable that strucs — at least in the linear form — would not have been possible without the grandiose road-building schemes the New York and London undertook in the 1970s. Today, it's as difficult to imagine London without its Ringways as it is to strip Paris of its Boulevards or Moscow of its Garden Ring. But the Ringways, and the Manhattan expressways, caused widespread dismay and protest when they were announced. A twist or two of local politics, and the whole network might never have appeared — and neither would the sites of the strucs.

Nothing about the strucs was inevitable. They were the product of determination and design. To accept any situation as inevitable or natural is to ignore the decisions and the ideologies that produced it.

Nevertheless, the next stages in the story of London's housing unfold with what sounds like the click of dominos. Housing costs tumbled in the 1970s and continued to decline in the 1980s. A couple of starter pods could be had for less than £200 in the first struc sections, a cost deliberately kept low to encourage uptake — and it worked. By the time the subsidies were withdrawn, production of pods had scaled up, and the entry prices stayed low. Even without starter deals, there was by then a lively market in second-hand pods. It is, just as the early prophets said, very much like buying a car: your first one is unlikely to be brand new. But unlike buying a car, a pod doesn't need an engine to provide shelter. What no one expected was the junked pods, stripped of struc certification, would still accommodate a few free spirits off-struc. Pop it on the back of a lorry, take it out to the plotlands of Essex or Kent, and live for free.

The growing availability of the new struc option drove down the price of other housing. In the first part of the century 'home ownership' had been a considerable marker of status. More than that, for people like my parents, having a house rooted in place in the dirt, unchanging apart from in the unappealing way they decay, symbolised a kind of security and solidity that it's now hard to understand. In retrospect it's obvious that housing should be as flexible as your living circumstances, and should easily grow or adapt to your changing family. The trad house is as ill-fitting and out-of-date as the Victorian frock coat. Imagine having to 'move house': disposing of all your rooms at the same time for an entirely new set, and having to move all your possessions at once.

But of course it was unlikely to be a move to a 'new' house — just another old one. And that's what really worked against the trad house — its expense. In earlier times, the cost of running a traditionally built home — maintaining all that dead plaster and inadequate wiring and hopeless plumbing — was offset by the accumulation of capital in the form of mortgage equity. With the strucs holding down house prices, and the banks chasing more lucrative short-term pod credit and losing interest in long-term mortgage credit on crumbling, depreciating assets, surface housing began to be a burden. The dilapidated, half-empty terraces of London we know today are the result.

If you're a middle-class bohemian or an architect, and you don't mind rotting floorboards or the smell of damp (and the associated bills), then there's rich pickings to be had from London's traditional housing stock. Hackney or Hammersmith council will give you a two-bed house in a terrace for five hundred quid, and be grateful to you. Ironically, this gives some Londoners the kind of flexibility that was once the preserve of struc-dwellers. Mobility within the strucs is dropping. During the 1980s, Londoners reSLOCed on average every four months, fully enjoying the freedom that the struc's designers imagined. That was certainly the way it was when I had my first couple of units, straight out of university. You'd reSLOC for a week, just to be near a friend's place for their birthday party, so you didn't have far to go home. You might reSLOC to be nearer a girlfriend on a third or fourth date. Today, Londoners reSLOC on average once every fourteen months. Desirable docks, such as the top level of Dickens Linear, overlooking Regent's

Park, are increasingly subject to 'camping', in which owners simply refuse to relocate. While perfectly legal, this is seen as being at odds with the spirit of the housing structures, and a reduction of their overall value. For sure, I keep a close eye on the top decks of Dickens, biding my time, hoping to be away from the Sickert's rather eccentric lifts — but if slots ever open up, I never see. I'm not organised enough. Sometimes it's tempting to look into that 'sniping' software you can get, which will jump in and reSLOC to a location of your choice as soon as it becomes available. In popular linear stretches, vacancy times are down to seconds. We know it happens, and it's technically legal, but most people consider it cheating.

Even less acceptable is 'multi-SLOCing', as increasingly practised by the more wealthy and sly struc residents: keeping multiple pod-clusters occupying docks in different locations. It used to be that even the most dedicated 'campers' would want to reSLOC eventually — for instance to enjoy a couple of weeks living in Brighton in the summer. But now they might keep a cluster year-round in a desirable SLOC by the seaside and simply travel there. Last year, County Hall announced it was looking into regulating multi-SLOCing, but it's hard to see how it can without introducing more bureaucracy and oversight into a system that is founded on simplicity and freedom. If I ever do luck into a SLOC on top of the Dickens, I'd be unlikely to want to let it go — so maybe I can't blame those neighbours of mine too much.

Meanwhile, costs are rising. Struc construction has slowed significantly since the beginning of the 21st century. In the 30 years to 2000, the number of available docks rose on average 30% every year. That pace of expansion could not, of course, be kept up indefinitely. The construction of the Ringway network — which cleared the ground for the Linears — was officially completed in 1991, and there are no serious plans for further expansion. The only Linear built since then followed the route of the high-speed rail link from the Channel Tunnel into Concorde Station, and after the delays and disputes that accompanied that project, there's little appetite for a reprise. Meanwhile, we are running out of appropriate sites for tree strucs. The central canopy is completed, and there are few opportunities for infill additions. Outside Ringway 1, there are thousands of hectares of under-populated, dilapidated surface housing that can yield sites, but not at a pace that can meet demand. Meanwhile an increasing proportion of the GLC Housing Authority's budget is taken up with maintenance and emergency repairs, both cost areas expected only to rise — finance for new strucs is tightening.

As dock supply fails to keep pace with rising demand, Londoners are also having to upgrade their rooms more often to keep pace with improvements in information technology. The average family used to upgrade its living room once every five years. That has now dropped to once every three years. My new Pyephone 12 simply refuses to connect with the command software in my Ikea living room and Hotpoint kitchen — and good luck trying to get a 10-year-old pod to connect to the Bennet at all.

What can be done? More strucs are plainly needed, particularly near the Docklands, Park Royal and Stratford thinkbelts, where most of London's new jobs are created. At the same time, the bright young things in those thinkbelts need to work less on the latest apps and gadgets, and more on making durable open-source strucware that won't simply glitch up within four years. In the meantime, perhaps pressure on the system can be eased by encouraging more people to live in traditional housing.

This might take effort. Trad housing is rightly seen as shabby, inconvenient and a bottomless money pit. However, if demand for surface housing can be increased just a little, a virtuous circle might be cause. The value of the old-fashioned houses and flats might begin to rise a little. This would be a welcome windfall for the owners, and in the long term might even amount to something like an investment. This rising value would give the owners an incentive to repair and improve their properties to further boost their value. If a trad house stopped being a miserable drain on resources, it might become more desirable, attracting more house-buyers and further raising prices. For a time, in the late 1950s and early 1960s, rising house prices were seen as a normal feature of what was then called a 'housing market'. It will be strange to see the provision of a basic need — shelter — as a 'market' with 'investments' and 'appreciation', rather than purely a technological, industrial matter of consistently exceeding demand. Utopian, even. But there was a time when mass-produced housing and residential megastructures were also seen as utopian and impractical, rather than the stuff of everyday life.

I'm prepared to do my part. Right now, I'm looking at a three-bedroom terraced house in Notting Hill — not the best neighbourhood, but Kensington & Chelsea only wants £675 to be rid of it. It'll cost maybe 20 times that to fix everything that's wrong with it, but I'm treating that as a new hobby. Next week I'll trade in my Sickert SLOC and binoculars for a toolbox and some plaster. It doesn't even have a Bennet connection — I expect to spend the next six months on the phone to the Post Office sorting that out. Back to the ground level. I don't know if my parents would be proud, or appalled.

Soft on the Inside

Noo Saro-Wiwa

If you're travelling on one of the buses going up the Essex Road in Islington, sit on the top deck of the bus and look to your left. Not too far from Angel tube station you'll see a shop window latticed with metal bars, shielding a bunch of animals. The bars aren't there for your protection, however; these animals can't move.

Some say taxidermy is a dying art; others call it the art of the dead. This particular taxidermist calls itself *Get Stuffed*, a name you may interpret as cheeky wordplay, or — if you're an animal conservationist — a middle-finger salute to the protection of endangered species.

A few years ago, somebody spied a pair of week-old tiger cubs on display at Get Stuffed and tipped off the police. The owner of this family-run business was subsequently jailed for six months after admitting he forged documents to get permits to buy protected species and sell them illegally.

Nowadays, the chastened boss only deals with specimens that have died of natural causes. His shop window bars are there to block the view of prying enemy eyes, and viewings are by appointment only.

Stuffing the dead is an interesting concept. It is said that we all have souls, and when we die our spirit departs to the afterlife, leaving behind a body. Yet though we are defined by our souls, we still get emotional about our outer packaging. To stuff a dead human being and mount them on public display is either an act of veneration or of gross disrespect, depending on the deceased's status. Lenin and Mao in glass boxes is okay, but an ordinary cadaver on public show is considered fucked up on all levels. Animals' bodies, on the other hand, are considered fair game. They can be pancaked by the tyres of road vehicles, hung from a butcher shop, mashed against a wall or worn around your neck.

Of course, no living person knows what happens after we or animals die. Only those of us who have reached the 'other side' understand that an animal's soul goes nowhere when denied a natural burial and decomposition. It is trapped in the body forever.

Take a look inside Get Stuffed and you'll see a lion, her face a crumpled, gaping rictus, roaring at nobody in particular. A zebra head is mounted on the wall, and a giraffe stands in the far corner by the window. Two squirrels — a red one and a grey one — are frozen in a holding-hands pose. The grey one is clutching a blank placard (someone thought this was a cute touch).

A Yorkshire terrier stands near the door. Her owner was an old Arsenal supporter who had died before he was due to collect the dog's stuffed incarnation. The taxidermist had removed the terrier's skin, applied some chemicals to it and wrapped it around a woollen, dog-shaped mannequin.

For a decade and a half this dog, known as Terri, had stood in this shop, staring at Zoe the zebra who was mounted directly opposite her. Looking at Zoe had been interesting, initially — her colouring was fascinating — but after a while the black and white stripes made Terri dizzy. Every day felt like one long LSD trip.

Day after day had Terri waited, hoping that each visitor to the shop was her owner. But they never were. Only voyeurs pretending to be serious buyers, poking at her nose and giggling. Other visitors were undercover conservationists sniffing around for illegal items. The animal activists got what they wanted: the two Bengal tiger cubs, Tanuja and Talib, who had been perched on a tree branch next to Terri. They were eight days old when the hunters came to the forest in Bandipur. Poor things, they had barely opened their eyes before being shot illegally. Their mother had tried to shelter them from the barrage of bullets, but to no avail. The twins each took a bullet in the abdomen. Hiding behind a tree, their mother watched the poachers lift her dead babies by the thighs and toss them into bags. She had to stifle her screams for fear of getting shot.

Someone called Don Galloway had sold Tanuja and Talib to a middleman who then sold them on to Get Stuffed. Galloway was a trophy hunter, a turd of a human being who loved animals in all the wrong ways. 'Population management' he called it. In truth, it was the thrill of the kill that got him going; each gunshot was like an ejaculation. Galloway administered a Facebook 'bragging board' page where fellow hunters could post photos of themselves displaying their prey. When he wasn't felling bears or posing next to colobus monkey carcasses, he was finding ways to shift his furry contraband across the continents. He always found a way. Not once had he been caught. The prosecutors hadn't even implicated him in the trial that led to the taxidermist's stint in jail.

On the morning the police raided Get Stuffed, they removed the tiger cubs and buried them somewhere. Although the other animals were sad to see the babies go, they were happy that they had been freed from their collective limbo. And everyone wanted Don Galloway's guts on a plate (quite literally, in the lion's case).

Then, one October evening in 2015, a strange thing happened: a whispering, disembodied voice told the stuffed mammals that they were now able to walk and talk, but that they had just 12 hours to make the most of it.

None of the animals knew who was behind this. Leon the lion reckoned it was the old Nigerian lady from Canonbury who had entered the shop one day and performed a *juju* spell (Leon knew about these things, he said, because he was born in the Tanzanian bush). In any case, the animals' glass eyes turned fleshy and began moving. They squirmed, shook their fur or (if they lacked torsos) puffed out their cheeks, their collective breath steaming up the shop windows.

The squirrels unlinked their paws immediately.

'Finally,' Red squirrel sighed, rubbing her wrist.

'Just be grateful you don't have to hold a placard too,' Grey squirrel huffed in his Philadelphia accent. He chucked the placard onto the floor.

'You've got nothing to complain about,' Red squirrel said.

'Oh god,' Grey flung his head back, 'here we go.' How many times had he heard about his ancestors 'coming over here' and squeezing out the native reds? Frankly, reds were their own worst enemy. They couldn't gather enough food to keep themselves going 'til dinnertime, never mind spring. As for their sex drive …

'You two, enough!' Terri the Yorkshire terrier said. 'Save your rage for the *real* enemy.' The dog panted excitedly at the front door. 'Look … they forgot to lock it properly!' The squirrels gawped at the entrance. 'You know what this means, don't you?' Terri squealed. 'We can track down Galloway.' For years they had been itching to avenge the twins' deaths. 'I'm gonna to deal with that prick,' she announced.

'I'm kamming with you,' said Goma the giraffe, her Swahili accent as strong as ever. She clip-clopped towards the door excitedly.

'Goma, you can't come,' Terri said. 'Look at you. You'll stick out like a sore thumb.'

'Yeah,' said Leon the lion, readying himself for the outing. 'You're too conspicuous.'

Terri laughed at Leon. 'And you're *not*?'

'Well … I'm not tall,' Leon blinked.

'You want to give the whole of London a heart attack?' Terri yapped. 'The police would order everyone indoors and you'd get shot. Just like the cubs.'

Leon tutted and lay back down on the floor. 'This was something I could've got my teeth stuck into.'

'I didn't know Galloway bothered you that much, Leon,' Red squirrel said. 'You normally don't give a toss about these things.'

The lion looked coy. 'Well ... it's been so long ... I just need ... there's a lioness around here, I can smell her.'

'She's in the zoo by Regent's Park,' Grey squirrel replied. 'You won't get anywhere near her. Just stay here.'

'Yeah, you'd better stay here with me,' Winston the wolf nodded — or at least tried to nod. His face was rooted to the floor since his torso was completely flattened. The taxidermist had given him a snarl that looked at odds with his pathetic prostration. Back in the day, carpet beetles sometimes crawled in and out of his mouth. Worse still, he only had the table legs to look at. He was bored shitless.

Goma the giraffe reluctantly agreed to stay behind with Winston. 'Can you get me some leaves, then?' she asked Terri.

The terrier smiled at her sympathetically. 'You don't actually need to eat, Goma. You *think* you do but it's just a phantom sensation.'

Terri motioned to the squirrels: 'Come on, you two, let's get out of here.'

Trying to conceal their smugness, the squirrels followed Terri out of the door.

'Rip Galloway's throat out for me,' Leon growled.

Terri and the squirrels were hit by the cool evening air. It smelled less polluted than Terri remembered, and it was a lot more crowded. Quite a few unfamiliar languages could be heard too.

They cantered down the Essex Road until they reached Islington Green. Red and Grey sprinted towards the trees, drunk with excitement. They chased each other around the grass and up a tree.

'Can you two get down from there, please?' Terri barked. 'We need to get to Galloway's house.' They remembered his address from the time he phoned for a taxi after his last visit to *Get Stuffed*. The squirrels scurried down the tree trunk.

Belsize Park was the destination, but getting there was tricky. How to use public transport without anyone noticing?

Terri hopped onto a 73 bus. 'Don't come in with me,' he told Red and Grey. 'You're too obvious.'

'So what do you want us to do?'

'Can you get onto the roof?'

'Sure.' Red and Grey scampered up a nearby tree and launched themselves onto the top of the bus.

The vehicle pulled away down the street. Passengers smiled at Terri like she was their long lost child. It had been a long time since she had got this kind of attention. She luxuriated in strokes and pats and tummy tickles, moving from one person to the next, responding to their beckoning: *Hello baby … hey little one … oh aren't you gorgeous!* People were wide-eyed and making silly noises. Terri moved from person to person, letting them massage her ears and kiss her snout while she licked their hands. Then she heard the words: 'The dog's got no collar'. An older man and his wife were speculating about whether Terry might be a stray.

'Shit,' Terri murmured, then scuttled upstairs before anyone tried to 'rescue' her.

On the top deck, near the front seats, someone had left half of a Greggs sausage roll on the floor. Though Terri enjoyed the smell of it, she had no appetite — her intestines were absent. They then switched to the 168 bus, which stopped on Haverstock Hill. Terri disembarked near the Somerfield supermarket and called Red and Grey down from the roof of the bus. They walked to Belsize Village. The little hardware store and the Oddbins wine merchant on the corner had gone, and fancy restaurants like ENO had sprung up. Somehow the laundrette had survived. So too had the newsagent, run by the good-looking Asian couple who owned the flats above — asset millionaires selling Mars bars for a living! Although still cosy and quiet, the village was scented with banking money, the kind that would have former resident Karl Marx spinning in his grave. The smell of lamb wafted from somewhere.

'Hmmm.' Terri's nose twitched. Red and Grey didn't get her obsession with meat. Nuts were so much better — great flavour, superb crunch.

Terri ordered Red and Grey to walk ahead of him (people would stare if they saw a Yorkshire terrier on the pavement, flanked by two squirrels). The trio turned off onto a side street and bounced past a tired-looking woman who, curiously, was clutching a scooter but not actually riding it. For some reason quite a lot of the men had beards, like the illustrated man in that *Joy of Sex* book Terri's owner used to keep on her bookshelf.

On Lyndhurst Gardens, Terri approached Galloway's exquisite Queen Anne townhouse. Crouching behind some bushes, they waited for Galloway to come out of his front door. Terri could smell him getting ready to go out. She was primed for a fight.

A few minutes into their wait, Grey spotted a female squirrel and ran towards her. Soon the pair were frolicking and rolling round among the leaves.

'You're not joining them?' Terri asked Red.

Red shook her head. 'Greys and reds ... we're not the same.'

'You look the same.'

'Nah,' Red shook her head, 'they're aggressive sex maniacs. We're also better looking than they are. I like Grey, but I'm not attracted to his sort. The feeling's mutual, by the way — I'm not a bigot or anything.'

'I'll shag *anyone*,' Terri grinned. 'Don't care what size, breed or colour. If I'm in the mood, I'm in the mood.'

Terri heard keys jangling in Galloway's hallway. When the front door opened, a grey whippet squeezed out of it and ran down the steps.

'Skinny bitch,' Terri frowned. Galloway emerged soon after. 'My god, that's him! Red, look!'

The man's coat smelled of fried eggs and toilet freshener. He closed the door behind him and descended the steps. His hair was whiter these days. Creakier in his movements, Galloway looked a touch fragile and avuncular at 75. But physical frailty was not be pitied in a person who drew strength from guns.

Terry shook her head. 'So unfair how he gets to keep his body *and* his soul.'

'Pffft, he lost his soul ages ago,' Red said. 'And all the money he made will never buy it back.'

Terri began pursuing him from a distance, motioning for Red to follow. Grey had also returned to join them. His face had a post-coital glow to it.

'You happy now?' Red asked Grey.

'Yup,' he smiled.

The three animals bounced along Lyndhurst Gardens with a sense of purpose that evaporated as soon as they realised they didn't actually have a plan.

'How are we *actually* going to teach him a lesson?' Grey asked. The other two stared blankly at Galloway's heels. 'We can't kill him. We're too small.'

'I don't want to kill him anyway. It's not my style,' Terri replied. 'I'm not a pitbull. And I don't have the stomach for it.'

'Alright,' Red said, 'let's just mess him up a bit, freak him out and ruin his morning. It's the best we can do. Let's just have a good time before the *juju* wears off. We've got one hour left.'

Everyone agreed. Red and Grey tried stuffing conkers up Galloway's car exhaust pipe but had to abandon the plan when they realized they had the hands for the task but not the height. Terri had neither the manual dexterity nor the height.

The trio caught up with Galloway as he continued down the street. Terri homed in, but within ten feet the whippet had clocked her.

'Who the fuck are you?' the whippet barked, yanking at her leash. Galloway had trained her well, apparently.

'I'm Terri. Who are *you*?'

'Willow,' she yapped.

Terri looked up at Galloway. He was staring at her lovingly and scanning the vicinity in search of her owner. She returned his gaze with fake affection. How could a man who got off on shooting lions be so nice to her? Willow sensed what Terri was up to, and when Galloway bent down to stroke the terrier, the whippet lunged at her. Grey responded by jumping on Willow and screaming insults, but she swatted him off with her paw.

'I wouldn't piss on you if you were on fire,' she barked at the squirrel.

'If you was on fire,' Grey sneered, 'I would stand over you and roast chestnuts in the goddamn flames!' Willow took another swing at him.

Red startled Galloway by running up his torso and clinging to his head for as long as possible. While she played rodeo on the man's skull, Grey squirrel pounced on Willow and clung to her snout by his paws and teeth, trying to ignore the strange taste of her fur.

Galloway grabbed Red's torso and squeezed. She shrieked and fell to the ground. Meanwhile, Terri was drawing blood from Galloway's ankles. The man tripped and fell, banging his head against a railing. Now horizontal, he groaned and rolled a bit. Terri tried to wee on him but nothing came out. 'Shit, keep forgetting I've got no bladder.' She jumped off Galloway's stomach. 'Let's get out of here!'

Terri, Red and Grey scampered off, leaving Willow bent over her master, whimpering and sniffing. Feeling bruised but victorious, the trio took buses back to the Essex Road.

Back at Get Stuffed, they received a hero's welcome. Leon, Zoe, Goma, Winston and the others whooped and cheered and high-fived (high-foured?) the returnees.

Terri and co. spent the last twenty minutes of free movement reliving their fight with Galloway. They gave the low-down on the world outside: the lack of dog poo on the pavements; those funny 'Oyster card' things people used; everyone wearing very tight jeans; lots more bicycles everywhere. The other animals were amazed. Still, Terri and the squirrels made sure to downplay the gloriousness of their freedom — no point in stirring up envy or resentment.

'Twenty seconds to go!' Zoe shouted.

The animals scrambled to their regular positions and froze up again.

SOUTH

Rose's, Woolwich

Paul Ewen

Woolwich, Friday lunchtime. The pubs are rammed with business folk, their eyes drooling, their hands rubbing with glee.

Business Folk: Oo-oo!

It's the Friday pub lunch frenzy. Meals are being rushed out, drinks urgently quaffed. It's like a flashmob, with condiments, spread over the course of an hour.

Meanwhile, at Rose's, things are more subdued. Rose's, too, is a Woolwich pub, open for Friday lunch. But no one's getting worked up here. With the exception of crusty rolls, served at the bar with a range of fillings, lunch usually comes in a glass. There's no manic rush, no flapping or flittering about. Even the jukebox is placid, lapsing into silence between the occasional gasp of retro pop.

Rose isn't a person. The pub's name is derived from the traditional English flower. Tradition is the order of the day here, this being a proper old pub, with dartboards, English flags, and mobility scooters. When you first enter through the main corner entrance, or the more discreet side door, you pass through thin coloured strips, hanging vertically, about 6-foot in length. Butchers use these strips to deter dirty flies, attracted by the smell of uncooked meat, but here, like a drive-in carwash, they appear to cleanse, washing people of their hustle and bustle.

Generally there's about six or seven old boys in Rose's of a Friday lunchtime, and they're never manic, never rushing about. Sometimes there's cricket on the telly, or horse racing, but the volume's always low, so you can hear yourself think. Today the horses are running hard through rain, and outside Rose's it's cold and drizzly. Inside is warm and pleasant, and in Ronnie's cage it's certifiably hot. Ronnie is the pub lizard. A couple of months back he shared his cage with another bearded dragon, called Reggie, but unfortunately Reggie died.

Me: Was Reggie shot? Was he thrown off the Woolwich ferry, with concrete-encased feet?

As I await the barman's response, the jukebox music stops, and the bar lapses into silence.

Barman: No. He wasn't.

My regular Rose's spot is a blue upholstered sofa alongside Ronnie's cage. It's a low-lying seat, and the cage, with its wooden sides, sits high on an old dresser. It's not possible therefore to see inside Ronnie's cage while seated. But because each end is slatted with mesh ventilation grilles, I can certainly smell him. Not him personally. More his lettuce remnants, his scummy water film, his excrement. When combined with their subtropical climate, it's no wonder it pongs.

The bottom of Ronnie's cage is covered in sand, and fake plants drape either side. He has a round plastic cactus for company (which he sometimes mounts), and a scattering of uninspiring rocks. A thin white bulb at the back of his cage projects both light and also heat, thus helping our central Australian native acclimatise on drizzly English days like this.

It's hot in there, it's warm out here, it's cold outside.

Hot, warm, cold. Hot warm, cold. Hot, warm, cold. I whisper this through the mesh grill, hoping to teach Ronnie human speech, like a bear might learn to walk on a barrel.

The old boys in Rose's are a lot like lizards too. Some have weathered, leathery skin; others spiky, bristle-like stubble. Like Ronnie, they tend to stare silently ahead without moving, for long periods. Pub regulars are often referred to as barflies, but this term is misleading. Flies, of course, are zippy and sprightly, full of zest, making the most of their precious little lives. They better resemble busy workers, like those currently rushing in and out of the other Woolwich pubs. The regulars in Rose's aren't like flies at all. They're like lizards.

When I run up to the bar on all fours, hand-feet flapping, head outstretched like a lizard of the frilled variety, the old boys barely bat an eyelid, just like Ronnie. The barman however, is more animated.

Barman: For Christ's sake! When are you going to grow up?

After warning him about my tempestuous lizard nature, he points angrily to a sign above the bar that reads:

Attention: Prices May Vary According To Customer Attitude.

Ronnie has spiky cheeks and holes for ears. Sometimes he opens one eye at a time. Like other bearded dragons, he'll bob his head to signal his domination, or wave his arm, as a sign of submission. Sometimes the old boys, the other lizards, come to life as well, and move around. Normally this is when they need a new drink, or when a piss is in order. Sometimes I follow them to the Gents, for a chat.

Me: Look at me, I'm the Woolwich ferry, unloading my cargo of piss. Soon I'll return to my table and load up with more. And then …

Old Timer: [Slowly shakes head.]

The Woolwich ferry operates between the southern and northern banks of the Thames, in the east of London. Woolwich itself isn't particularly flash, but because it's near Canary Wharf, certain bankers live here, residing in segregated, gated communities with maximum security. Their riverside apartments, I'm certain, have terrific views of the Woolwich ferry, along with its small journeys across the short width of the water.

Despite the coloured strips draping Rose's entrance doors, there always seem to be flies buzzing around in the Gents. Sometimes I pummel them with my wee stream. It's a mystery how they get in. Perhaps they're specifically bred as lizard food. Unlike most pubs, Rose's still offers toilet soap in bar form, as opposed to messy dispensing liquid. Using the well-worn bar of Imperial Leather is a real treat, and when alone in the Gents, I'll often hold it up to the mirror and pretend I'm the front person for an old-fashioned advertisement, eagerly extolling the soap bar's charms.

I'm sitting on the blue upholstered seat when an old boy approaches Ronnie's cage and taps on the glass.

Old Boy: Hey there, Godzilla. You poking your tongue out at me?

Me: Yes, he is. Because you keep tapping on the window of his house. And because you always get his name wrong.

Old Boy: I wasn't talking to you, smart arse.

Soon afterwards, a young woman rushes her little girl past, seeking out the loos. As they're walking back, they stop in front of Ronnie's cage and the mum lifts her daughter up, who bangs on the glass.

Mum: Iggy, hello Iggy. Say hello Iggy.

Daughter: Hello Iggy.

Mum: Iggy the iguana.

Me: For crying out loud!

The word Rose's appears backwards on the frosted glass, highlighting the fact that we're on the inside, in the warm. Ronnie's cage, as mentioned, is hotter than inside the pub, which is warmer than outside. The inside of his cage is like a hot cage inside a warm cage.

After finishing my cool drink, I go outside, into the cold, and look back into the warm.

There are no cacti or rocks on view, but I can see a wall-mounted jukebox, and a dartboard with a black backing board. I start banging on the window, trying to get the lizards to move.

Yes, it works. They turn, cocking their heads, nervously shifting their arms. They've come to life, their cold blood is flowing. Now their attention shifts, towards the barman. He too is moving, but in a very un-lizard way, darting quickly around the side of the bar. He is literally flapping about, his face reddening with heat as he strides towards the coloured butcher strips on the warm side of the cold-warm entrance door.

In the Vauxhall Pleasure Gardens

Sunny Singh

Graham has always been wary of honey traps. After all, he's spent nearly four decades paying for them. They always show up the same way, even now, starting with some extra receipts for drinks, in nice pubs. In fashionable cocktail lounges and low key, offbeat bars. Then over time, there are gaps in spending, or an odd receipt for a night or two in a cosy, picturesque, out of the way inn. Finally, and he knows this is when things go very wrong, there are the unexplainable, unexplained holes in operational funds.

The guys in the field think they are being discreet, will never be caught, but Graham learned early to identify the signs. Simply because he must ensure he isn't paying too much for similar activities by his own operatives. Although that's stretching the truth — it is Her Majesty who really pays — his job has long been to make sure that her money is appropriately spent. He looks through carefully at all the receipts, from Budapest, Baghdad, even Bogota on one occasion, though he tries to forget that that operation had gone particularly poorly. He knows the exchange rates, prices for drinks, meals, and coffees in cities around the world. His eyes sharp for any treats that the boys in the field may want to slip through.

At the beginning, when they were still in the old offices, he had checked against the guidebooks in the office library, laboriously estimating price rises against economic indices. Now he just needs a few clicks on his computer. Not that he needs to do that anymore, he has a whole team these days, albeit constantly depleted by the ongoing budget cuts to monitor Her Majesty's expenses. Still, one likes to stay in form and keep an eye on the young ones, who seem to grow more feckless with each new intake.

When he was younger, he sometimes would wonder about far off places: Moscow, Delhi, Kampala. Not that he had any desire to go to them. He always took his three weeks of annual leave on the Cornish coast, just as he had as a boy. But perhaps he would need to change that now. The old lady who managed the cottage had died just the year before, and he didn't think her flighty daughter would quite manage to keep things just so. And soon, he'd have more time than the annual three weeks. Graham tried not to think of the change that loomed not so far ahead.

As a born and bred Londoner, he was at home in the city that the world clamoured to make its own. Or perhaps he was just a creature of habit, like the suits that he always bought in the same colour every second year during January sales from Marks & Spencer. He waved that thought away. No-one who lived in a shapeshifting city like his could ever be a creature of habit. Even less so given his professional affiliation. So he liked things to be calm, ordered. Just as he liked the daily brisk walk across the bridge from his bachelor flat in Pimlico. Then down Albert Embankment to the new building, and then up to his office. He had preferred the old offices, a bit run down and grey, and draughty. They fitted him better, like his painstakingly polished but battered old brogues, each scuff and fold of the leather a sign of history. Of character — as his grandfather had often said.

The new building seemed hollow, its shining facade a proclamation of power that all knew had ebbed away. In a secret, never to be spoken part of his mind, Graham thought of it as a folly. Worse still, all these years later, he had not grown accustomed to crossing the river each day, to the daily trips south. His few prejudices ran deep, though he refused to consider them thus. It was just the healthy disdain of a decent man for the decrepit remains of the Pleasure Garden. In the early days of the move, he deliberately did not look across the street where shabby, colourful denizens congregated under the dark arches. Walking briskly, his nose would curl nose unconsciously, imperceptibly, at the faint scent of mildew he was sure hung over the neighbourhood. Occasionally, he feared that they were much like the people he paid to do Her Majesty's work but he quickly pushed away the treasonous thought.

For quite some time, Graham avoided crossing under the railway. He pretended that nothing existed beyond and returned across the river for his after-dinner pint before heading home. Of course, he varied his routine, and his routes, as the training manuals instructed. But then slowly, imperceptibly, as the surroundings gentrified, the Vauxhall pretty boys vanished from the shadows, and shiny new builds replaced the shabby old streets, he began to settle in.

Graham's walk across the river and down the Embankment is still brisk, intended to get his heart pumping a bit better. He has even grown accustomed to looking out the window and at the city from an upside down perspective, remembering only occasionally to note how it looks quite different from the south, and across the water. If he still feels a sudden occasional panic at being outside the city, gazing at it from afar, that is only normal for someone who had never crossed south of the Thames till his 18th birthday.

He discovered The Black Dog a few years after the move to the new offices. None of the others from his section liked it much, finding little of interest or comfort in the shabby pub. After work, he began to cross under the tracks, and then to the small garden. He always sat on the bench for a bit, working on the daily crossword puzzle in his paper, always facing the tea house. That has changed as well in the past couple of years. It is a theatre and tea house now, and antiseptically pristine. The pretty boys, the prostitutes, the peddlers are all gone. Graham wonders occasionally if he misses them, but is quite sure he doesn't. There is more pleasure now in the shabby garden than had been before. The benches are clean, and he likes hearing the young men play in the caged-up basketball court as he painstakingly completes his crossword. Before things were cleaned up, people would stop to ask him for cigarettes, or money but not any more. Yes, he prefers the Pleasure Gardens of now. There is sense of purpose to people walking straight through, to the theatre-café, to the pub, or the basketball court. No lingering or malingering, he tells himself, repeating a phrase from his childhood.

He finishes his crossword and pops into The Black Dog for his usual pint, always taking it to the little table in the corner, nearest the door to the beer garden, almost invisible from the glass windows and prying eyes. There's something comforting about the old-fashioned wall paper and vintage sconces. The silent Bakelite radio reminds him of his mum's stories. They used to have one at home when he was growing up but it had disappeared somewhere once he left home. Just the one pint, and then the walk back across the river. It's a comforting routine, and increasingly, in the moments when his thoughts stray, he recognises that he'll miss it. But not till the year after, not till retirement, or 'freedom' as some in the office call it.

*

Graham saw her on an early day of spring, though of course he'd seen her before. Weeks before, noting her presence as only a slight disturbance that first time. Or rather the second week. Casuals came through the park regularly. He'd learned to clock and discard them instantly. But he noticed her that first day, and then through the week. She looked like a woman who could have been beautiful once, if she had tried. Her features were even, and there was dignity in her bearing, in the measured steps, in the squaring of her shoulders as she stopped to choose a bench. He noted that she deliberately turned her eyes from the train line and the shiny glass monster beyond as if she found them unseemly.

Then as she settled to read on the bench next to him, he noticed that her fingers were long, graceful, with unpainted, clean short nails. And around the book she held, her hands were steady. She hadn't come to the pub afterwards, walking off into the street to the south.

He'd expected her gone after the weekend like all those staying at the affordable business hotels that edged the gardens and had felt a sudden frisson when she appeared on that drab Monday. And again on the days that followed. They never spoke beyond the initial greeting, though he thought he could recognise her voice anywhere. Soft with flat vowels, something that could have been an accent, but unrecognisable. Or at least he would recognise her voice if she said 'good afternoon.' But he'd grown accustomed to their half-hour of silent companionship, seated side by side on the bench, his crossword, her books. He never quite caught the titles that she read but had sneaked enough glances to know that she preferred old editions with dark hardcovers and brittle cream pages.

He wasn't sure when he began looking for her, when he first felt a nervous flutter as he settled himself on the bench and wondered if she'd come. But he remembers that first moment as he ironed his shirts for the week ahead, watching the news on a Sunday night, when he had found himself smiling. Monday. He'd see her the next afternoon. Then an unfathomable wave of sudden terror swept over him and his stomach had felt hollow. What if she didn't come? He'd shaken himself angrily, telling himself off for being an old fool. But as the man on the telly droned on about bombs in one of the places he knew only from the office receipts, he'd found himself wondering what her grey hair would feel like through his fingers. She wore it up, in one of those severe twists at the back of her head. He had seen it catch the afternoon light and knew it would feel soft, full in his hand. Just like the rest of her.

He learned her name one afternoon when she answered a phone call. Graham had been a bit annoyed at the intrusion of sounds but she was brief, with many yeses, nos, and of courses, walking away a little from the bench for privacy. But he had noted the first sentence she had spoken. 'This is Catherine.' He liked the sound of the name, turning it in his mind, relieved at its stability, yet vaguely disappointed that it was so commonplace.

'I'm so sorry.' Her voice low when she returned to her place on the bench, her lips twisted wryly. 'Family.' He had smiled and nodded, too shocked to respond with anything more. But later he remembered that her eyes were warm, with tiny laugh lines at the creases.

*

Spring turned to summer, and Graham lingered longer over his crossword. They seemed to grow harder to solve in the warmth of the sunshine, though he knew it was more because he couldn't stop watching Catherine from the corner of his eye. He wondered if all her skin were as soft as it seemed on her forearms. She shed her winter coat for a mac and he would find himself wanting to span her belted waist with his hands. He thought he knew her scent now, musky with something floral and clean but that may have been his mind playing tricks. But they were the kinds of tricks he wanted more of each day.

*

They say goodbye now, Catherine and Graham, though he has never told her his name. He finishes his crossword, taking a bit longer each day, folds his paper and stares ahead at the young people crowding the theatre-café. In the summer light, he can almost feel the heat from her. Sometimes, when he lets his eyes stray a little, he knows the distance between them grows imperceptibly smaller, the glossy dark span of wood between her beige mac and his grey suit just a little narrower each day. But then perhaps this is a trick his mind plays as well. Catherine now reads a little longer, just a couple of minutes, then marks the page in her book and puts it away and they sit there for a bit. She is always first to rise off the bench and waits for him. 'See you tomorrow,' four times a week. And then, 'See you next week,' on Fridays. Her teeth small, very even, and her smile warms him up from the inside. They walk side by side, a few steps, almost like friends or lovers, to the edge of the Pleasure Gardens, till she turns south into Laud Street, and he steps into the shadows of The Black Dog.

Some nights, alone in his flat, Graham wonders what it would be like to speak to her further. Perhaps he should ask her to join him for a drink. Or perhaps tea. Perhaps they would come back to his flat. Or hers? Would she be soft all over? But that near inaudible hint of accent makes him wary, though he tells himself times have changed. This is London, his boss had said some days ago, everyone has an accent now. But old habits are too deeply rooted and he has seen too many good men falter to take a chance. Sometimes he wonders if he should ask one of the others to run a check on her. It should be easy enough with all the money they have put into databases over the years. But the thought of sharing her with anyone, even, especially at work, fills him with horror. Even worse is the thought of empty afternoons, of nothing but his crossword, of sitting alone again on their bench.

This is also why Graham has been increasingly afraid of

this afternoon. He is to go away on Monday for his holiday and is too afraid to even wonder if she'll miss him. Yet he has caught himself worrying that she won't think of him, or find other company for her evenings. Or worst of all that she will no longer come to the park, when he returns. That she will disappear forever. He plans to ask her for a number or an address. He has always wanted to send someone those postcards they sell in the village off licence.

As always as he crosses the Albert Embankment, strolls under the train tracks, through the tunnel, he feels a sudden surge of excitement. The essence of the Pleasure Gardens, even though little remains of all that was once glorious and louche. She is there first today, seated already on their bench. As he walks along the winding path, he can feel his stomach knot. Her arms are bare today, he notices, with a sudden lurch. A summer dress that makes her seem younger, lighter than he has ever imagined. As he nears, he sees she has placed her mac next to her, almost as if to reserve his spot.

Her eyes are warm, her smile wide as she looks up from the book, moving her mac to her lap to make room for him. 'Good afternoon.'

Graham can feel his heart thump. Even to his own ears, his voice sounds like a croak. He can think of nothing to say as he pulls out his crossword. Her arms look as soft as he has imagined. Under her dress, he can see the shape of her thighs. He wants to run his fingers on the skin he knows will be as soft, fill his palm with the curve. They stay longer than ever before, almost till the park starts to empty and dinner tables fill up. He hasn't finished his crossword and she keeps reading, the edge of her mac almost flush against his thigh.

'We won't see each other anymore. Not after today.' When she finally speaks, her voice is low, soft, almost a question.

'Yes, not for three weeks.'

'Graham, you must know.' She has turned to him. He can smell her now. Something floral and musky, and expensive. His eyes catch at the hollow of her throat, where a web of lines crisscross her skin. He wants to reach out and run his tongue against it. His breath catches as her lips seem to draw closer. Then he feels her hand move, light against his thigh. Warm, gentle. Then something fleeting and sharp.

'How do you know my name?' he wants to ask but her scent fills his nose. Her lips are moist, slightly parted. A bit blurred perhaps because they fill his eyes so completely.

'This is just a message. Nothing personal.'

Her breath is warm against his cheek.

Graham wants to move, lift his hands to pull her close. To draw her in for a kiss but his body has frozen. No words push past his tongue. She reaches up to pull the clip from her hair, freeing it. Streaks of grey flood past her shoulders, a tendril reaching out to his face.

'But this is. This is personal.' Her lips touch his gently, quickly, just once. As soft as he had imagined. Then she is moving away, her mac in her arms, to the left on the path and then south. He watches her leave, his vision blurring as she recedes into the distance, his head growing ever heavier, and breaths increasingly slower and harsher. As he slumps, he thinks she turns around and smiles.

Nightingale Lane

Stephanie Victoire

When you ascend the escalators of Clapham South tube station, a mighty gust helps you forth. It sends the loose strands of your hair scattering about before your face like dancing vines, or the eager spindly fingers of a witch. The pages of your newspaper flap and flutter, sounding like a flock of panicked pigeons. Hold on to the rail of the escalator, and when you reach the top, this gust of wind helps you around the corner and through the barriers. You think of a dinner party host, merrily pushing you into another room where new people and new pleasures await. But you are not going into something; you are blasted out, like a pile of leaves blown from a front-garden path, or a child shot out of a tunnel on a wave at a waterpark. 'This way! This way! Hurry!' you believe you hear.

Perhaps you do, because it is not simply the air you feel beating against the corner and rushing through a hollow-bellied building, but the sylphs. Like mermaids and mermen of the sky, they are the air spirits, twirling and swirling above. They are celestial in their appearance, wearing white, almost diaphanous gowns, long, fine and flowing hair and faces that hold a certain bliss, a kind of peace glowing gently in their cheeks. They have come to greet you and speak to you now. They swim on the wind like fish, rather than fly like birds. There are very few sylphs in London, but they are the keepers of the special places, the soft places. They want to show you what it feels like to experience a sliver of enchantment in a large city. Keep hold of your senses, they say. Don't shut them off. You are on Nightingale Lane and it has a magic that won't be found in Tooting or Leicester Square or Camden. Noise is not its speciality; there is no bustle or buzz, but serenity, if you allow yourself to find it. Little has changed around here, save for the small parade of shops over there, the Sainsbury's Local and the Costa. If you follow those shops all the way down that hill, it will lead you on to Balham, but a different sort of spell is cast over there.

Look up. The building there that strikes your eyes at the crossroads? Mark it. It sits like a guard at the gate of the Lane's end, a large and flat-faced building with little embellishment to its structure, but it emits a great presence. After decades of abandonment, the arrival of Tesco on the ground floor was an anti-climax. In the year 1984, South London Hospital was shut down, locked up, and the death of it was an eerie thing for the residents of Clapham South. Empty and black on the inside, it spooked passers-by. All longed for something bright and fresh to take its place. Year after year passed and hope dwindled. Nothing would come — no beautiful, tall houses to match The Mansions, no school, or even a new hospital that allowed men inside. But the sylphs say that if you were to look up into those dark little windows and focus, you can sense women and children in there, still roaming those halls, still believing they are in our world. South London Hospital — such a generic name. But special births took place here, though lonely deaths outweighed them.

Cheer up, turn your back to the high street and come this way, left of the station. What sits here is Dover Florist; still here long after the wars with the most beautiful and elegant bouquets you've ever seen. Folks have been buying the finest peonies here for years, a delight to the eyes and the nose, a fine little row of colours tucked into the corner, to remind you that beauty isn't always obvious. Breathe in the perfume of the flowers, let the fragrance ripple through the freshness of the wind. The sylphs enjoy this spot in particular — they bathe in the scent as one would in bath oils. Family owned and always will be, even through the terrifying Blitz that obliterated the roads so dangerously close to here. One child born deaf in the family, and one stillborn, they've never stopped holding onto the solace and life they find in flowers.

When one sense is lost, the others are heightened, don't we all know, and Nightingale Lane has birthed many children with no experience of sound. Three schools for the hearing-impaired have been built around here, and it is they who feel the presence of the sylphs and smell the aromas of the flowers the most. Look at their faces; they know true peace when they feel it.

Across the way is the common, a wide plain of pickle green that stretches across to the other Claphams. Its openness invites you to run across it like a giddy child. But watch for all the people now who use it for Sunday picnics. They meet with their friends to eat bread and cheese and drink supermarket wine. In the summer, they lay on their backs almost body to body, and bring rowdiness to this calm and quiet space. They won't remember how it once was. They come in crowds to the November 5th display — a tradition the common has kept up — but all of them strangers. They won't know what it was like when we all still called it Guy Fawkes Night. 'Penny for the Guy?' you would often hear young children say, as they passed by with a wheelbarrow full of straw and a dummy of the Great Gunpowder Plotter himself. They'd collect pennies from the greengrocer who always enjoyed the joke, and from the baker from whom they'd buy their iced-doughnuts after school. The neighbours knew each other by door number and block. They'd pass each other sparklers, having brought spares for those who had none. 'It's really nippy tonight,' Number Four from High Trees House would say. 'It's supposed to be the biggest bonfire yet,' Number Two from Holmside Court would chime in. After it was over, they'd filter out of the common and walk home in groups, inhaling the thick, but not unpleasant, fug of gunpowder smoke that lay over the crisp autumn air. They'd see each other again in the newsagents, or at the bus stop and talk about the next local event.

They used to start the London to Brighton race here, did you know? Once a year on that Sunday morning, the residents of Nightingale Lane would rise early to lookout through their windows, or come out onto the street with a thermos of tea to see the excited cyclists begin. This place has always known such morale. The mother and daughter of Number Ten at The Mansions used to hand out biscuits to their neighbours. They've lived here ever such a long time and it's likely they'll never leave. They miss the gatherings and the chats they would stop for − it made their day, being remembered. The mother, now old, and the daughter never married, could tell you a thing or two, maybe more intimately than I. They know that this road has always been special, and they are bound to it, like a genie to his lamp.

Let's move along now, we'll get to the heart of it all. Have you ever heard of genius loci? A spirit animal or guardian that attaches itself to a place, a watcher, or keeper, if you will. Perhaps you've heard of hellhounds guarding the gates to the underworld. They are not seen with the naked eye, but they are there just as much as that squirrel is, over there, running up that tree. Well this road has plenty genius loci and lives up to its name in more ways than one. Aside from the sylphs, there is a bird, the beautiful, singing nightingale herself. She is the sylphs' companion; she sails with the elemental beings. Glide down the lane with her, whistle a little tune and let her catch it on the breeze. It puts you in a good mood, doesn't it? Uplifting because the usual cacophony of London has fallen away.

The honking and swearing and bus roars have gone. Have you noticed? It's quiet down here. You've come in the autumn, before the earth takes her slumber, but you should see it in the spring. The blossoms bloom well and bow down from their branches to give little pink kisses on the crown. Nature isn't the only glory here, you mark those buildings, they impress you. Tall and handsome — those mansions

— and you wonder who first lived in them before they were hacked into flats. You think of oil lamps and grand pianos, parlour songs sang facing out to the large windows where the glow from the inside was lost to the black of the common. It is true, there has been good money here, and there still is, but only very few families have kept up such opulent tradition. They have been wise to pass these houses down from kin to kin.

Look here to the right at Holmside Court, tucked in by black railings and shadowed by its larger and much less attractive sister block, High Trees House. Holmside Court, ah now, that's the humble and quiet little gem that has taken in poor and newly emigrated souls and has held them in its bosom. Florence Nightingale is another guardian who springs to mind; she is bound to this place by name; a devoted nurse to soldiers — a tireless nurturer.

Let's step into the courtyard for a moment. Here a soldier once lived with his beloved wife and their six children who then bore their own and flew the nest, but always returned. This soldier could sense there'd be safety here for his family, who found their way across the ocean from the tiny island of Mauritius. Whilst he was serving in the African Allied Forces in Italy from 1940 to 1945, this road was being equipped with deep bunkers to save as many lives as possible. Often, when the Mauritian soldier passed the abandoned bunker on the common, it would set off memories he didn't like to remember. Yes it was safe here, and he would march up and down Nightingale Lane at any hour in his well-practised sergeant's stride, and never encounter any trouble. He knew the milkman by his first name and would greet him as he chugged his float into the courtyard at six in the morning. The soldier would say good morning in Gujarati to the Indian family next door. He spoke fluent Italian to the lady who ran the Nightingale Patisserie, and all knew him in return as the kind Mauritian man from Number Six, Holmside Court. He was often seen in the yard tinkering on a second-hand car or sat under the roundabout tree to take a rest. Yes, they've paved around it now. Cars used to creep down the path and take a turn around this tree if they needed to go back on themselves. A shame so much concrete has locked this tree in, but perhaps it is to serve this tree, or rather, preserve it — keep it tidy and upright, like a statue. If it could speak, it would tell you much of what it has seen. The little one, the granddaughter, whom he fathered more than any of his own, comes back here sometimes, and walks around this courtyard with such nostalgia in her heart. She'll remember her grandfather sitting under the tree, and she'll put her palms to the trunk and retrieve the stories that it has stored.

The medical students who bought their flat will never raise their children here. They won't come down to the courtyard and rollerblade up and down the path with their kids, like the soldier did with his grandchildren. They won't have children who will learn how to ride a bike here and take several, wobbly turns around the roundabout tree. No, the time of children has passed.

Look up to the kitchen window of Number Six. The medical students who live there now cook their pasta in a rush and never sit down to watch the sun rise over High Trees House, which hits the right spot on the kitchen table where one can enjoy a slow, pleasant breakfast. They won't know how rich and exotic the food used to smell in there when the soldier's wife was cooking for her large brood; Mauritian curry spice, dhal, ginger, rich tomato and coriander sauces wafting out through the open window and down to anyone walking through the gate. Sometimes, back then, you'd hear her hollering at them to wash their hands, come for dinner, or to come and blow out their birthday candles on the cake she'd spent all day making. I believe the students painted the kitchen blue and it cast the homeliness out, leaving the room feeling cold and vacant − all trace of spices, pots and pans, cakes, pictures on the fridge and noisy chatter, gone. It has never really been the same in this block since the soldier passed away. One of the very last things to take a turn around this tree before the concrete was put down was a pair of black horses adorned with purple plumes, pulling a carriage that came to mark his death and lead his heartbroken family to his grave.

Let's follow the hoof prints of those horses, walk as if in the wake of that carriage. Turn right out of the courtyard and continue the path back down the lane. You slow your pace in respect. The tree branches whistle softly in the wind and scatter leaves about your feet, like devotees who sprinkle flower offerings to their gods. Pass the Nightingale Patisserie and smell briefly coffee and toasted paninis. The owner smiles at you as she serves a slice of cake to a customer outside; she's always been so friendly. Come to the turning of Endlesham Road where the grandchild remembers walking down to school with her granddad. She'd skip about at his side as he carried her lunchbox for her; he'd tell her stories and jokes and sing to her his favourite songs in Italian. Heard now, the opera that complements the sweet song of the nightingale bird and the movement of the sylphs and the breeze in the treetops — picture the theatre this place is, see the light on the stage, the curtains draw back. Feel the emotions rise.

We're coming up to The Nightingale pub now, passing the estate agents that used to be a fun stationery and knick-knack shop, run by husband and wife — both artists. Their passion for prints and notebooks couldn't quite pay the rent, and off they went to who knows where. Estate agents have been hungry for the properties around here, and they swooped in like vultures when the little shops went, to tear off juicy pieces of commission from million-pound sales. And the new money that brought them this business all file into the pub on a Wednesday for Quiz Night, something the man at Number One-Forty, Nightingale Lane, doesn't enjoy. It has changed too much for him. After all, he's been coming to this pub for decades, especially during his days of working for British Gas with the Mauritian soldier, just before retirement. He was one of the first to hear the news of his cancer, and it had hit close to home; he had lost his wife to it in the Christmas of 1995. The soldier came into work one day with a letter from the doctor and he stopped coming to work soon after that. When the black carriage passed by on that grey afternoon, Number One-Forty raised his pint and silently toasted the spirit of his old colleague.

Follow it all the way down now, the road is narrowing, do you see? Almost at the end. Take in as much peace as you can before you cross over. Breathe in deeply, elongate and march now, down the slight incline, past the mixture of period properties, the blocks, and the semi-detached. They sit all along in a row like the teapot collection of a great-aunt — each random in style and appearance, but all orderly and perfectly in line.

You've reached the crossroads. The sylphs hover over and

wish to bid you farewell. Do you feel the air suddenly turn still? The nightingale turns back on herself and flies away, her birdsong carried away in one direction, and the echoes of the horses' hooves are carried away in the other. Across the road is Wandsworth Common. We won't go any further with you, but we will always be here should you return. We keep all stories for all time; just remember how we taught you to see them, hear them and feel them. Go now to where the green grows thick, and the branches tangle. The wood nymphs will take you from here.

Babies From Sand:
A Guide to Oliver's Island, Barnes & the St Margarets' Day of the Dead

M John Harrison

1. The Water House

A permanent exhibition of water paintings at the Holst House Gallery features *Crossing the River Styx* by Joachim Patinir, as well as some small canvases by John Atkinson Grimshaw, including *In Peril,* in the foreground of which several figures are seen running towards the sea at night across a vast, sloping, otherwise deserted quay. 'Though he is not known for his seascapes,' the catalogue remarks, 'when we re-examine Grimshaw, everything he painted seems to be located near water — wet estuarine streets in Leeds; Hampstead depicted on bluffs above a shallow sea at night.' Gericault's *The Raft of the Medusa* can be found in a side-room, along with a Philip James de Loutherbourg, *The*

Flood — sometimes known as *The Deluge* — the composition of which eerily resembles that of *Sea Idyll* by Arnold Böcklin (1887). Loutherbourg died in Chiswick in 1812, having all his life 'pursued interests in alchemy, faith healing and the supernatural'. He was a follower of Cagliostro.

2. The Dogs of St Margarets

The 26th of June: Cultural Day of Bad Luck all along the river as far as Windsor, but especially in the small enclave of St Margarets. A hot breeze moves the baskets of trailing flowers on the lamp posts. Faded looking men in red t-shirts, a little bald, a little grey at the edges, gather outside Edward Fail Solicitors, across the road from the bowel cancer charity. Later they will go down to the water, where every high tide briefly strands three lumps of wood known as 'the Three Maries'. These — large, black, asymmetrical, sodden as much with age as with water — are celebrated as the estuary's gift to the land, in a traditional call-and-response. (The dogs of the enclave howl: not just today, but on the anniversary of every one of the borough's many more private, more primitive tragedies. Each year when the light is right these animals remember events of five, ten, fifty years before. They remember not to the day but to the season. Things spread out. Whole months fill up with overlapping disasters.) Among the amusements on offer to visitors are: dream incubation, ritual bathing, and divination by the Lots of Mary.

3. The Reverend Harry Price

During the late 1990s, especially at high tide, the familiar figure of Harry Price could often be seen ascending the water stair at Hammersmith Bridge, dressed in dirty cotton chinos and an old-fashioned Belstaff waxed jacket, and carrying on a plastic strap round his neck the Polaroid Sun 600 camera with which he recorded much of his data. Nightly excursions to the astral plane had emaciated the ageing psychogeographer, and his incomplete masterpiece *The Potassium Channel* — written in 200 black Moleskine notebooks as he pursued, yard by yard, dérive by dérive, his minute investigations of the Brent River and its surrounds, from the boatyards at its confluence with the Thames, past Wharncliffe Viaduct and the zoo, towards the A40 at Greenford — lay abandoned.

'If the disaster can be said to be unevenly distributed,' he wrote to his wife, Fanny, by then a permanent resident in the old Barnes Fever Hospital, 'Brentford is one of the places it has been distributed to. Boatyards and their horrible refuse. High water one minute, the next only mud. Sudden drops bulwarked with rusty metal.'

4. Transformation Reach

'Oliver's Island', open six to seven most evenings, May to October: a small wood, frequented by foxes and wildfowl driven upriver by population pressures in the Barnes wetlands, has grown up on a late-Victorian dreadnought abandoned in midstream. Its iron plates have turned to stone. All down this stretch of the Thames, islands are becoming boats, boats are on their way to being islands. The boats fix themselves in the mud. They settle in the mud. Over the years they become mud. In the final stages of transformation, they support a thicket of buddleia often too dense to navigate.

Between the bushes the old decks can sometimes be glimpsed, covered in rabbitcropped turf and little winding trodden-down paths. Suddenly a passer-by makes out a new shape — planks! the curve of the bow!

5. The Human Footprint

'Squalls of rain pursue each other southeast, the latest accompanied by a lurch of pressure and humidity that encourages waves of scent from the narcissi in the vase on my desk. Between squalls, light strikes half-opened petals, which, though individually white, wrap themselves round a smoky yellow tinge. It races in like the epileptic aura, at a surprising angle from the broken edge of the cloud cover, leaving the air quick and transparent against a dark sky. Ideally one should experience this kind of light on the riverbank near Putney, four o' clock in the afternoon; and perhaps remember later that the person who walked towards you was gone too quickly when you turned to get another look. Look for what rises to the surface in light like that! Not so much ghosts as visitors from the future, the past, or somewhere that is, simply, never quite there. People from under the water, who lose something of themselves on the shore. Babies from sand, at a loss beneath water. To us they seem robust, but their hold on reality is tenuous.'

— from *The Seizure Journals of Fanny Price.*

6. *The Potassium Channel*

Notes for the incomplete final chapters of this work present as a sheaf of media reports and scientific abstracts. A seminar on ancient human migration (tracked via mitochondrial haplogroup); the Gnostic foundations of 20th Century Russian science; computer software designed to identify unknown locations by matching them with 'a library of 60 million landscape images': Harry Price's obsessions run together, hardening into unconformable layers of time and data. From a study of studies, robust evidence surfaces of a pre-Cambrian micro continent along the Laccadive-Chagos Ridge; paragraphs from Wikipedia shed new light on metabolic byproducts found deep in the Juan de Fuca tectonic plate. Body parts wash up on a beach east of Southampton; while ('almost simultaneously' Price notes) in the Borough of Brent, a man of about 40, naked and with an inexplicable greenish tinge, is observed by passers-by to drag himself out of the Grand Union Canal near Gallows Bridge then run straight into heavy traffic on the nearby dual carriageway of the M4, where he is struck and killed by a black BMW Alpina with Swiss registration plates before being dragged for some distance underneath an unmarked Volvo FMX D13 truck painted Mediterranean blue.

7. Arnold Böcklin, *Sea Idyll*

Perhaps the best but least-known of the Holtz House collection. The Swiss symbolist, known for his dream paintings of the English Cemetery in Florence, produced this item quite late in his career. In it, three figures — a woman and two children — are depicted sprawled on a lumpen, almost-submerged rock barely large enough to accomodate them; while a fourth — perhaps a man, perhaps some more powerfully ambivalent creature of myth — emerges waist-high from the water nearby. Their tenure on the rock seems anxious and marginal, their poses are awkward and strained. The woman, in yearning towards the man, is carelessly allowing her baby to fall into the sea; while the dwarfish older child, its enlarged buttocks stuck up into the air as a result of some deformity of the spine, appears to be trying to mount her from behind. The painting is too fraught to be any kind of idyll. A sense of confusion — of failed allegory — infuses the drab palette, the deformed anatomy.

8. The Seizure Gene

Somewhere along the Brent between the Thames confluence and the Fox Inn, for reasons unexamined or perhaps even unadmitted, the Prices became, in the days leading up to Fanny's illness, obsessed with the meaning of human gene Kv12.2. This gene originated 'more than 500 million years ago in the genomes of sea-dwelling species' and has a decisive role in spatial memory. A final note for *The Potassium Channel*, written some time in the early 2000s: 'Yesterday I watched a heron eating a live eel in bright sunshine on the South Pier mudbank. Today it was foggy: the mud was almost awash: the heron still waited there. I fear the hidden channels of the confluence and hate low tide as much as I hate the partly-foundered lighters.' And later: 'Kv12.2 is a very old gene. Even the fish have it.'

9. Eulogy for the Ageing Hauntologist

Mystical sunsets behind the troubled roofs of East Sheen, the overgrown gravestones of Barnes Common, the grim Edwardian silhouette of the Elm Guest House. A smell drifts down the river which can't for a second be mistaken for that of the brewery. The tide is low, the water fast and turbulent between the piers of Barnes Bridge. Eddies thicken with the matted stuff left at high tide — bottle caps, tampon applicators, condoms in a matrix of sodden interwoven twigs rarely more than five or six inches long — it's a substance in itself. (The sexual health of a nation can always be judged by the state of its rivers.) Like the smear of light on the wet tiles under the bridge, it is a language, a signal from those who have gone before. It is what they have to say.

They remember being alive, they remember a slick of light on old tiles on a wet day, the pavement becoming wetter and blacker as people track the rain into it and the human footprint blurs to black. They remember the cold draughts. Everything thus becomes more itself, or what people have understood it to be. The departed swirl forever under Barnes Bridge, a cultural attraction which draws visitors from all over the world. Come for the sunsets, we say in West London: stay for the funeral!

10. The Lots of Mary

Further along the tideway, the old Holst House fills up with depictions of people in the throes of some cultural stress you can't quite understand. They recoil from one another and yet seem intertwined; they are bent back in the shapes of change, of seizure, of a body language of transformation which can have no meaning to the carefully groomed and dressed art tourists who pass in front of them. In his rooms directly above the Middle Gallery, Harry Price, puzzled by some implied but not quite demonstrable consonance between the celebrations of the St Margarets Day of the Dead and the central anxieties of Arnold Böcklin's masterpiece, which he feels as a powerful astral 'presence' in the hanging space below him, falls asleep thinking about the agitated gestures of the woman and her son, the smiling but curiously unreceptive expression of the older male. His dreams are filled with sounds both human and marine. At three in the morning the phone rings. A throat is cleared at the other end, but no one speaks and in the end it is Price who, looking down at hands, feels he must whisper: 'I'm becoming something else.'

Thy Kingdom Come

Koye Oyedeji

It's difficult to call Walworth much of anything these days, far less home. At first look, we could all be interlopers. I struggle to tell a Walworth resident apart from those that are simply passing through. The smell of city diffidence clings to us all. The fashion sluts that walk along Walworth Road in bold blazers, skinny jeans and brogues could just as well be from the east side of town. The young Arab man in the designer suit bears the hallmarks of a foreign graduate student on an executive fast track. Even the homeless man, who's trying to sell an Oyster card to anyone that might give him half a chance to explain the deal he's offering, is likely to have roots elsewhere. He wants a tenner for a card that's got just over 20 quid on it. Someone ought to tell him you can't put a price on trust.

Our origins have never been as open to interpretation as they are today. Details flee from us as quickly as they are gathered. Accuracy is expendable. Truths are dependent on the people willing to get behind them. The emperor's new clothes have been commodified, mass-produced and sold cheaply to us all. And Walworth has had its string of emperors; like the actors Charlie Chaplin and Michael Caine. They proved you could be raised in Walworth and become more than just a person. They were symbols for the working class white man, a source of pride, a sign that you too could reach for more.

Emcee is Walworth's modern emperor. An award-winning rising star who, like Caine and Chaplin, was raised in Walworth but cements his local legend by featuring the south-London neighbourhood in his work. When *Late to the Game* hit bookshelves in 2011 it depicted Walworth as a dreary backdrop for gangs and guns, bitches and bravado. Publicists, bereft of any imagination, plastered their press releases in lazy adjectives, and the magazine reviewers followed suit. It was 'gritty', it was 'raw' it was 'edgy' — and it was critically received. By the time the follow up, *The Walworth Wars*, arrived the next year, only the purists grimaced at Emcee's banal leap from council flat beginnings to a career carved out of urban iconography.

His most recent project, *Thy Kingdom Come*, was released

earlier this year. It's been marketed as an autobiography of sorts. A copy was spotted in the hands of the rapper Jay Z as he took a selfie with a fan in a departure lounge at JFK. Social media did the rest. It's been a tidal wave ever since. New Line Cinema has optioned the rights to what they're now calling a 'trilogy' with a 2019 release date set for of the first instalment. Rumours have followed; is *True Detective's* Nick Pizzolatto's on board to produce a screenplay that moves the setting from Walworth, London to Yonkers, New York City? Has F. Gary Gray, fresh off the success of *Straight Outta Compton* been attached as director? The noise has risen around Emcee. His Wikipedia page has been protected, as a result of edit warring. He was the subject of a recent BBC documentary. *Vanity Fair* sat down with him for a feature and then *The Atlantic* and *Ebony* followed suit. There were others, one publication after another until his name came up at one of our editorial meetings. I felt it was my professional duty, at that point, to raise my hand and confess that Emcee was a close childhood friend of mine.

We grew up just a couple miles away from Westminster and the Houses of Parliament, to the south of the river, at the north end of the London borough of Southwark. Walworth's loosely agreed upon borders are the Walworth Road to the west, the Old Kent road to the east and southwards to Burgess

Park, an expanse of green that runs along the entire length of Albany Road. Walworth is no bigger than two square miles and most of it had been swallowed by the Aylesbury and Heygate council estates — two networks of maisonettes and high rise matchbox-shaped buildings conjoined by a network of bridges. The estates were once an architectural wonder of the 1970s, set apart by their amenities — grocery stores, bakeries, and laundries on mezzanine floors — as well as their scope — the Aylesbury Estate once housed over 7,000 residents and was considered the biggest in Europe. By the late 1980s the estates became typical examples of urban blight, unkempt and graffiti-riddled, crime and drug infested. They remained like this for the next two decades. Even long after Tony Blair, as new Prime Minister, turned up on the estate steps in 1997 delivering a speech to both the press and public, promising his government would tackle the resident's social disillusion. 'The Forgotten People' is how he described them. I don't think he's ever remembered them.

I wait in front of the Morrison's on the Walworth Road. It was once a Safeway where, at 16, I landed my first part-time job. I've no doubt Emcee thought of this when he sent a text message asking for me to wait there. It was a 15-minute walk to our old neighbourhood where Emcee still resides.

As alien as I felt, I had not lost the geography over the years. He could've given me an address. I could've made my own way. It makes sense only when I spot the young man that arrives. Emcee has sent someone to meet me simply because he can. The acolyte dresses like a walking museum of our time. A classic sense of Walworth is in his threads, a Stone Island anorak, stone-washed skinny blue jeans and an all-black pair of Nike Huarache. He turns to me once I make myself known. He has a slim head and baby goatee, a wisp of hair above his top lip and a flattop haircut that, during my day, I did not have the confidence to wear. He shakes my hand as he sizes me up. Close to two decades older than he, but perhaps not as old he thought. I'm wearing a fedora. My woollen blazer and white shirt are fitted, the shoulder bag is tan leather, my trousers are straight and I know he would wear my black plimsolls if they were in his wardrobe.

'You don't look American,' he says.

'I'm not.'

He introduces himself as Fire. Such names don't surprise me. He carries on a tradition of birth and rebirth: you take on a graffiti tag, keep the stage name from the days when you thought you were a rapper, or embrace a nickname. I was once known as Fox Mulder, because of my love for *The X-Files*. Before 'Emcee' there was just Mark Charles. We have other friends with old 'new' names and whether the etymology is unremarkable or the stuff of folklore, I've found that each name bears a story.

Fire wants us to hurry. He tells me what he wants me to believe are his own stories as we walk down East Street towards Old Kent Road. 'There's bare man around here looking to do me something,' he says. He offers an example, a story about following a bredrin to a house party and feeling a tense vibe amongst some of the other boys there. I smile. I don't know why he is telling me all this; if it's some sort of crude welcoming concocted by Emcee. At the party he had turned to calm a third friend and took a bottle across the back of his head. He collapsed. A cheap shot, he says, his reward for trying to play peacemaker. He flashes a grin. His right canine is higher than the other. 'We got rushed that day,' he says. 'I came away from it all with a concussion and 12 stitches.'

He says he doesn't remember much from that night and yet he has plenty to say. By now I am only half listening to him, doubly stunned by the way history can be stolen out from under your feet as well as the way it has been plastered over in Walworth. The market on East Street used to teem with foot traffic, a lively strip, where the stalls on the road used to line up so close to one another you could hardly see the pavement or the shops behind them. Now the street is half empty. There are gaps between the stalls, vacant lots that go unoccupied. Some of the tradesmen do not bother to hire stalls, setting down containers in the street that brim with goods. Behind the stalls, beside pawn shops and pounds shops, it warms me to see Charlesworth of East Street, a longstanding luggage and handbag retailer, is still there. There are some halal meat places left, the plucked boiler chickens that my mother was so fond of still hang in their windows, but the shoe shop Barrie Howard, that used to always be the first to sell the latest Kickers, is a shell of its former self.

'What's happened?' I ask Fire.

'Road's dying,' he says. He tells me there are different reasons, depending on who you talk to. Like gentrification and the opening of the Asda superstore on the Old Kent Road in December 2004, the austerity measures passed by the Conservative-Liberal coalition of 2010 and the new parking laws that make it difficult for drivers passing through to stop and take a look around.

This erasure of place and the sense of loss it creates is compounded with the knowledge that the Aylesbury Estate is also disappearing. It is in the process of being demolished and residents are being systematically rehoused. In 2014, the last buildings on the Heygate estate were toppled and they have begun to be replaced by the first of the new buildings that will make up Elephant Park, a sprawling £1.5 billion property development project over 28 acres of land around the nearby Elephant and Castle thoroughfare. It is set to be rolled out over the coming decade and in the end it will offer 3,000 new residences. Southwark Council and its partner, the property developers Lendlease, call it regeneration. A recent report by the Independent stated just 79 of the new homes will be flats available to rent as social housing. This, for longstanding locals like Fire, is not regeneration.

The sallow hue of gentrification saturates the surroundings and the spaces that young men once occupied, like the stairwells and underpasses on the Aylesbury Estate, are being bulldozed. Because of this, Emcee has a small army of young men who will follow him without question. He feeds their need to remain relevant, quenching their thirst for representation. They find something gladiatorial about his work. They guzzle on the shots of hyperbole in his tales, they crave the flavour of a milked truth. Then off they go, empowered and everything. They tell stories about the stories he tells, punctuating their retellings with guessing games and the names of who they think Emcee's gangstas and victims are based on.

Emcee builds them a better estate, better blocks and better stairwells. And even though they cannot touch these places they agree that the depictions are an improvement, if only for their notoriety. He spins a series of tales based on an organised network of pushers on the Aylesbury estate selling coke, crack and weed and all that comes with that — high stakes, deceit, betrayal, paranoia. He gives them a world full of territorial gunfights, kidnaps and murder, a rivalry between the mafia-like Aylesbury boys and other nearby gangs, like the North Peckham boys, the New Cross 'Ghetto Boys' and a gang of white boys from Bermondsey filled with racial hatred.

It's all codswallop. These gangs were never as systematised as he makes them out to be. Walworth didn't really do gangs. True, there were a bunch of boys on the Aylesbury Estate that aspired to be more, but Emcee and I were a part of a group that didn't really know much about that. I always thought Walworth was insignificant when it came to that sort of thing. In a way I embraced that insignificance, we were centrally located yet an anonymous part of a world famous city.

'Man, we should pick up our feet,' Fire says. 'You don't keep man like Emcee waiting.'

"Man like Emcee,' I say. 'What does that mean? That he ain't like the rest of us?'

He baulks at that offering. 'Whud' ya mean? Emcee 'a big man y'know.'

I smile. I'm tempted, so I ask. 'What happened to those

guys then? The ones that jumped you?'

His smile comes alive again. 'I see. Ya wanna know if man's big time too.'

He explains how they eventually caught the guy that took the bottle to his head. They had received a tip-off that he had been spotted outside the Borough St. police station, in the line of young black boys who were queuing up to work a few hours as stand-ins for line-ups. They had 'tooled' up and driven there, waiting over a good hour for their ambush.

'I jooked that boy up,' he says. I regret encouraging him. He is demonstrative in his retelling, he swings his arms, leaps back and forward to mimic a stabbing motion. The entire sight is disturbing, the way he is thrilled by it all, the way he attempts to claim history. But at what cost do we do this? At what cost do we tell a story? I watch Fire mimic all these thrusting motions and make a jester of himself. I realise how badly he wants to hold on to this story and how deeply embarrassed I am by it.

I've asked Emcee the same question a number of times, during rare phone conversations or during a WhatsApp text message exchange dragged out across international times zones. At what cost do we tell our stories? He's accused me of sanctimony more than once. He says it's always been my drug. 'So hey,' his reply read, 'what I wrote wasn't my story, but at the same time it was. The person that owned a gun wasn't next door, but you could be sure there were less than six degrees of separation that stood between us and them. Growing up, there were six degrees of separation between us and every kind of danger.'

I did not want him to diminish the space and opportunity those degrees of separation afforded us. Space for us to attend, for instance, Thursday Boy's Brigade meetings where, as part of the 168th Company, he and I would learn how to play the bugle, to march and stand at attention. It's there where we heard our first bible stories, where we participated in regional bible knowledge competitions, where we'd learned to memorise the Lord's Prayer.

Fire and I pass the East Street Baptist Church — where the 168th Company meetings used to be held. It's a small traditional building with window frames, wrought iron fencing and a side door that have always been painted and repainted in aquamarine. I don't stop for memories. I am two strides ahead of Fire, propelled by my disappointment with it all. The second half of the market appears to have thinned out even further, with only a sprinkling of stalls and traders, among them a Nigerian man selling Nollywood DVDs, and a South Asian man flogging faux leather pastel coloured handbags. I'd always thought of East Street and its market as the neighbourhood's major artery, as something that would outlive me. It had survived already for more than a century, moving from Walworth Road to East Street in 1904 to make way for tram lines. It was a place that didn't always have everything you wanted — you weren't going to find the latest pair of Air Jordans there — but it always had everything *you needed* — like underwear, batteries, food and soap. Yams were sold alongside potatoes. Okra alongside cucumbers. Now it looks like it might not even last another decade.

Fire attempts to break the silence. 'So what do you do out in the States?' he asks.

'I work for an entertainment magazine.'

'Oh yeah? Doing what?'

'I review film, music. Books.'

He gives up after that, just as we come to a point where there are no stalls whatsoever, just tables piled with clothes and signs that read '£3 each or two for £5'. Then the market spits us out, and I am in an even more familiar space, the last quarter length of East Street, where aside from a handful of shops it is solely residential. The Aylesbury Estate Taplow building still stands, a 12-floor modern relic dotted with satellite dishes and anti-pigeon netting. On the side wall that runs along the building's foot ramp are the words 'Migrants Welcome Cops Not Welcome Here!' spray-painted in black. A little further up East Street, where the estate's old Wolverton building used to be, the first few floors of a new building stand behind wood panel construction with lettering that reads 'Harvard Gardens is coming'. On my side of the street the family-owned fishmonger's still lives beside the William Hill and the best kept shop-front on the strip is still the gravestone display in the window of the Francis Chappell & Son's Funeral Directors. Death is recession proof.

I find myself too distracted to focus or revel in the nostalgia of the streets I once took to school. I am disappointed even more so with Emcee and Fire than I am with the loss of living memories. Their distortions only help reinforce the foreign sense of unbelonging I already feel whenever I return to London. They are active participants in this transformation.

I slow down and let Fire lead us the short distance we have left, just as we begin to pass the brown bricks of Innis House, the post-war three-winged block of council flats where, for almost 20 years, Emcee and I had lived two floors apart. Fire would not suspect it held any significance to me. I hardly look at it as we pass. I wouldn't be able to enjoy it today. I have already had a mouthful of memory.

Marcia Road is tucked behind the Old Kent Road, a small street with limited access, lined with terrace houses and little else. Half-a-dozen young black men loiter outside the entrance to one of these houses, in Moncler and Ralph Lauren coats, H&M and True Religion Jeans. They make way for Fire. They grunt and bump fists with him. They nod at me with a quick flick of the head. Fire leads me in and towards the rear of the house, past a staircase and into what must be the living room. It's a decent size for central London real estate but not the extravagant setting I expected it to be. The walls are painted white, there are wood panel floors and a stone-coloured mid-century modern style sofa sitting off the wall. It's all more understated than I imagined, but then I remind myself that Emcee is in the publishing industry where income, even for the most successful, pales in comparison to film and music. Fire tells me to wait here, and then he is gone. I stand at the fireplace. The built in bookshelves to either side are completely lined with copies of his books. Above the fireplace is a blown up poster of the cover art to *Thy Kingdom Come*, a black background with gold lettering above the gold skull necklace, minus a lower jaw, that he has made a fictional sign of membership amongst the Aylesbury Boys. Staring at it, I am reminded of another case that Emcee makes for himself, that I ought to be pleased he is bringing young men to books in a way that hasn't been done before.

Just as I begin to believe that he is intentionally keeping me waiting, Emcee walks into the room. 'Koye,' he cries. He is genuinely excited as he moves towards me and pulls me into an embrace. 'Seven years,' he says, 'and all you give us is a couple Christmases here and there.' I forgot how baritone his voice is without a phone to dull its reception. I forgot how tall he was too. He holds me at arm's length by the shoulders and takes me in. He is barefoot in jeans and a white top that clings to his upper muscular build. His hair and beard are salt and peppered.

'How's the family?' he says as he gestures towards the sofa and we move to sit. His tone is avuncular.

'They're good. Mum's good.'

'And your stay so far?'

I remove my hat as I sit and, as always, I run my hand across the keloid scarring on the back of my head, as though attempting to pull some of my hair over the marking. It's a futile but instinctive habit I've developed over the years. 'It's been interesting,' I say. 'Your man Fire. You've fed him some stories. He can spin a good yarn. Anyone else would've been convinced.'

EAST

Heavy Manners

Tim Wells

Much as I know what rap is, but know nothing about rap, you can stand on the same streets and hear the same music but they're not the same streets anymore.

At the time I'm writing about me and my mates were on our first jobs or unemployed. We mostly did unskilled work, warehouse or, as I was doing, building. Hard graft but cash in hand. Being young we laughed at people who worked indoors. Soon enough I was learning a trade: silk screen stretching. But as soon as I'd mastered it and put in a bit of time the process was automated and we were out on our ear. Pull up … that situation has been getting a rewind all through our lives.

The concrete is there, the stains are different. The urgency is strident, the pace is different. The rain still falls, the reflections are different.

It's a market. It's right that it shouldn't be the same. It never was. Last week's fruit is mush, and last season's fashions are for losers. We've lost plenty, but losers we ain't.

Looking up Ridley Road from Kingsland Road there's still a crush of people, ever a mixtape of voices and languages. I could show you where Mosley was punched to the ground, where my mates got cut, where my own blood spattered. It's a market, all cut and thrust.

Come Saturday at home it was a scramble to get into the bathroom early. It was always a busy day. Breakfast, shmatta and out. Shmatta was all important, looking a nebbische was death. You'd wanna look better than the grebos, better than the office bods, better than your chinas.

Clean pants — we weren't savages — fresh shirt, matching socks, tank top, Harrington in the warmer months — Crombie when it's 'tatoes. Frank Wright loafers, cherry red or black depending on the tank top. Either way there'd be a gleaming penny tucked into the band across the front of the shoe, hiding behind the tassle. Shweet as.

From home it was a brisk walk to the bus stop on Stamford Hill and dahn to get records. This was where the day really started. Don't be at the back of the crowd and don't miss any killers.

Record shops were a world to themselves back then. You

could spend a day there drinking beer, chatting rubbish. It's where everyone met up, debts would settle, news would share, rumours spread.

The etiquette of a record shop was all it's own. Choons were limited, many coming over from JA on a white label pre so if you weren't tipped to it, or had an ear for it, you'd miss out. Conversation dropped to a hush every time the needle hissed onto the kick of a new choon. The selector would only play a few seconds, enough to clock who the singer or DJ was, who the producer was and what the riddim was. The trick was to shout 'Mine!' and bag the choon before anyone else.

Older records and those currently hitting would be lined up on the walls, the title, artist and price written across the sleeve in heavy black felt tip. Sometimes I'm asked where I get the titles for my poems from: should anyone take a dip in my all killer/no filler box they'd know.

The air of anticipation as the needle hit the groove was akin to a horserace, and if the record delivered there'd be the same exhilaration and thrill. People shouting, jumping about and the selector pulling it up as sold copies flew over the counter to the people who'd yelled for it first. But then there could be the DJ cut: Dillinger? Trinity? Ranking Joe? Maybe a horns cut, and always the dub.

You'd need an ear, honed at dances and from listening to

reggae repeatedly. An ear that'd know who the DJ was, and more importantly, who the producer was. Kids into guitar music would follow bands, know their songs and albums. With reggae we categorised our music by producer. Dennis Brown might cut killer 7s on several labels but we'd classify as Joe Gibbs, Junjo Lawes, or Linval Thompson before we'd check the singer.

There were several shops locally, Regal dahn Lower Clapton, a stroll away on Stoke Newington Road was Third World, Body Music up in Tottenham, 36A Dalston Lane's M&D to name but a few and several market stalls too. The shops had a few constants. There was a Jamaica tourist board of a busty girl in a wet t-shirt with 'Jamaica' emblazoned across the front of it. I don't know if it portrayed Jamaica's best attributes but it certainly showed off hers. Jim Reeves was another. Most of the guitar music crowd don't believe me when I tell 'em there was always a selection of country at reggae shops. Jim Reeves was always there, and Marty Robbins' 'Gun Fighter Ballads' was perennial too. This was the kind of music popular with the older West Indians, as well as ska they had an ear for country, soul and jazz. Country and reggae both spring from the struggles of working people. Even in the more divided 70s and 80s there was some harmony on the record shelves. Leave people to get on with it and there usually is.

Sticky carpets was another constant, carpets sodden with slops from beer cans and the sweat from the hot press of a load of people in a small room and nervous sweat from jumping to get the best tunes. Back then there'd be a pall of smoke too. I really haven't missed coming back from a Saturday and having me clothes pen and ink.

We'd usually meet up at Rupie Edwards' stall on Ridley Road. That was a thriving street market in the heart of the area. Rupie was a producer himself had been making records from ska days, through skinhead reggae and into dub. He'd put some killer choons out on his Success label: 'The Return of Herbert Spliffington' and 'Promoter's Grouse' being particular faves of mine. In 1974 he got the first dub single into the top ten, 'Irie Feelings'. Rupie was always good for a chat and he'd always do a good deal. As well as reggae he sold a lot of gospel, we didn't buy that but we liked to chat with him, hearing his tales and sharing some beers. Sat halfway up the market, Rupie's stall led us right into Kingston, JA. It was said that King Tubby, who'd never left Jamaica, could actually give directions around Dalston; that's how close we were.

From Rupie's we'd hit M&D just past the Four Aces on Dalston Lane, that was better for current reggae. You'd get the new records there. We'd usually scan Echoes on a Thursday and check the reviews of new choons and take note of what we wanted to get over the weekend. There were pres too. White label records put out to test the popularity of a choon before it was released proper. These were real gold, you get a good choon way before it was released and there'd not be loads of copies. Definitely a way to get your chinas jealous.

Then it was on to pie and mash at Cooke's opposite the market. Easily the best nosh on Kingsland Road, not Amhurst Park, obviously, but definitely the best on offer on Kingsland Road in daylight. Conversation was usually about an upcoming dance, football, or what cinema allnighter we'd be hitting: kung fu or horror?

Outside of Cooke's were several tin trays that contained slithering live eels. You could pick one and they'd chop it and stew it there and then. The pavement in front was spattered with blood and sawdust. We used to take girls there and show 'em the eels. This was a time before sexting.

Pie and mash fair sets you for the day. Pie crust down, mash spread on the plate with a wooden spoon, plenty of liquor and then a dash of vinegar. Chili vinegar for the adventurous. The healthy lads went for double double, or two and two; that being two pies and two servings of mash. All downed with a fork and spoon. Knives were for shmegeges.

The inside of Cooke's was tiled and there were thick

wooden benches to sit on. There were coat hooks on the walls and these were shaped like eels. As it happens they're still there. Cooke's is now a Chinese restaurant, a good one at that, and the pie and mash front of the building has been listed and kept as it was.

A bit of a larf, vinyl and a belly full of grub. That was a Saturday morning.

There's a new record shop in Dalston. It's full of wankers.

Tayyabs

Nikesh Shukla

Conversation #1: Epiphany

'I didn't like Indian food before,' he tells me. 'It was all tikkas and vindaloos and naan breads. This,' he says, pointing at the air before sniffing it emphatically, pushing then pulling his hair back into its tight circular bun, 'this is authentic Indian food. I fucking love it.'

I don't correct him. We're standing in a queue in a Pakistani restaurant. Naan means bread. He listens to the tail end of an anecdote from one of his friends. It's about a synthesiser malfunctioning and sounding better than its original tones at a gig.

Realising he has missed the bulk of the story his friends are telling in the time it took to give me, a stranger standing by himself, idly scrolling through Twitter, an aside, he turns back to them. He then returns his attention to me. I may have made a new friend. I ask what he recommends, what his favourite dish is.

'The fucking lamb chops mate, they're out of this world. Literally.' He points to an A3 framed print on the wall. It's of a charred lamb chop framed against the curve of the earth. One of those stupid hipster projects where people attach food items to Go-Pro cameras and send them up as high as they can, into near space, with a drone or a weather balloon.

'Tasty?' I ask.

'They're delicious. So delicious. I have had several life epiphanies eating the things.'

'Really?' I ask. 'Sounds delicious. What sort of epiphanies?'

'I realised, eating one of their lamb chops, so succulent, so dripping in mustard seeds and oils and chilli and every single spice known to man, I realised I'll never be David Bowie. Ever. I'll be like him. But I'll never be him. But there is another David Bowie out there. And I'm going to find him. So I developed an app called Star Man, which allows male artists to upload videos of themselves doing acapellas, singing, rapping, doing poems, whatever the bloke wants to do, and they'll be rated by their peers. Anyone with a 4.5 rating or above gets to audition for my management company. We have a monthly showcase. Only costs them

£50 each to be in the showcase. You sing?'

I shake my head.

'Shame. I haven't had any ethnics yet.'

'Maybe we're not as talented?' I offer. 'Or confident.'

'I bloody hope not,' he says, turning his body away from me, back to his friends. 'My Arts Council funding depends on me getting five fucking videos from five fucking ethnics.'

*

He turns back to me after another ten minutes and ten feet of advancement. He still hasn't managed to engage in his friends' conversation. They've moved on to the trials and tribulations of fucking on Molly. Apparently, Molly can make you go for hours if you're able to get hard in the first place. Best to drop some Viagra before you go out, someone suggests.

'You eating by yourself?' he says to me, almost scoffing at my misfortune. I nod. 'Definitely have the lamb chops,' he says. 'It'll be like dining with a bunch of friends who'll help you re-evaluate your life choices. I decided I was going to try heroin when I was sat in here once.'

Conversation #2 Resurrection

My lamb chops arrive, sizzling in their fat and oil. I can see bubbles on their surface from where the barbecue has sweated the meat. I pick one up by the bone and bite. It burns my mouth.

A man in a suit sits alone next to me but opposite me. It's like we're on an awkward date, given the proximity of the tables in this section of Tayyabs, where they cram in enough bodies to ensure the clientele get what they want and the only people who need to snake between the tightly-packed tables are the inversely-hipped waiters. 'What are those?' he asks. I tell him. 'Can I try one? I'll pay you back if I order a plate.'

I pick the plate up by the wooden block it's been placed on and lift it towards the man. He stares at the lamb chops, still sizzling and picks up the biggest one.

'No,' I say. 'That's the best one. Take the smallest one. You might not like it.'

'Why did you leave it on the plate?'

'The best one? So it would continue to cook in its juices.'

'It's fair game as far as I'm concerned.'

'I could retract my offer.'

'You'd be breaking a binding contract.'

'How's that?' I ask.

'We established a binding contract. I made an offer. There was consideration for the offer. You accepted the terms of the offer and are now in the process of delivering the first batch of terms.'

'Are you a lawyer?' I ask.

He shakes his head. 'I have a law degree,' he says, smiling.

'Me too,' I say. 'You just regurgitated the first lecture we ever had on contract law.'

Smiling, he takes the biggest lamb chop off my plate, the best one. Before I can react, he has taken a huge bite, leaving behind the tasty gristle. When will white people learn to eat meat off the bone correctly? He regards the taste in his mouth. I keep the plate hovering, almost in grief at the loss of the best chop.

He swallows and looks at the chop. He places it on his plate. He looks at it. He picks it up and places it on the table, to his left, further away from me. 'Too oily,' he says. 'Not for me. What else do you recommend?'

Before I can react, he has taken out his phone and is tapping away. He then places it to his ear and waits. 'Jean,' he says, 'there's a problem with the numbers. They just don't add up.' I don't know if he's acting for my benefit, talking management bullshit until I get bored and carry on with my meal, or to drive home the point that he's much more important than me. I place my discarded chops on his table, and call over the waiter. I order another plate. I tell the waiter in pidgin Hindi/Urdu that the man next to me is a idiot. 'Want me to spit in his tikka masala?' he asks.

'Is that what he ordered?' I ask.

The waiter rolls his eyes.

Conversation #3 Early

She shows me the first photo of the lamb chops on her Instagram. Between the selfies and photos of funny graffiti, there are many grainy murky photos of the same dish. She comes here every week.

'It's starting to feel staid,' she says.

'Eating the same dish week after week?' I offer.

'I've eaten 500 of these lamb chops over the years,' she says.

'And what have you learned about yourself in all that time?'

'I'm a greedy fucker. I don't think I'll come here again. It's like everyone and their mum is an expert about this place. It's just lost its edge for me. Remember when it had edge?'

'No.'

'When did you first come here?'

I tell her the approximate year. 'I came here the year before that,' she says, forgetting she just showed me an

Instagram photo that disproves this. Her first visit, the year before mine, pre-dates the app.

'I remember,' I tell her. 'Looking at the walls and thinking, half of these desi heroes, none of you hipsters will ever know who they were. Talvin Singh, man, what a legend.'

'Such a great MC,' she says. 'I love the one where he samples *Knight Rider*.'

Conversation #4 History

She tells me that the proximity of Tayyabs to the East London mosque is no mistake. She tells me that magic happens here. It used to be a café, a typical east end caff, where occult magi gathered to talk strategy. She tells me 9/11 was an inside job. She tells me that yoga was invented by ostro-goths. She tells me that the recent ebola epidemic was the first strike in a religious war. She tells me that Jai Paul doesn't actually exist. She tells me that the recipe for the lamb chops was stolen from a nearby stall. The owner of the stall was a simple man who used to stand outside the mosque after Friday jummah. The recipe proved so successful, he was murdered and left to rot in the streets as a warning. She tells me that the flat she lives in backs on to the back of the restaurant and the extractor fans are sending her slowly crazy. She tells me she loves my skin tone □ it reminds her of yoga retreats in

India. She tells me I can kiss her.

Conversation #5 Statement

It feels like a moment of gravitas when Wasim comes to sit at my table and sip from his can of Fanta. He doesn't look at me. He's pinpointing different waiters, ensuring they are operating at optimum efficiency. He talks out of the side of his mouth, almost as if he is disregarding everything I say.

'My father,' he tells me. 'He would be proud. The recipe is nothing special. It is how we cook back home. Here, everyone has burned their mouths off with vindaloo for so long, they forget we like to taste our food. There is actually very little chilli in the marinade.'

'When did he die?' I ask.

Wasim tells me about his father's last week. He hadn't come to the restaurant in months by this point. He was more interested in stillness than noise. He was barely eating. He couldn't taste anything, he said. Hot tins of chopped tomatoes, with chilli powder, he lived off that. On his final day he told Wasim to start taking bookings; the business would crumble without it.

'My father doesn't understand, people will queue for his food. He didn't understand,' he corrects himself. 'And if they queue, there will always be others to stand behind them to see what the fuss is. That is the way of the British.'

Conversation #6 Self-Reflection

I lean forward to let the gas out. I crush the can in front of me and add to the pile. My friends are talking about the new *Star Wars* film. I haven't seen it. They do not care about spoilers. I want to do something that people will queue for, I think. I want to do something that transcends the page. The singe of burnt mustard seeds, the piquant persistence of lemon, the pops of cumin and coriander and the demonstrative tang of barbecued onion — that is what I want my work to be. Food is complex in the way words can never be. Because the more you chew, the more sustenance you get.

Broadgate

Tim Burrows

The Banker reflected upon the lit faces of the passengers, the dull blue-white glow hinting at a communion that was never more than implied on the 21:18 from Liverpool Street. But it was there. A communion of behaviours, of desires, always unspoken yet still evident. A communion of trivial obsessions and recriminations, infidelities and repetitive pathologies, neatly sewn up and somehow made sense of by a series of social media apps and communication tools.

Friday night; faces sagged with a mix of fatigue, relief and drunkenness. He had spent another day working in Broadgate, which to him had become more than a workplace. Its architecture was causal geometry, as if the grey blocks, wrought iron girders, prisms and circles had shaped him as the highly successful, highly sexed, man he was today. His sense of self-worth percolated through the air-con systems and security-guarded rooms of his building. Around it, the City was a set of shapes which poked into view from different vantage points in Greater London's further reaches, lights twinkling amber, standing for attention.

He never felt more alive than when he pulled in to Liverpool Street station. When it was built, it was dug 17 feet under the ground. Carved into the earth. The Banker felt lucky to be born on the Thames Estuary in the 1970s. Grew up in Chatham on the Medway river valley in Kent; moved to Snaresbrook and Wanstead on the other side of the river, and now Brentwood, Essex suburbia. The pride of the South East, aided by the M25 and the clogged arterials that connected retail parks to suburbs.

Broadgate felt like home more than Brentwood did. He approached Saturday with fear, time with Sandra like a cavity after a week's febrile communications back in the heat of the city. At the corner of the carriage, loud talk of work drinks that got out of hand. 'Got absolutely wrecked in front of my boss bruv. Shit, we were paralytic but it was all right in the end — he bought the coke.' Many were listening in. They'd all been there, and some wanted to be there right now.

Broadgate was built around Liverpool Street on the site of the old and unloved Broad Street station next door, and the development squeezed in at the station from all sides. Of all the pubs there, the Fleetwood was probably his favourite. Low-lit and authentically inauthentic, with a digitally printed blown-up detail of an old photograph of Liverpool Street on the wall. The City spoke to a heavily regarded truth about the south-east English lifestyle, a lifestyle of banter, concealed obsessions and serious drinking. Everything was a barter for trade while jockeying for position. Conversation rumbled, growling regurgitations of a day's sparring, brains spaffing their loads. A lads' holiday fuelled by lines: the bravado-laden one-liners traded in bars, and the powder unwrapped to fuel them.

His was the usual self deception. Just pop in for a couple on the way home. Text Sandra to say you'd be late. The constancy of the buzzing pocket, the innuendo; outside-fag chats presaging tonsil-to-torso formalities back in the office. Fumble for the train before recriminations at home. He thought his wife might know what he was up to, but he took that as a signal to ignore all that and concentrate on his interests in Broadgate, on the chase into different tunnels of anticipation. But it wasn't simply these different women he craved. Communication had become his fetish, his smartphone a constant provider of escape routes, burrowing out to nowhere-roads, a deferral hidden in the shorthand of animal instinct.

Some had already been caught out. He'd heard about a bloke at UBS, who'd synced everything — Facebook, Google Hangouts, Whatsapp, Skype — to his laptop. 'One day he'd accidentally left his computer at home and his missus used it for something,' the story was told to much amusement in the pub. 'One of the temps from work he'd had a thing with started messaging him stuff and you can guess what she thought about that. In the end she read all his messages to different birds, been goin' on for months it had. She smashed up his car with a hammer, totalled it. Took a photo and sent it to his Facebook. It went viral! As you can imagine, he was not happy.'

The Banker retold the tale to Pavel, who ran a greasy café perched precariously just outside the ancient wall of the City. He ate lunch at Pav's on the rare occasion he left Broadgate's embrace — it was his last link to his idealistic youth, the days he used to visit lesser cafes for ideological reasons. He liked to watch how Pavel held court to anyone who listened, duly imparting advice like an agony uncle. Upon hearing the story as told by the Banker, he shook his head, but with the suggestion of a grin glinting out of the side of his mouth. 'My mother's brother was a priest, but he didn't care how he spoke,' he yelled over the fryer (his advice was never exclusive). 'And he said man is like the rat, he is always looking for a new hole! He never satisfied with what he's got!'

*

Daniela was a new cleaner at the company. England, to her, was still a secret. Even though she had lived here for 11 or so years, she felt she never knew how to behave. She was 20 when she left Bogota after a successful uncle became her benefactor, funding her master's in English. Her publishing dream fizzled out years ago, but estrangement still felt too strong a word for her predicament — too isolating. She regarded the gang of assorted exiles in London she'd spent her twenties with as a silent majority, an invisible republic of kitchen parties fuelled by cheap booze and good music. But, as friends left after visas had run out and dreams faded, she felt like she had figured London out, its compromises and the temporary surges of epiphany it can often provide, epiphanies unmasked as false dawns as soon as you try to hold them in your hand.

The previous year she'd moved to Southminster, a relatively isolated town surrounded by fields and marshland at the end of a railway line in the Dengie peninsula in eastern Essex. She'd first visited on a glorious summer day with her boyfriend Giovanni, making a pilgrimage up by the mudflats and salt marshes, to the ancient church of St

Peter's on the Wall, stopping to watch oystercatchers from a grassy bank. When their landlord told them he was going to double the rent, they decided to make a drastic, romantic break from east London, and moved to Southminster. After their relationship began to disintegrate, he blamed it on the place – 'It's too fucking quiet Dani!' – but she stayed, unable to stand the thought of moving back to London.

Most mornings after she had arrived into Liverpool Street she sat on a bench in Broadgate Circle, smoking a cigarette, mulling over the effects of this decision, how she had hardly made a single friend in the eight months she had lived in Southminster. The Banker began to notice her, the way the smoke fanned out of her straw-like bob, dark freckles piercing through a white haze. He took it upon himself to borrow a light. He liked the way she talked. 'Any fool can work, all he needs is a job,' she told him early on in their what turned out to be daily meetings.

They talked about his job, her job; his obsession with women, her obsession with marshland; his dying relationship, her dead one. He said that the only real comfort he felt in life was within Broadgate's embrace. She talked of how she felt its hold was suffocating, and digressed into a monologue about how Bogota claustrophobia is very different from the London variety. The latter is entropic, born of comfort and order and stasis; the former jabs and shouts and dances. 'In Bogota, roads clot with traffic and addicts die in the street; some of the city's homeless are encrusted in a dirt that you might call Victorian. But London is still the filthier metropolis to me. It's an invisible filth, tidied away and locked in some vault, or memory, safely underground, incognito. London's scars are worn inside.'

After a while, the Banker tried to remedy Daniela's unhappiness and offered her money. She looked at him witheringly. 'Money doesn't seem to have put you in an especially good place, wouldn't you say?' But she still found there was something interesting about him that she couldn't let go of.

*

One Wednesday after Daniela had finished for the day she suggested the Banker visit the Dengie with her. He agreed they should set off right there and then, even cancelling his meetings and phoning his boss to say something had come up with Sandra, something serious.

It wasn't often the Banker felt this urgent. Grubby as the carriage was, it encased them, a bullet shell shot towards the sea, away from the City's bunker and into the lightness of fantasy. He felt a kind of release, as if some forgotten synapses were being recharged. Daniela held his gaze as they talked for much of the journey to Wickford, where they changed to catch the train to Southminster, a smaller service with fewer carriages. After stopping at her place to get him some of Giovanni's old walking boots, Daniela and the Banker walked to Bradwell, skirting fields lined with comically bulbous pigs, and spinning with their arms out, taking in the horizon. All was sky. The steamrollered landscape appeared so still and sedate. A dalmatian horse in a ruddy-green field glowed like an emblem.

'It looks so calm,' said Daniela. 'But look closer and all is tension, like gritted teeth.' She had read in an old book that the preponderance of sky over the land led a zealously religious fervour in these parts. 'It is a kind of culture that isn't a culture, or if it is it fits somewhere between my memories of flat American landscapes in Hollywood films or TV series I have seen, and there's some grim puritanical thing about the place, I don't know.' They stopped in a pub in the village of Tillingham to be told they had been noticed in a field by the locals, who looked his mud-flecked suit up and down.

Daniela and the Banker approached St Peter's by the grassy sea-wall path that hovered above the spongy marsh, separating or indeed saving the land from the churning North Sea. They stopped to sit and look out to to the water. The wall reminded her of Cartagena on the Caribbean coast where she'd worked during tourist season in her late teens. The Banker told her he had been there on a gap year: Christmas day eating ceviche, looking over the ocean from the bar that had been situated on top of the wall that surrounds the city. She replied matter-of-factly that the wall in Cartagena was built with the blood of slaves, many of whom died cutting up stone in the heat. The new skyscrapers and apartments there were built with 'laundry' money, she said, and many of the old colonial buildings had swimming pools on top of them that hardly anyone could use. But for Daniela it was always the sea, not the wall, that held the most dread. It was a wash of definitions, an ocean of disputations, one that could be interpreted a million different ways. It reminded her of London itself, a great confusion within a wall, its secrets perpetually unknown. To her, it was the sea that was inside the wall in Cartagena, not the city. 'On land, we are always outside looking in. My country was built on slave ships, but it's the same as your slave streets, slave suburbs. My ship of slaves is the early-morning train we all catch, to and from, to and from, every day for our little piece.'

Daniela lowered herself down the grassy bank and walked over the marsh, towards the point where the water began. A surge of wind prompted her hair to take a shape around her akin to a basking jellyfish caught in a wave. A flock of migrating birds billowed in the sky, reminding the

Banker of the animated ident that greeted him when he turned his smartphone on. He looked back to the shoreline and she had gone. Gulls rested where Daniela had been, but there was no sign of her. The Banker got to his feet and bellowed her name. Panicked, he looked at his phone and dialled the emergency services. No signal. He looked out towards the sea and beyond the green marsh he thought he could see something in the water. He staggered down the bank towards the water, but his legs gave way to the uneven, bouncy ground. Trying to crawl on his chest, he noticed a worm powering out of the soil, up and into the light.

He exhaled, buffering into a delirious stasis, comforting himself with thoughts of clean lines, glass and steel. After a little while he pulled himself up the bank and back over the other side. Dry land's horizon glowed at its seam. It was the most beautiful dusk he'd seen in a while.

Spluttering, he reached for his smartphone. What time was it? He was relieved when the clock on his phone said it was almost 4pm. If he could get back to Broadgate, to the Fleetwood, it would be fine. It wasn't his fault, all this, and he couldn't have helped her anyway. Wherever she'd gone, she did it herself. She was obviously troubled. Whatever this was, it wasn't his fault. And besides, he had work to do.

He carried on away from the sea and towards Bradwell

village. He never looked back. Early evening stillness stirred into something more irascible, the wind beating the flat horizon as if to punish it. He got to the end of the track and could see a collection of mean looking houses in the distance. He met the road and heard a car approaching from behind, waving it down. 'You look rough mate.'

There was a faint whistle as the train approached Southminster station. The cursed rumble of its engine flatlined with a hiss, a hot frying-pan splashed with water. Finding signal, he sent a text: 'Pint?'

Warm and Toasty

Yvvette Edwards

I noticed her when she was walking back on her own. She was on the other side of Chatsworth Road, and there was no sign on her face of the rage I'd seen so many times before when she glared at Warm and Toasty as she passed by. Her head was down, her shoulders hunched. She seemed preoccupied, troubled, and was probably cold. It felt bitter today, colder than the 4°C indicated on my iPhone. Maybe it was because we'd been lucky this year with the long warm autumn, and were only now experiencing our first proper winter snap. Or maybe it felt colder because of the lashing wind. She was wearing a macintosh, and the thin material, fit for keeping her dry and little else, flapped about her lean frame like a flag on a pole.

It was just after 11, and quiet in the café, probably would

be until lunchtime, the bulk of my day's business already done, though I'd be open as usual till five. My only customer was young man in a pin-striped suit who sat at the corner window table nursing an espresso con panna over a yoga laptop. Huge Bose headphones hugged his ears. He was absorbed as I strode to the café door, opened it, stepped out and shouted, 'Hey!'

Though a number of other people on the street turned around, she did not. A dapper elderly man, looked at me, pointed to himself, and when I shook my head and pointed at the woman, walked quickly after her, caught up with her outside the haberdashers, said a few words and she stopped and looked over at me, at Warm and Toasty. I smiled and beckoned. She stood still, watching me with suspicion. I smiled again, shouted louder, 'Please!'

There was a delay before she began walking towards me, pausing at the kerbside for a break in the traffic, then crossed, watching me with an expression on her face that made it clear she had no idea why I was calling her over.

'Would you like a cup of tea?' I asked.

'You taking the fucking piss?' she answered.

'No. I'm not. I've seen you, and your son, passing by, in the mornings. A cup of tea, or a coffee, hot chocolate if you like. It's cold today. And it's on the house.'

'Free?'

'Absolutely.'

'I won't be buying any of your toast,' she said.

I stepped back, holding the door open for her to enter.

'I'm not trying to sell you any,' I said.

She paused a moment then stepped inside and I closed the door behind her. She looked around, and for a moment I looked around as well. The interior walls had been stripped back to expose the brickwork. I'd grown up just a couple of hundred yards from here, on Kingsmead Estate, with my mum. Chatsworth Road was where she'd shopped when I was a child, back in the days before the road had changed beyond recognition, when the market was a fulltime bustling, teeming strip of inner-city culture, before it had evolved into a weekly crafts and farmers' market. Back then, no-one could've guessed that making our flat look decent didn't require years of scrimping and scraping for wallpaper and paint, that the only thing needed was a chisel and some black bags. The walls were littered with framed black and white prints of actors, old-timers like Richard Roundtree, Dorothy Dandridge and Rudolf Walker. There were record sleeves from LPs and singles, the kind of music I grew up on, *1000 Volts of Holt*, Roberta Flack, Bob Marley's *Exodus*. Then there was the random stuff, like the rusty bicycle my guest was staring at, suspended from the ceiling above the front window. I'd spent weeks scouring dumps and Gumtree for cheap tables. Shaded lights dangled low above them. Instead of chairs, I had old benches and stools. Splashes of colour came from the vibrant African-print cushions strewn on top of them. The floorboards were bare. I'd been aiming for shabby chic and had ended up with classic Hackney gentrification.

'You're doing alright for yourself,' she said, her tone at odds with any compliment I might have taken from her words.

I shrugged then indicated the high stool on the customer side of the bar, went around to my side, all stacked white china and chrome and glass, stood in front of the polished percolator, grinder, juicer. She was looking over my shoulder, at the huge blackboard that covered most of the wall behind me, which had my menu and prices chalked onto it.

'What would you like?' I asked.

'Tea.'

Normally I would have asked what kind, listed a handful of the wide selection of choices I had — green, decaf, rooibos, chai? — but I knew the bristling woman before me would not be impressed. She hated me, hated Warm and Toasty. She didn't need to explain; I got it.

'Milk?' I asked.

'Yeah.'

I put a cup of tea on a saucer down in front of her. 'Sugar's there,' I said. 'Help yourself.'

She ignored the tongs in the kiln-cooked, hand-painted bowl, used her fingers to pop three rocks of raw cane demerara into her cup, stirred, then sipped.

'He's a bit old, your son, for you to be taking him to school,' I said.

She'd folded her arms, was massaging her elbows with her fingertips. 'And?'

'He's what, 11? 12?'

'13.'

'I started walking to school on my own when I was six,' I said. My mother had been a single parent, always had two jobs on the go, trying to make ends meet. She left the house in the mornings before I did, after she'd done my hair. I had my own key even then, kept it on a piece of string around my neck so I wouldn't lose it, sorted myself out for breakfast — when I could find it — dressed myself. In those days, schools prepared meals on site, and after first break, the building was filled with the smell of cooking lunch. Most days, after first break, I did little learning. I passed the time focussed on my grumbling stomach, fantasising and trying to work out from the aromas what I would soon be eating for lunch.

'Well your mum probably thought you'd actually get

to school if she didn't take you. If I don't take Justin in, he doesn't go.'

'How comes?'

She was about to tell me to mind my own business, when the bells of Big Ben began to toll. Her fingers stopped moving. We both looked over at the young man in the corner as he raised his mobile phone to his ear with one hand, and wiped his handlebar moustache with the back of the other.

'Drake and Hallister,' he said, paused a moment, then, 'Speaking.'

The new gentry knew the power of talking. They gathered together around huge tables in designated rooms at home, in gastropubs, established delis, trendy wine-and-cheese bars; at genteel coffee mornings, breastfeeding support groups and yummy-mummy playgroups, with therapists and counsellors, in groups and forums and committees, they gathered together and they talked their bloody heads off. This woman lived outside their smear-free, pristine windows, on her own, looking in.

She sighed, looked back at me, rubbed her arms more slowly. 'It's a long story ...'

'I've got loads of time.'

'You don't wanna hear my problems.'

'Yes, I do.'

She looked at me steadily, assessing, weighing my

sincerity. I did not look away.

'Fine! He hates school, that's what he says, but it's not school he hates, it's me … not me, our life, this life.'

'That's pretty big.'

She rummaged in her bag, pulled out a packet of pills. I immediately realised that what I had taken for anger was actually pain, well some of it, anyway. I watched as she swallowed two tablets, closed her eyes, felt her relief that it would soon begin to abate. She gently rubbed her thighs with her flat palms. Though she was younger than me by a couple of decades, suddenly, she reminded me of my mother. After a moment, she opened her eyes, saw me watching, seemed embarrassed.

'Sickle cell,' she said.

My mother had had sickle cell disease. She died 12 years ago at the age of 52, four years younger than I was now. She suffered with it for all of my life that I can remember, getting worse as she got older, more frequently in crisis, especially at this time of year when the weather was on the change, her condition badly affected by the cold and dampness in the air. It wasn't the pain that finished her off though, it was the slow, relentless shutting down of her vital organs one by one. I already knew more about her life, what it must be like for her and her son living it, than she could have guessed. The gene is hereditary, passed on from generation to generation, though lucky ones, like me, carried only the trait. I'd never had children of my own. It wasn't something that particularly bothered me, but occasionally when I did reflect, I found myself wondering how big a part in that decision having sickle cell trait had played.

'Morphine?' I asked.

'Yeah … I'm a regular druggie.'

'I'm sorry,' I said.

It was her turn to shrug. 'It is what it is.'

The guy in the corner was clicking his raised fingers to get my attention. He came here a couple of mornings a week and always clicked his fingers for the bill. It was unnecessary. Arrogant. I checked myself before nodding and printing out his receipt, putting it on a bill tray with a wrapped mint, then took it over and handed it to him with a smile. I used to work in the council call centre. Dealing with rude customers was my forte. He picked up the bill and put a tenner on the tray.

'Keep the change,' he said without looking at me, zipping his laptop into his rucksack.

I said, 'Thanks.' By the time I got back to the counter, he had exited the café.

Now it was just the two of us. As I looked at her, she laughed. The sound was harsh. 'I've gotta take my hat off to you! You must be laughing all the way to the bank with this place.'

'I can pay my bills. I wouldn't say I was rolling in it.'

'I'm surprised. It's packed in here every morning. I've seen whole families coming in, mums with two, three, four kids. They could afford to buy a frigging toaster with what it must cost for one breakfast, a toaster and a loaf of bread … fucking yuppies!'

She was right. I had about 30 families who were regulars, who came for breakfast two or three times a week, many more who popped in ad hoc. I even took table bookings some mornings, usually on birthdays, and the demand for children's breakfast parties on Saturday and Sunday mornings was so high at the moment that I was completely booked up over three weeks in advance, had had to turn customers away. They came with their Bugaboo buggies and Storksac nappy bags, often paying for their kids to do little more than lick off the jam.

'They sent me for a job,' she said.

'Who?'

'The DWP. Sent me for a job at Iceland's.'

'Did you tell them about your sickle cell?'

'Yep. I can't tell you how many letters my doctor's writ. They know, they know all that and they still sent me to Iceland's, said if I never went, they'd sanction me. So I went. Exactly what I knew would happen happened. Same night

I had to call out the ambulance. They wannid to take me to hospital, but I said no. I go into hospital, Justin goes into care, and he can't handle it. I said no and they had to give me the transfusions at home. Didn't wanna, but I didn't budge. Was in bed for nearly a week. And you know what they did after all that? Sanctioned me. Said I left suitable employment. Cut my benefits for six months …'

'When? When did they do that?'

'Six weeks ago.' She shook her head. 'We're eating from the foodbank, and you've got people paying you two pound bloody fifty for toast, toast; a frigging slice!'

I had to agree with her, it was incredible. I'd worked for over 30 years at the Housing Department call centre, talking to callers about their points on the Housing Register. I'd been cussed out, screamed at, threatened on a daily basis. It was a routine part of the job, expected. Not every call was like that, but enough of them were to make me yearn for something different as the decades rolled by. I'd always paid into the pension system and I retired as soon as I got the chance, at 55, on my actual birthday, took a lump sum from my pension pot, leaving just about enough of a pension to pay my bills. I used the capital to open this place. My friends thought I'd gone mad.

'I watched a programme on TV,' I said, 'years ago. It was about a guy who worked as a professional cat psychologist.

My mum told me about it. She was spending most of her time at home then, watching telly. She couldn't believe her eyes, made me watch it so I could tell her what she was seeing was really true. Back home, in the Caribbean, someone owned a cat, they didn't even give it a name. You'd be lucky if people who had mental health problems could find trained professionals to help them. This whole country's filled with people with mental health problems who can't get the help they need, and that man was making a living as a cat psychologist, not just any living, a seriously good one.'

She said, 'And?'

'While I was watching, the idea for this place just came to me.'

I serve eight kinds of bread; soda, brioche, multigrain, pumpernickel, rye, gluten-free, wholemeal and my bestseller, good old regular white. I had an amazing array of artisan jams including strawberry and pepper, hot banana, and ginger and rhubarb. You could have your slice of toast with butter, margarine or olive oil, peanut, almond or cashew butter, Marmite or chocolate spread, and if you were particularly famished, you could have two slices for the bargain price of £3.75, three for £5.00.

'Your prices are nothing but a rip off,' she said.

'My customers are happy with what they pay.'

'I'll give you that, but it don't make it right.'

'Look at the biggest companies in this country. You think they've got to where they are worrying about whether what they're doing is right?'

She stands up. 'Thanks for the tea. I still don't know why you gave it to me.'

I'd had enough hungry mornings when I was young to recognise the look of a schoolchild on their way to school with an empty stomach. I wanted to feed her son. That was why I'd called out to her initially. But our conversation had moved me on from my starting point. She reminded me of my mother. I saw my childhood being played out in the life of her son. I wanted to help them. Both of them. She sat erect in the seat opposite me, her posture as much a response to pain as a declaration of pride. She would no more appreciate an offer of charity than I appreciated that tip left with such poor grace by my last customer. I spoke slowly, carefully selecting my words.

'I need an assistant, for the mornings, ideally seven days a week, two hours a day, more at the weekends if you can manage it. I'll pay you the going rate. And you can bring Justin. He can have breakfast here before he goes to school.'

'Why? Why are you doing this?'

'Because right now it's really busy during breakfast and I'm struggling to cope on my own.'

'Staring when?'

'Tomorrow. At 7am. Seven till nine.'

'I thought you opened at eight?'

'I open to the public at eight, but I need you here at seven.'

'Don't you need references or anything?'

'I just need two things; for you to be here on time, and for you not to call my customers 'fucking yuppies'. Do you think you can do that?'

She laughed. 'Yeah, I can do that.'

'What's your name?' I asked.

She laughed again, 'Bit late for that, after you've already given me a job. It's Latisha. Latisha Wilson. What's yours?'

'Josephine Allen. Phin. Most people call me Phin.'

'I'll see you in the morning at seven, Phin.'

I said, 'Thank you.'

'You're serious, aren't you?'

'Yes,' I said, 'I am.'

I had already opened the front door by the time Latisha arrived with Justin, though she was about ten minutes early, serving the schoolboy in front of me, four others patiently waiting for their turn.

'Morning,' I said. 'Justin, why don't you join the back of the queue? Have a think about what drink you'd like, and what you want on your toast.'

Latisha stared at me, at the queue of schoolchildren, confused. I said, 'I told you it'd be busy,' as another child entered. 'Chuck your stuff under the counter. It'll be fine there. Maybe I can leave you with the toast and I'll sort out the hot drinks.'

She did as I suggested. 'Wash your hands, please. There's an apron for you beside the juicer.' I cut the two slices of toast with Nutella on the chopping board in front of me in half, put them into a paper bag, handed it to the young man with his hot drink in a disposable cup. 'You said tea, didn't you?'

He nodded.

'Have a good day, Olu. See you tomorrow,' I said.

'Thanks,' he answered.

Latisha materialised beside me, knotting her apron strings across her stomach. I pulled two slices of toast from the toaster. Put them down in front of her, smiled at the young girl in front of us. 'Morning Keira. Strawberry jam and a cup of hot chocolate?'

'Morning. Yes please,' she said.

I looked at Latisha. 'Can you do the topping please? I'll get her hot chocolate.'

'Sure.' She turned to the girl in front of her. 'Hi honey. You want just jam, or marg as well?'

'With marg please.'

'Sure. Two slices coming up.' As Latisha began to butter the bread she asked me, 'Takeaway?'

'They're all takeaways,' I said, tipping the hot milk into a disposable cup, stirring it, then putting on the lid. Latisha was easing the toast into a paper bag as I handed Keira her drink.

'Has she already paid?' she asked.

'They don't pay. It's a kind of members-only breakfast club.' I grinned at the expression on Latisha's face. 'You should never judge a person by the price of their toast,' I said. 'We'd better get a move on. They've got to get to school.'

She watched me for a moment, reassessing me, shook her head then smiled. Keira had already taken a bite from one of the slices, was folding the top of the paper bag back over. 'Mmm ... thanks,' she said.

'See you tomorrow,' Latisha replied. 'Have a good day.'

There is Something Very Wrong with Leyton Mills Retail Park

Gareth E. Rees

There's something wrong with Leyton Mills Retail Park. I didn't notice it in the old days when I used to go there with my wife to shop in B&Q. In need of a bit of wood, or a thingy to fix an object to another thingy, we'd drive from Clapton across the Lea Bridge, then follow the railway lines along the back of the Hackney Marsh. A solar system of mini-roundabouts slung us like space probes past a Eurostar depot, allotments and petrol station, up a ramp into a car park surrounded by chain stores (Asda, Next, Pizza Hut, KFC, Costa Coffee, TK Maxx, you get the picture) built on a former railway goods yard.

B&Q means *Boring & Quiet*. They don't say that on the big orange sign, but that's what it means. It's the size of a hangar with impossibly tall aisles that go on forever. I'd trail forlornly behind Emily as she picked out rawl plugs or rollers or wallpaper paste. She knows what she's doing when it comes to DIY. She knows the gauges of things and what kind of paint adheres to what kind of surface. ('Oh shit you're not using gloss on the walls are you, Gareth? Give me the roller!') Mostly I'd glide on the trolley behind her or mess around on my iPhone. Sometimes we'd rush across the car park to Asda afterwards to pick up some things for tea. Then it was back in the car for home, B&Q quickly forgotten.

That was the old days. It's now six years later. I'm fatter, wrinklier, and a large portion of the ice caps have melted. Numerous people have died. An even bigger number have been born. The London Olympics have come and gone. In Switzerland the Hadron Collider started, stopped and started again, revealing evidence of the Higgs Boson particle. The scientists' theory is that there's stuff in the universe that you can't see. Dark matter and the like. It definitely exists because the stuff you can see doesn't make any sense otherwise. A boson is a force that acts on particles, giving them mass. Most probably. They think.

While they were scratching their noodles over this conundrum, Emily and I moved away from London, leaving our B&Q paint on the walls and our B&Q wood stain on the floor. Occasionally I return to the Big Smoke for meetings, usually on the cheaper train to Charing Cross. But today I'm on the fast train from Ashford to Stratford International, like a City high flyer or a famous actor. The train has a bullet nose and feels as if it's about to lift from the rails like a jet plane. Under the influence of a can of gin and tonic I remember that B&Q, sentimental for those old days when life was simpler. As the last lemony dregs slip down I resolve to walk all the way from Stratford to Clapton, passing through Leyton Mills Retail Park for old times' sake.

I come out of Stratford International into a neo-Soviet landscape of residential blocks overlooking fenced play areas and micro-orchards. A marble wall is engraved with Tennyson's line, *'to strive to seek to find and not to yield'*. Street names like Liberty Bridge Road, Prize Walk and Cheering Lane are emblems of a committee-decreed Games mythology superimposed upon industrial land. Other than a couple of workers in yellow jackets sliding poles from a van there's nobody on the streets. A threadbare green stretches towards silent stadia, the Westfield shopping mall and scaffolded tower blocks grazed by cranes. A sketch of a place waiting to happen, tainted with the melancholy that it might not.

Approaching Leyton, hoardings around the 'East Village' apartments proclaim a New Neighbourhood for *real people* and show images of actors playing the parts of those real people. Colour pictures of the proposed communal areas have features sketched onto them: swings, benches, bird houses and — inexplicably — hot air balloons. In Drapers Field a playpark is bustling with kids. To make sure everything stays friendly, signs are bolted onto the concrete:

> **Is this your first time here? I hope you are loved for the rest of HUMAN LIFE.**

> **Whenever you tip your head back and LAUGH, the whole street falls in LOVE with YOU.**

> **Is everything you love FOREIGN, or are you foreign to EVERYTHING you LOVE?**

I don't understand what the questions mean, or who the questioner is supposed to be. It's like the irritating copy you get on packaging that says 'Please recycle me!', or buses with signs that read 'Sorry, I am out of service'. You're supposed to imagine the consciousness of manufactured objects speaking to you, as if the constant nagging voices in your own head aren't enough to contend with.

After the signs I'm in familiar London terrain. Leyton High Road is a terrace of Victorian worker cottages with shops: **NOORUL ISLAM Books, NEMO SHOP & FASHION,** and **MOULOUDIA Pound Plus Super Market**. As the road bends, the dome of TK Maxx rises like a mosque on the far side of a bridge over the railway lines and M11 link road, the latter for which locals were evacuated and houses demolished in the 1990s, amidst the protests of a resistance movement who boarded themselves into the doomed properties. Cars hiss down a tarmac strip where their battle was lost, a victory parade of street lights marching over the hill's brow towards the motorway.

I pass loiterers smoking fags outside the tube station and descend into Leyton Mills Retail Park. At the bottom of the steps is a steel water fountain with a man hunkered beside it, staring at his phone. I walk down a tree-lined pedestrianised street with Subway, TK Maxx, Pizza Hut and KFC on one side and a row of fake independent shops on the other, their frontages painted onto the back wall of a building. There's a pretend shop called **Your Fashion**, another called **Musica** with a door that's been painted ajar as if to lure you in, and a café called **The Leyton** where they've painted pretend graffiti onto the pretend exterior. An entirely fabricated boutique called **b'Leyton Fun** has a sale on, which is great fictional news. In its window there's a gigantic biplane that looks like a penis with wings. **Marshall Music** has guitars floating in its window. *'Waltham Forest: it's happening here'* says a fake sticker on the fake door.

Two real human men in matching baseball caps sit on the

doorstep of the non-real **Leyton Gelato** ice cream parlour, drinking cans of lager, which spoils the conceit and I'm surprised they've not been moved on by the cartoon police. Next door is a place called **Livo Jazz** — 'open daily from 5pm' — but they've painted shutters onto the painted door to show that the non-existent venue is closed. I should come back at five o'clock with a saxophone and start hammering on the fake shutters, crying, 'Open up you fuckers!'

At the end of the row of fake shops is an alleyway full of cans and sleeping bags. The homeless here are real enough. A sign on the wall says:

Counterfeit DVD vendors are trespassing and may be prosecuted

This seems a bit rich bearing in mind the street I've just walked down.

I peer into KFC where there's a scrum of teenagers by the counter. Signs assure me that they use '100% real chicken'. To prove it, the wall is covered with a photo of a farm with fields of rapeseed blazing in the sunshine. I assume you're not supposed to imagine the sound of slicing blades and the spatter of hot blood on steel in a shed just out of shot.

Pizza Hut is next door. Outside is a shallow amphitheatre for people to sit and stare back at the Pizza Hut sign. A woman with a severely taut ponytail is sat with an Asda bag, smoking a fag beside an empty Fosters multipack carton. A nervous youngster in a suit hovers near her with leaflets for Sky Television from an open-sided van where his partner encourages him by flapping his clipboard forwards, as if to propel him on a breeze. Skilfully swerving the salesman, I enter the car park where the big wide world of retail opens out. Costa, Carphone Warehouse, Burger King, Next, Sports Direct, Currys and my beloved B&Q are arrayed down one side. Asda takes up the right hand flank, its windows adorned with photographs of giant ASDA people with perfect skin and hair, clapping their hands, or leaping over invisible objects in well-creased trousers. An eight foot Asda boy stares out from the window with his mouth open. He looks like he's discovered a portal to another dimension, through which he can see tiny people moving between tiny cars. He presses his face against the glass, amazed to see me staring back at him with tired eyes in my strange, non-Asda clothing.

Hung on the wall next to the boy is a banner advert for air freshener: *Smell the Scents of Autumn. Not the odours.* It puzzles me. The artificial smell of autumn they've created will rid us of the odours we smell in the actual autumn? Is that the idea?

All this fiction is making me queasy. It wasn't like this in the old days, looking for beading or a spirit level in B&Q. Choosing an angle-poise lamp. Picking up light bulbs. God no. We just drove in, drove out. I never thought to take a walk around. Has anyone, for that matter? Who decides to explore a chain store car park? But now that I have, I understand that there is something fundamentally, totally fucking wrong with Leyton Mills Retail Park. It's not what's inside the shops.

It's what's happening in the car park.

To the *people*.

They're reading papers at the bus stop. Waiting by Belisha beacons to cross the road. Sitting in cars without their engines on. Milling at the Asda entrance. Ignoring their kids in the playground by Costa. Drinking outside pretend cafés. These people are not passing through. They're *dwelling* here. As if this is a real town.

Drizzle starts to come down and I go into Costa for a coffee. The customers seem normal enough. But it's busy. Really busy. A damp smell is coming off hair and coats. The baristas are young girls with Eastern European accents. In a large, funky mixed font, the wallpaper lists a series of coffee subcultures — 'the cappuccino crowd', 'the espresso enthusiasts', 'the latte lovers' — and poses the question, which one am I in? When I look closely at the tables around me, the people are drinking matching coffees. Latte opposite latte, cappuccino opposite cappuccino, flat white with flat white. Only I am drinking espresso, and I feel isolated. Unwelcome. It's time I left.

Outside it's spitting with rain. I head past B&Q but don't bother to go in, not even for old time's sake. I've realised that you don't need to go into the superstores.

It's the car park that's the place.

I cross onto a grass verge beneath steel fencing, scattered with debris: a plastic toilet cistern, a chaise longue, a football wrapped tightly in black plastic, a window frame, bottle of Ribena, sodden carrier bags. Loud squeals drift from Eurostar's Temple Mills train depot on the other side of the access road. This is the perimeter. Here's where everything breaks down. Cars are few and far between. There are rows of empty slots, their white stripes fading. A driver eats lunch in the cab of his truck. A man in an Audi stares dead ahead, as if he has logged off. None of them acknowledge my passing. Out by the perimeter, you're not anywhere. You're not really seen. Only the gravitational pull of your recent card payment in B&Q or Asda suggests your existence in the universe.

Finally, I reach the car park exit, through which Emily and I drove all those years ago. The allotments are still there in the scruffy land beyond the fence, by the mini-roundabout that used to spin our Peugeot along the railway lines. An overhead sign thanks me for shopping with Asda and a smaller sign says: **Trolleys will automatically stop if taken beyond the red line.** The words 'red line' are coloured red, to make sure I know what red looks like. At the bottom of the sign, written in a cheery font is: **happy to help every day.**

The hedgerows by the sign are beautiful. Trimmed in a rolling wave of autumnal browns, bursting with berries. I turn my back to Asda and B&Q, looking beyond the railway lines and marshes to the Shard on the City skyline, like a radio transmitter. It feels like I am on a moon colony staring across at earth. Ground control. Funny how far you can travel in a place you thought you knew.

The sound of heels clopping behind me. Someone else is out walking in the nether regions of the car park. It's a woman in an elegant black coat, carrying a Next carrier bag. She looks a little uncertain that she's going the right way, and when she sees me, she baulks. I turn back to the City skyline, so as not to embarrass her. The sound of heels slows but doesn't go away. I turn again to see she's drifting to the hedgerows by my shoulder. As she reaches the **trolleys will automatically stop** sign, her legs lock and her torso lurches forward with the momentum. For a moment she is bent over double. Then she flips herself right. She looks confused, staring down at her legs, shaking her head.

'Excuse me,' she says to me in an accent I can't place.

'Yes?'

'Which way's Costa?'

It's a strange question. She only has to turn around. I raise my finger and point towards the car park. That's when I see the sign of B&Q has changed. It now says BOSON & QUASAR and pulses with a furious energy, emitting orange waves across the tarmac, shoppers manifesting in its glow.

'Back there …'

She turns and walks back into the car park, flicking her hair into place, weaving expertly between wing mirrors. Light shimmers and flexes at her passing, as if she's disturbing sheets of liquid dark matter. It strikes me that to continue my journey I need to pass beyond the red line of the *trolleys will automatically stop* sign. I feel queasy and uncertain about what might happen if I try. Will my legs be locked-out like wheels?

Across the road there's movement behind the allotment fence. A man and woman in overalls stare at me intently through the slats. They clutch pitchforks and spades. They seem angry, frightened. Waiting for me to make my move. Waiting to see what I am. What I am not.

Hoping against hope that I am not like all the others, I step towards the red line.

Filamo

Irenosen Okojie

The last monk told the tongue that holding a naked sheep's head underwater would undo it all. Some time before that, prior to the madness beginning, old Barking Abbey loomed in the chasm; grey, weather worn, remote. Inside the Abbey, a tongue sat in the golden snuff box on an empty long dining table; pink, scarred and curled into a ruffled, silken square of night. The previous week, the tongue had been used as a bookmark in a marked, leather bound King James Bible, page 45 where the silhouette of a girl had been cut out; loaded with words like *high*, *hog*, *clitoris*, *iodine*, *cake*, its moist tip glistening in temporary confinement. The week before that, the tongue had been left in the fountain at the back of the Abbey, between winking coins. There, it pressed its tip to a stray ripple, cold and malleable, shaping it into a weight, pulling it down, under, up again. Several weeks back, it had been in a hallway window, leaning into Mary's hands, whose fingertips tasted of a charred, foreign footprint from the grass. Her fingertips had sensed a change in the air before the monks came, when the corridors were quiet, expectant. Molecules had shifted in preparation for a delivery. The monks arrived through a hole in time on a cold, misty morning, transported via a warp in space that mangled the frequencies of past and present. They arrived curling hands that did not belong to them. Unaware that this would have consequences none foresaw, except a tongue bending in the background, unaware of the repercussions of time travel.

Each time the tongue was moved, it lost a sentence. The monks missed this in their ritual of silence. They had done for weeks; walking around rooms with arms behind their backs, bodies shrouded in heavy brown robes, shaven, sunken heads soft to the touch. They trod this new ground carrying yolks in their mouths, hardening as morning became noon, noon became evening, and evening became night.

One morning, the monks found a miller's wife gutted on the stone wall enclosing the allotment, a white felt cap shoved into her mouth, her husband's initials embroidered in blue at the top right corner of her bloody apron: V.O. They threw salt on her skin. The tongue tasted the sharpness, and that night, Dom Vitelli made the noise of a kettle boiling in his sleep. He began to tremble covered in a cold sweat. He fell to the floor, stuck.

The next morning, the monks rose to discover the empty well near the stone outbuilding surrounded by plump, purple jabuticaba fruit, tender and bruised, the colour dwindling in areas as though a god was sucking it through a crack in the sky. Lonely figures in their heavy brown robes, the monks held their hands out as they circled the abbey. They heard the sounds of buses on the high street, car doors slammed shut, trains grinding to a halt. They caught items that fell through noise, things they had never seen; a white adapter plug from the sound of a plane speeding through the sky, a black dog muzzle Dom Oman later took to wearing when sitting by the fountain, a knuckle duster that fell from the sound of a baby crying. They placed these items at the altar in the chapel, flanked by candles on either side whose blue flames bent, then shrank sporadically. They took turns holding their palms over the flames. By the time the monks began their chores, the cockerel that had fallen over the walls from a car horn began to smash its beak into a jabuticaba fruit. Afterwards, it jumped into the stream connected to the Roding River, following a thinning, yellow light it attempted to chase into the next day.

The tongue was warm in Filamo's pocket, pressed against

a copper coin bearing the number two in Roman lettering. The musty taste of old items passing through lingered. Filamo, a cloaked figure, a betrayer amongst the monks, stood outside the prayer room, fingering a swelling on the tongue, listening quietly. Dom Emmanuel paced inside, the only other place speaking was permitted aside from supper during this imposed period of silence. A slightly forlorn figure, he shook. The bald patch on his head looked soft like a newborn's. Light streamed through the stained glass window where three naked cherubs wore angry, adult expressions and had changed positions again overnight. One lay on its side holding an ear, the other was eating stigmata injuries and the third at the bottom-left corner had tears running down its cheeks into the jabuticaba fruit growing through its chest.

Dom Emmanuel faced the silence of the cross on the nave wall without the figure of Christ, which had turned up at supper two days before, bleeding between slices of bread. There were three deep, wooden pews behind the Dom, half-heartedly built, scratched on the seating. Dom Emmanuel began to walk back and forth. Then, he paused momentarily as though to catch his breath, chest rising and falling. He held his arms out, confessing that lately he had begun to worry about his lover withering in a wormhole. The man Dom Emmanuel loved had not made it through this time, stuck in a winter that would quickly ice his organs and distribute the seven languages he spoke into the orbit for other monks to grab and stow away along with new disguises.

Dom Emmanuel could feel that cold in his bones, an absence of language, lightness in his tongue. Recently, Dom Emmanuel had dreamt of them running through lush, sunlit fields naked, penises limp at first, then turgid, moist at the tips, till thick spurts of sperm dribbled and their irises glinted. He missed the warmth of holding another body skin to skin, the innocence of early youth, the freedom of making mistakes. He moaned that his hands ached; that they had begun to talk to him, consumed by restlessness, till he sat up in bed sweating, tense, listening to a distant mangled cry travelling towards his organs, to his hands. For days the cry had come to him each night while the others slept, on each occasion, magnified by the constant silence, taut, suffocating. The cry grew in volume, weight, intent. Till he was led by it, until he found himself stumbling outside into the grounds, disrobing by the darkened stream gleaming in the night. Naked, covered in bite marks, he hunched down to catch things from the water; Siamese green lizards who shared an Adam's apple, a piece of jabuticaba fruit which grew another layer of purple skin each time you touched it, one cherub whose eyes had blackened from things it had witnessed upstream, a lung wrapped in cling film. Surrounded by his discontented small audience, Dom Emmanuel removed the cling film, crying as he ate flesh. It tasted like a man he once paid four gold coins in Tenochtitlan to keep him company, to be rough then tender with him afterwards, who had stuck his curious tongue into his armpits as if digging for his body's secrets using a pliable instrument.

Dom Emmanuel did not turn around when Filamo moved towards him lifting the blade. The cut to his neck was swift. He fell to the floor, blood gushing. The cry from his lips was familiar. It had been chasing him for days. He pressed his hands desperately against his neck, attempting to catch one last item rising through the blood. Dom Emmanuel died thinking of his lover's sour mouth, praying into it. The wound on his neck a cruel smile, clutching the lines of an old rectory sign bearing Roman number two in the left corner, his talking, gnarled hands slowly eroding. And half his body purple from a winter he already knew. While the monks scattered in shock, the tongue inherited Dom Emmanuel's last words, *El Alamein*.

When the saints arrived through their time cannon, continuing their ancient tradition as watchmen over the monks, the night was onyx-shaped. A faint howl followed them onto the tower. The Abbey was formidable in the moonlight; imposing, damp, grey, surrounded by high stone walls. The saints were orange skinned from the Festival of Memory. Each had a feature missing but something to replace it within their bodies. Saint Peter was missing an ear, yet had a small, translucent dragon's wing growing against a rib. Saint Augustine had lost a finger on his left hand but had two hearts; one pumping blood, the other mercury, so much so his tongue became silvery at particular angles. Saint Christopher had lost an eye and gained a filmy, yellow fish iris that cried seawater no matter his mood. This time, each had been fired from a cannon. Temporarily deaf, they clutched instructions for short transformations in golden envelopes. They wandered the cold halls lined with carvings and paintings on the walls, while the monks were gathered at supper, oblivious.

The saints deposited the envelopes beneath their beds. Each individual instruction for transformation sealed, yet written in the same long, right leaning handwriting by the same white feather dipped in blue ink. Each slip of yellow paper wrinkled at the corners, worn from weather, prayer, silence. Then, the saints fashioned three flagpoles from sticks they found in the cellar. They planted them on the grounds. The blue flag for go, red for pause, breathe, green for transform. Afterwards, on their journey back to two golden towers erected between wormholes, the saints became infants in the wind.

Later that night, the remaining Doms filed from the front

of the abbey holding their golden envelopes. Dom Ruiz led the way, stopping to take his position at the green flagpole. The other Doms followed. Dom Mendel, slighter than the rest, took a breath on the steps by the Roding's stream. The white hexagon several feet from the flagpoles spun seductively. In the library window, old leather bound books nursed the wisdom of hands slowly erased by time.

The Doms took their positions on all fours. Light trickles of dark rain began to fall. They uttered pater tollis peccata. Their mouths distorted. The bell rang. They darted forward, towards the centre and each other growling. A sharp, splintered pain shot through their heads. Spots of white appeared in their vision. Bones cracked as they expanded, organs grew, teeth lengthened, fur sprouted, hooves appeared, nostrils widened. Their sense of smell heightened. Dom Ruiz became a boar lunging at Dom Mendel the centaur, chasing him with an urgency that had his teeth chattering. Dom Kamil became an epicyon hunting Dom Augustine the procoptodon between all three flagpoles, through the other side of the white hexagon where the static hissed, then back up again. They snarled at the skyline, leaping, rushing; following the strong scent of old flesh emanating from the soil. They buried their faces in it, dug leaving large prints around the abbey that had a peculiar beauty from above. Three hours later, they retreated back to their starting positions becoming men again, exhausted bodies heaving. Speckles of blood fell on the golden envelopes, over the lines in foreign hands that had arranged into blueprints.

There were always injuries during a transformation. But the small, morphing nuclei they had generated would flatten in their brains, rising again when necessary, mimicking the silhouettes of tiny watchmen. As their breathing steadied, they studied the red flag flapping in the wind for stop.

After the transformation, the silence within the abbey was heavier, loaded. Having been banished by the saints for the fallen monk in their midst, each monk was busy dealing with the repercussions of their borrowed hands. And who knew what that could do to a man? Seeds of doubt and mistrust had begun to take root in this fertile ground of the unspoken, watered by the saliva of sealed envelopes. The monks did not venture beyond the abbey, afraid of being sucked into a vacuum of noise they would not recognise. Noises of a future they felt unprepared for, frightened that the influences of an outside world would somehow shorten their time at the abbey. Everything they needed was within the abbey's walls. They grew their own food using the allotment out back. At least 12 chickens were enough to feed from for a while, producing eggs for breakfast and the occasional comic attempt at escape. One chicken laid ten eggs that would not hatch, each filled with a finger of a new monk poking through deep red yolks. Somehow the Jesus figurine had found its way to these eggs. Stained by mud, it sat amongst them as they rolled and the other chickens leapt over the sound. Fed on bits of sullied bread, little Jesus waited patiently for a different kind of resurrection.

The saints made several visits back to the abbey through their time cannon to deliver items; salt, a bow and arrow, a television remote, nails, a hammer, three serrated knives. Several days after the transformation, Dom Augustine woke in the middle of the night barking like a dog, tongue slightly distended, skin clammy. The next morning, he began to set animal traps around the grounds; one on top of the tower, one in the allotment, one behind the middle pew in the prayer room, under his bed, one on the white hexagon slowly fading from damp and cold. After all, who knew what a man's shadow would do while he pretended to look the other way? Dom Augustine felt a panic rising inside him. Each day his tongue loosened further, as if it would fall out at any moment. He did not know whether it was his increasingly intensified barking at nights that was the cause or his particular kink from banishment, from flight. There were always complications. He had arrived in the main chapel, between two tall marble grey pillars, deposited on the alabaster altar, naked and wrapped in a thin silvery film reflecting past angles of light. His limbs had hurt, his head throbbed. His breaths were slow, deep, attempting to acclimatise. He had broken through the film, instinctively grabbing at items from a past that would never appear, knocking over two large, white candlesticks on either side. Famished, he scrambled along the cold altar. He looked down; his gaze met the knowing blue eyes of a cherub who jumped up and down excitedly, showing him its scarred back from repeatedly falling through stained glass windows. Its mouth was purple after eating a combination of plump fruits and unidentifiable things. He'd broken his hands in just like all the other Doms; carving a small Jesus figurine, fixing the hole in the cellar roof, building a pantry. The ache in his hands never fully left, only dulling with time. His fear of items and sounds from the outside threatening to infiltrate the abbey had become so potent, one afternoon he had been washing his hands in holy water by the pantry when the sound of an axe lifting, falling, chopping, breaking, smashing had almost deafened him. Slow at first, coming from afar. Then closer, louder, heavier till he curled up by the metallic bowl of water screaming then barking, breaking the silence.

A week after Dom Augustine set the animal traps, parts of his body were found in each one. Pieces in the traps by the fading white hexagon looked like an offering. The axe the saints delivered had vanished. The tongue in Filamo's pocket dined on splattered blood.

It was a chilly evening on the occasion Dom Kamil decided to perform his act of rebellion against the silence. A light frost covered the grounds, more jabuticaba fruit from the well scattered. Large pillars at the abbey's entrance bore tiny cracks oozing a sticky, thin sap. The intricate, golden chapel ceiling depicting Old Testament scenes began to shed tiny specks of gold from the corners. Only an observant eye would notice the figures had began to head in the opposite direction. Metallic bowls of holy water carefully placed outside room entrances collected reflections as if they were a currency. Dom Kamil awoke to find himself doused in kerosene and Doms Ruiz and Mendel absent. Throat dry, he trembled before swinging his legs over the bed onto the floor. The smell of kerosene was acrid. He did not call out. Instead, he slipped his dull, weighty brown cloak on, briefly running a hand over the length of wooden flute he'd kept close during the daytimes. For weeks he had found the silence unbearable, craving the joy music brought. He had resorted to wandering around the abbey with the flute he'd made secretly, rubbing his hands along it when his fingers curled and flexed with intent. Beyond the abbey walls, an ambulance siren wailed. Dom Kamil rushed outside; at least 50 yellow notes were strewn on the frosted ground. He scrambled between each one, eagerly opening them but they were mockingly empty. Distraught, he pulled the flute from his pocket and began to play. When Filamo set him alight he did not stop, playing urgently until he fell to his knees, the heat of the flames licking his skin, veins, blinding him. The sound of the flute hitting cold ground reverberated in the abyss, the ambulance siren shattered. A dark curl of smoke shrunk into the tongue poking out from Filamo's pocket contemptuously.

The next morning, the two remaining Doms wandered the halls with the taste of kerosene in their mouths.

On the fated Sunday that followed, Dom Ruiz and Dom Mendel began their last set of chores for the week orchestrated by the saints, setting scenes for destruction; ripping the pages of books in the library, defacing the expressions of religious figures in paintings hanging on walls, smashing up the organ in the chapel nobody had been allowed to play, flinging the black and white keys over the bodies of ten monks in the deep, open grave tucked behind the stone steps. They sprinkled salt on those bodies. And when those monks' mouths were sealed shut again by snow from a future winter, they fed the chickens communion. After dying the underside of their tongues purple, they fished out the animal traps, assembling them into a circle at the abbey's entrance because their hands could not help themselves. They danced within the circle until sweat ran down their backs, till their legs ached and the skyline became a blur. The nuclei embedded in their brains rose, bubbled, spat. They danced for what felt like an eternity until finally they crawled indoors. Heavy eyed and wary of collapsing in their sleeping quarters, they sat across from each other at the long dining table, watching, waiting. They dared not sleep, until the saint in their peripheral vision began to scream, burning bright, burnished orange smog into their heads.

Dawn arrived to discover Dom Ruiz slung over the bell, hands clinging limply to a thick, white rope, face battered beyond recognition. He dangled like a grisly gift a god had despatched. Meanwhile the tongue ran its moist tip along the bruises on Filamo's hands.

Spat out from another chasm, Dom Mendel lay sprawled on a wide patch of the Abbey's green surrounded by concrete paths. Time travel flight had occurred again. He knew it from the trembling in his knees, the ache spreading in his chest, the blockage in his ears slowly thinning, popping. His bruised hands were numb, stiff after being curled in the same position for hours. As though he'd been inserted into a corner of sky trying to balance, fingers instinctively wrapping around the shadows of lost items. Every junction fell off the map each time. A severed organ floating in white smoke till it disappeared. He sat up gingerly, taking small gulps of air. It felt like spring. Bright sunlight shrouded everything. The abbey was a carcass of its former self, its high walls reduced to mere remains. The sound of cars on the roads around it was jarring, alien. Mouth dry, barefoot, he stood slowly, noting the curfew tower in the distance. Exits at either end of the gutted, green gladiator-like pit beckoned. He decided to take the exit in front rather than the one behind him. He crossed some stone steps before landing in the graveyard. St Margaret's church stood to his right behind the tower a short walk away, bearing a flimsy white banner that said Café Open. People passed him throwing curious looks. Their clothing appeared odd and unfamiliar. He ran his hands over a few gravestones. The rough stone was cold to the touch. He grabbed sprigs of grass lining the bases, placed them on his tongue.

Chewing, he made his way over the zebra crossing and onto the tail end of the market on East Street, drawn by the buzz of stalls, the cacophony of voices, the smell of meat hissing and spitting over a barbecue. He ran a finger over the tongue in his pocket as he heard the words *Bell End, Mango, fireworks, truncheon*. It curled against his finger as though acknowledging receipt. He walked along the market in shock, throngs of bodies spilling, multiplying and scurrying in every direction. On the high street, a man held a snarling Alsatian back from him. He could smell what it had eaten hours ago, a rotten, pungent scent. He resisted the urge to bare his teeth. Something lodged in his chest. His blood warmed. His heart began to mutate into the shape of the snarling dog's mouth, knocking against chest walls. He stumbled away from them. Trapped light in his retina split into tiny grains. Everything felt intense, gauzy. A bearded man bumped into him. He entered the sliding red door of the shopping centre almost by accident. Things bled into each other; the mannequins' mouths pressed against their glass confines, stitches from their hands coming undone, grazing his retina. Along the way his footsteps were dogged by sightings of familiar faces; Dom Emmanuel appeared on the raised stage for a concert, holding the knife that had killed him, slicing his neck repeatedly at the microphone. Dom Augustine's head lay in the Asda supermarket freezer, one animal trap snapping over his lost limbs as they reappeared. Dom Kamil sat engulfed in flames in a barber's chair. Dom Ruiz lay slumped over a Thomas the Tank Engine train, clutching one yellow note.

Dom Mendel passed a line of monks on an escalator, touching their shoulders but each one vanished. He was consumed by a loneliness so vast it was unknowable in this lifetime. He followed the exit out and back onto the streets. He kept walking, filled with a slow hypnotic wonder, wiping the dew off a car side mirror, becoming a small figure in its contained distances. Then on all fours, he scavenged in the bins outside the Yaki Noodle bar opposite the station. Afterwards, he walked around back streets staring at houses. He walked to Creekmouth, passing the mural of two men vomiting water, coddling ships while the land flooded. He studied the parked HGVs on industrial roads wondering what they contained, noticing the small factories and recycling stations. A veil of bleakness cloaked it all. The ghosts of Creekmouth swirled. Workers for the Lawes Chemical and Fertiliser Company emerged from rows of cottages attempting to stuff items into his pockets. The Bluebird and The Yellow Peril aircrafts of the Handley Page Factory hovered above, between the rough marshland of Barking Creek and the north bank of the Thames leaving white trails in the sky. Children ran from the school, mouths turning to dust as their cries faded. Debris of old lives tumbled through the nearby tidal barrier. The sound of ships sinking filled his ears. An ache in his hands intensified. Laughter from Romanian weddings rang at the entrance of The River Restaurant. He almost entered to search for hands he could borrow. He stood in the midst of it all listening, to marshy land rising, urged by the echoes of the Thames, to the sound of a great flood coming. He did not notice his feet were bleeding. His teeth began to chatter, his tongue distended. The tongue in his pocket started talking.

The last Dom, Dom Mendel, stood on the bank of the river Roding, disrobing to reveal breasts jutting, her nipples hardening in the cold. Pregnant with another bloody season, her new name carved on her stomach from a serrated knife read: Filamo. She had left behind the abbey in the chasm; its entrances spitting Bible sheets, its lines leaning against a distant prayer, the faces of saints morphing into bruises. A different transformation was occurring; malevolent cherubs chased the cockerel, the limping cockerel drunk from holy water chased the Jesus figurine, squawking 'Amen!' Rolling jabuticaba fruit chased the hatched monk's fingers. And the abbey chased new burial ground. Dom Filamo listened to the symphony of cars, human traffic, the beauty of noise. She dipped her left foot into the water. After fishing a hammer and tongue from her robe pockets, she started to bludgeon her head, hitting the ring of hair. As another yolk broke and blood ran down her face, she slipped the tongue into her mouth howling. The tongue of a saint. That first kill. The reason for the punishment of a period of silence. Her skin mottled. She leapt into the river gripping the hammer, chasing the sheep's head that had surely become a different animal by now.

Market Forces

Kit Caless

1. Abhiman

David chooses the spiced lamb wrap from the Moro street stall. He wants meat sweats. He is sick of the diet his personal trainer put him on. This is a rebellion. David normally eats with clients or investors at the bricks and mortar restaurants on Exmouth Market. He's well known at Caravan, Santoré, and Paesan. David eats most regularly at Moro's sit-down restaurant because his personal trainer approves of their cuisine; couscous with authentic ras al hanout seasoning, lentil salads, babaganoush, vegetable tagines.

'David, please. It's on the house,' says Brahim, refusing the five pound note being waved in his face.

'Nice one!' says David, taking the box in one hand and

stuffing the fiver into his back pocket with the other.

'See you soon.'

'Definitely.'

David walks up Exmouth Market and cuts into Spa Fields, a precious slice of green space in the concrete coppice of Clerkenwell, where the office workers take their street food for lunch. Walking past the outdoor fitness gym on the west corner, David waves to Jenny, one of the marketing girls at his company. She is sat on the bench press. She is not lifting anything other than her homemade sandwich; wholemeal bread, tomato, hummus, beetroot and carrot. She waves back, mouth full, wishing she had bought a bento box from Neki's instead.

David employed Jenny fairly early on. Back when Steam Interactive was a start-up, instead of the award winning digital agency everyone knows it as now. Back when it was just David, his wife Claire, his best friend John, some investor mates and an idea. David feels avuncular towards Jenny, unlike a lot of the other girls in the office. Now the company has over 300 members of staff, David doesn't bother to get to know anyone. He has a good memory for faces, but a particularly good one for nice arses.

On to Bowling Green Lane, David walks to the NCP car park fondling the lamb wrap in the box. Still warm. He takes a big sniff. The meaty, smoky smell rides all the way down the back of his throat. He hasn't eaten meat in three weeks.

Inside the NCP the ground floor has maybe ten, 12 cars parked. Most of them are SUVs, there is one Ford Ka and one Jeep. David takes the stairs. The first floor has two vehicles in it. The second, one. The third and fourth, none. He arrives on the roof, short of breath. David clocks the CCTV camera and pulls his cap down to hide his face. Skirting the wall on the east side, he sidles past the CCTV camera. It doesn't move. On the other side of the roof, David sits down on the floor and opens his Moro box.

David stares at Claire's office window across the road, shoveling perfectly spiced lamb into his gob. The meat squelches under the grind of his small teeth, spitting juices onto the inside wall of his cheeks. Gulping down the piquant mush, David knows that one day he will own the land underneath his widened arse. He has big plans. A vision.

It happens quicker than he thought it would. A flash of movement inside and the office door opens. David pulls a pair of binoculars out of his bag. Adjusting the focus, he can see right into the room as if he is sat at Claire's desk. Then, as expected, John comes in. He locks the door behind him and checks his watch. Claire sits herself on top of the desk, with her back to the window and pulls John towards her. They kiss, hard, full, greedily. John pulls off her jacket and bites her shoulder. She reprimands him with a tight slap, but then digs her hands under his belt and into his crotch.

David remains calm. He even feels a twinge in his groin, a sense of excitement. He carries on watching. Waiting for the right moment, chewing more mouthfuls of lamb. He needs to get the timing right, for full impact. He needs as much leverage as possible.

David wants the NCP car park so bad. Imagine the landmark office he could build here. Imagine how Clerkenwell would look at the Steam offices and think, 'David Browning is running this spot.' Imagine knocking down a car park to build an office that you could see from a plane high in the sky. Imagine those poncey little studios and pokey design agencies seeing that and thinking, 'I should have let Steam buy me out when I had the chance.' The NCP are playing hardball. David is determined. I will own this end of Clerkenwell by the time I am 50, he promises himself each day, when he is on this roof watching his best friend shag his wife.

David pulls out his camera and takes some photos of the action. He has over ten gigabytes of this stuff now. He's watched them do all sorts, more than he's ever done with her. Click click click.

David picks up his phone and calls Claire. He sees her look at it. Like most days, at this time, John stops thrusting and Claire picks it up. They appear like they almost expected it.

'Hi darling,' she says, barely controlling her breath.

'Hi pumpkin, would you like anything from the market?'

The same conversation, every time.

'Oh no, it's fine love, I've got something to eat.'

'OK. See you in a bit.'

'Bye.'

John's pelvis returns to full pelt. David carries on watching.

One day soon he will tell them to look out of the window over to the car park roof and he will wave his binoculars and camera at them and say, 'You are both done for.'

Then he will be free to buy this land.

2. Kreng Jai

Tuma parks his truck on Tysoe Street outside Budgens. He walks down Exmouth Market to the German Barbecue stall. He queues behind two young men wearing indigo jeans, brogues and plaid shirts. They are talking about a difficult client forcing them to use a chartreuse colour scheme. Tuma lights a cigarette and marvels at how clean these two are, how clean everyone on Exmouth Market looks.

Tuma orders a giant bratwurst in a roll with onions,

mustard and a gherkin. He sits on the bench at the end of the market facing the junction opposite the Royal Mail building, people watching. A pigeon bobs and weaves on the pavement as Tuma takes bite after bite of the taut sausage. The mustard produces waves of heat evaporating out through his nose.

The next job is in a brick office opposite the Budgens. Usually about 20 sacks of white paper, ten newspaper and ten cardboard. It's a big job for one guy. Used to be that Tuma would down a double espresso in the morning with couple of Marlboro reds and race through the rounds like a mad man. Lifting and shifting recyclable waste isn't hard, but the sacks get heavy. Years in the job now and the rounds only get bigger.

Tuma used to enjoy being awake before everyone else. On the daily 5:30am drive to the West Ham recycling plant. He appreciated the empty roads. He felt freer than he had at any time in Free State. He gets backache most nights now, in bed by 10pm with a cup of chamomile tea. He understands why his father used to fall asleep after dinner.

'Hard work makes you tired, boy,' his father would say.

Back at the truck, Tuma opens the cab and puts on his gloves. The rear door of Steam Interactive is open. Some sacks are already at the bottom of the stairway. Tuma feels a heat rise up from his stomach to his throat. He runs up the stairs, two steps at a time. At the top, Sophie — a woman from marketing — appears with another sack.

'What are you doing?' says Tuma, 'why are you doing this?'

Tuma's Bloemfontein accent is still strong, though friends back home would tell him otherwise. Sophie looks at the bags and back at Tuma. She cocks her head and gives him a smile she normally gives her children during their school nativity play.

She spins on her heel and goes back into the office. Tuma stands at the door watching her walk all the way to the other end and start dragging the blue sacks towards him.

As a child Tuma would wonder why his father worked so hard for men who didn't seem to work at all. They just drank beer and cooked themselves red under the South African sun, while his father toiled with the earth. As he grew up he understood it wasn't by choice.

Usually, Tuma always enjoyed getting white people to work for him. From simply packing his shopping bag at the supermarket, or serving him a pint in the pub, the novelty, after 23 years had not worn off. But as he watches Sophie drag the sacks towards him, Tuma thinks about his sister for the first time in many years.

Sophie is getting close. Some of the others in the office are watching Tuma watch Sophie, wondering why he isn't helping her out. Tuma feels their stares a little too keenly. His scalp prickles and before he can stop himself he shuffles forward a few paces to intercept her. Annoyed at his feet for taking action without consent, he grabs the top of the bag from Sophie's hands.

'No,' he says.

Tuma's voice is as close to shouting, without shouting, as you can get. Sophie screws her face up, drops the sack and turns on her heel.

'Fine, take the damn thing.'

Tuma knows she is offended and that, professionally, he should apologise. But he says, 'good,' picks up the sack, takes it outside and throws it in the back of the truck with the rest of the day's collection.

3. L'appel Du Vide

Sohini dangles her legs over the balcony on the 24th floor of Michael Cliffe House, the tallest block on the Finsbury Estate. On the streets below, packs of successful young things walk from their offices to Exmouth Market, to Spa Fields and St John's Churchyard. Fully haired heads and hats move like 8-bit computer game Pacman splodges up and down the roadways of Clerkenwell.

Sohini has been up here for two hours. She has been living here for 25 years. She's got nine red letters from the council demanding rent payment in a pile on top of the microwave that no longer works. She hasn't been able to go to the bank for a month because each time she steps out of Michael Cliffe House to do so, a panic jumps on her chest and pushes it in like plunger.

Two years ago she was up here dangling her feet with a different mood. She had just been promoted to senior administration officer at the construction company and had started looking at houses to buy in places like Forest Gate and East Ham. Nice two-beds with a little garden and an open plan kitchen/living room. The space was always slightly smaller than Michael Cliffe but it would be hers and she wouldn't have to take a lift to get to her front door.

It's one and a half years since the company went bust and she hasn't been able to find a job since. She always gets to interview stage, but never makes the final cut. Too old, she suspects, and too brown.

That feeling. You know the one. The part of your brain that says, 'go on, do it'. That feeling is rippling right through Sohini. The itch that you hope you will never scratch. The squeezing horror that you might actually give in to that siren call one day. The call of the void.

Sohini looks between her legs, directly below the

entrance to the building. She sees Mr Uddin, the owner of the Cinnamon Tree restaurant, run into the block. He's been here longer than she has. A minute later he runs back out. She follows his path along Myddleton Street to the back of Exmouth Market. He runs to the street food slalom, until he reaches the Cinnamon Tree stall. He unwraps a roll of kitchen towel and pulls some knives and forks out of his coat pocket. He could have bought the roll and some plastic forks from Budgens.

Sohini decides to pay Mr Uddin a visit at the stall. The food is excellent, but it seems they could do with a few logistical pointers. She pulls herself away from the balcony, dropping her feet onto safe ground, slides the door across and looks for some socks in her bedroom.

The pile of letters remains unopened, but she has a chance to open them tomorrow.

4. Saudade

Sue leaves the stall with her usual box of Chicken Pad Thai. She asked for sweet chilli sauce and the man poured it in the corner instead of spreading it over the food. It's £5.50 now. Sue always buys from Simply Thai because she can't see a boss or bigger restaurant attached to the stall. The two men working there seem to own the means of production.

Walking back to Clerkenwell Green from Exmouth Market via Rosoman Street, Skinner Street and Sekforde Street, Sue thinks about the Victorian workhouses that populated Clerkenwell. Work at these places was for the most impoverished. It consisted of breaking stones, picking hemp from telegraph wires, crushing the bones of deceased workers for fertiliser. All those bodies at capitalism's mercy bounce off the walls and rattle in Sue's ears. The digital agencies and the marketing companies that now occupy these buildings are just as bad, only work is not forced on the workers. They have managed to build a culture that means you stay beyond 5:30pm voluntarily. These people work harder and longer hours because they want to get ahead of their rivals, but they never get paid overtime. There are no prizes for being the last to leave the office, but if you're the first, it is noticed. These days she sees workers playing home time chicken with each other. The first to leave loses; the last to go eats a microwave dinner at their desk. Sue believes they are complicit in their exploitation; they are lost to the machine. Pretending it is 'realism' they refuse to think they could build another world. *Wat Tyler didn't die for this*, she thinks.

Sue buzzes the door to the Karl Marx Memorial Library and Workers' School. Graham comes down to let her in. She gives him the handwritten receipt from the Thai stall. She may volunteer at the Library but at least they cover her lunch expenses. Sue heads down the corridor away from the main book room. She passes Jack Hastings' fresco, *The Worker of the Future Upsetting the Economic Chaos of the Present*, and the Spanish civil war room, with its ¡No pasarán! solidarity banner depicting the Siege of Madrid. Entering the room that overlooks Clerkenwell Close, Sue moves a laminated copy of *Iskra* off the desk and sits down next to Vladimir Lenin.

'How's it been today?' she asks him.

He doesn't reply because he's a bronze bust. She rubs his bald metallic pate fondly and opens the Thai box.

'Couldn't have got this stuff in your day eh?' she chuckles. The food is still warm. The sweetness of the chilli is offset by tart lime juice, salty peanuts, bitter tamarind and umami fish sauce. It's delicious, as always.

Lenin stares out over the Close. It was in this very room that he edited and published seventeen issues of *Iskra*, wrote call after call to revolution and developed his own unique understanding of economics, capital and communism.

Sue traces his eye line and looks out the window. It must have been so exciting back then, she thinks. The fever, the promising ferment of change, men and women challenging every structure of power imaginable. The workers were different then, she was sure. Made of tougher stuff, willing to put their bodies on the line for their brothers. A sense of solidarity across all the battle lines against capitalism. They had an understanding of wage-labour relations. The knowledge that unless they take over the means of production, they will forever be exploited. Sue imagines the cries from the streets below in 1901. The turn of the century, the Queen is dead! Only another 15 years and Vladimir would be in charge of the largest country in Europe, liberating so many of those who had toiled for capital. Oh for sure it was a better time, at the edge of potential, at the precipice of transformation. She felt she was born in the wrong era. She could have been working class, she could have been a suffragette, she could have been somebody instead of a librarian, which is what she is.

Sue volunteers in a library no one visits, full of books no one reads, in a part of London that houses the most architects per square kilometre in Europe. The past is another country, of course.

5. Ilinx

Tawiah cannot believe it's there. Spinach and Agushi. Exmouth Market has never been so appealing. Fresh jollof rice everyday, if she wants it. Since she moved from her parent's house in Pollards Hill, to LSE student halls on Rosebery Avenue, she hasn't had time to cook, or find freshly made jollof. It better be good.

The man who is serving it is fit, too. Got that nice trimmed beard look and a fitted, ribbed black t-shirt that shows off his muscles. He's not muscly in that gym way though, thankfully. He's toned, but like a tennis player, or footballer. The sort of body you can lie next to without feeling like a dwarf.

Tawiah got a part time position at the Mount Pleasant Royal Mail branch a few months ago to help cover the maternity leave for one of the sorters. For five hours, three times a week, she stands in front of a hundred shoots all with different parts of the country written on them, divided by postcodes. It's not a bad job, but she's the only student on her course works a job to support herself. Her parents are wealthy but Tawiah chooses not to take their money. She wants to teach herself independence, feel like she's earned her way through. Even though they pay for the fees and accommodation and sneak money into her bank account on regular occasions, Tawiah likes earning money because she feels less indebted to her parents.

She's studying International Relations, getting good grades and great feedback from her tutors. Tawiah is all over it, basically. On top of everything. Apart from right this very moment. It's quarter to two and Tawiah is on the 2-7pm shift. There are an impressive number of people looking curiously at the food on offer. She barges ahead of a dithering couple. The attractive man boxes up beef bell pepper stew, plantain and jollof and Tawaiah is next.

She asks for the jollof and agushi stew. The man smiles at her and she pays her fiver with an equally broad grin. The box has that beautiful peppery, seeded, tomatoey, warm smell. Suddenly she realises misses home much more than she thought she did.

Tawiah quick steps to Mount Pleasant.

In the staff room she gobbles down the food in the box with a plastic fork that breaks as she scours up the remaining juice and flecks of rice in the corners. Her head rushes with heat and flavour. She glistens. She walks into the sorting office and grabs her first post sack of the day. Elated, giddy and alive from belly to fingertips, a kind of voluptuous panic sweeps over her; a spinning, falling rollercoaster-riding emotion rattles her body.

Before she can stop herself, Tawiah is picking up the sack, emptying it out all over the floor and kicking the post all around the room with joyous laughter.

About the authors

Chloe Aridjis is a Mexican writer based in London. After completing her doctorate at Oxford in 19th century French poetry and magic shows, she lived in Berlin for six years. Her first novel, *Book of Clouds*, won the Prix du Premier Roman Etranger in France. Her second novel, *Asunder*, is set in London's National Gallery. Chloe was co-curator of the Leonora Carrington exhibition at Tate Liverpool in 2015 and is currently working on a film project as well as her new novel.

Three of her favourite London books are *High Rise* by J.G. Ballard, Ian Nairn's *Nairn's London* and Robert Louis Stevenson's *The Strange Case of Dr Jekyll and Mr Hyde*.

Her favourite little-known London location is the Swedenborg Society, with its own magic lantern.

Unfortunately **Gary Budden** was born just outside of London, in Watford in 1983. He now lives very close to the spot in Willesden where his mum was beaten up by 'bigger girls' in the late 1960s. He is the co-founder of Influx Press and writes in the tradition of a made-up genre called landscape punk.

As a boy, his father gave him the warning, 'don't go south of the river son, it's bandit country', advice he has tried to stick to.

Some of his favourite London fictions are 'Looking for Jake' by China Miéville, *Savage Messiah* by Laura Oldfield Ford and any of Alexander Baron's London novels (*King Dido, The Lowlife* and *Rosie Hogarth* especially).

A favourite odd London location is Horsenden Hill, a conservation site and popular cottaging spot near Wembley.

Tim Burrows writes for *The Guardian, The Quietus* and *Vice,* among other publications. He grew up in London's slipstream, in the Essex seaside town of Southend-on-Sea at the mouth of the Thames Estuary. 'Broadgate' is first work of fiction.

Three of his favourite London fictions are *The Slaves of Solitude* by Patrick Hamilton, *Savage Messiah* by Laura Oldfield Ford and the films *London* and *Robinson in Space* by Patrick Keiller.

His favourite current London location is a toss up between that spot between the memorials of Blake, Defoe and Bunyan in Bunhill Fields and inside the Stratford Centre shopping mall when it's filled with skaters and music at night.

Kit Caless lives near Hackney Downs. On his mum's side, the family hail from deepest, darkest Bermondsey. On his dad's, the pirate place of Penzance. He is co-founder of Influx Press and writes non-fiction on the side for cash.

Some of his many favourite London fictions are *The Black Album* by Hanif Kureishi, *Remainder* by Tom McCarthy and *Mrs Dalloway* by Virginia Woolf.

According to Kit, one of the best London locations is 'suicide bridge' on the hill between Highgate and Archway.

Yvvette Edwards is a British writer of Montserratian origin. Her debut novel, *A Cupboard Full of Coats*, is based in Hackney where she grew up. It was nominated for the Man Booker Prize, the Commonwealth Writers' Prize and the Writers' Guild award. Her second novel, *The Mother*, was published in 2016. She continues to live in east London with her family.

Three of her favourite three London books are Dickens' *Great Expectations*, *The Elected Member* by Bernice Rubens and Bernardine Evaristo's *Mr Loverman*.

Her favourite little-known London location is Hollow Pond, Epping Forest.

Paul Ewen was born and raised in New Zealand. He moved to London in 2002, living some years in Tufnell Park before moving south of the river to SE, where he is today. He is the author of

The London Pub Guide and *Francis Plug: How to Be a Public Author*.

Three of his favourite London fictions are *New Grub Street* by George Gissing, *Twenty Thousand Streets Under The Sky* by Patrick Hamilton and *Remainder* by Tom McCarthy.

His favourite London location is Hermit's Cave, Camberwell.

George F. is the author of *Total Shambles* (Influx Press, 2015). He moved to Streatham Hill in 2006, but since he starting squatting in 2009 has lived in innumerable parts of the metropolis as he constantly seeks new places to find refuge and finally sit down to write. He has lived in abandoned furniture shops in Homerton, old offices in Borough and Bermondsey, been arrested skipping food in the Waitrose bins on Holloway Road, blockaded Tower Bridge with a mob of anarchists on May Day and fought cops outside a squat party in High Holborn. He looks forward to further adventures in the belly of the beast.

His favourite London location is the mural of the Battle of Cable Street, in Cable Street.

Three of his favourite London fictions are *Keep The Aspidistra Flying* by George Orwell, *The Man Who Was Thursday* by G.K. Chesterton and *V for Vendetta* by Alan Moore.

Salena Godden is an author, poet and broadcaster. She moved from Hastings to London in the early '90s. She has lived off the Finchley Road and around Tufnell Park and Hampstead Heath and frequented in pubs in Camden and the secret members' bars of Soho and ruled North London for two decades but has just recently moved East to Stratford.

She is the author of *Under the Pier* and *Fishing In The Aftermath, Poems 1994 – 2014*. A literary childhood memoir, *Springfield Road*, was successfully crowd funded and published in October 2014 by Unbound Books. Salena is the lead singer and lyricist of SaltPeter, alongside composer Peter Coyte. She has appeared on BBC radio as a guest on various shows including Woman's Hour, From Fact To Fiction, The Verb, Saturday Live and Loose Ends.

Her favourite London fictions are *Night Walking* and *Mrs Dalloway* by Virginia Woolf and *Down and Out in Paris and London* by George Orwell. She also loves Peter Ackroyd's books and *From Hell* by Alan Moore.

Her favourite location is still her magic tree on Hampstead Heath but she doesn't live up that way anymore so cannot see it as often as she used to.

M John Harrison lived in London for 35 years. Three of his favourite London books are Elizabeth Bowen's *The Heat of the Day, Hawksmoor* by Peter Ackroyd and the A-Z.

He'd prefer his favourite little-known location to remain little-known.

Juliet Jacques was born in 1981 and grew up in Horley, a small town on the Surrey-Sussex border which has recently, and staggeringly, been incorporated into the London Travelcard area, presumably as Zone X. Since then, she has lived in Bethnal Green, Leytonstone and Dalston, as well as Manchester and Brighton. Her memoir, *Trans*, was issued by Verso in 2015; she has also published a monograph on English author Rayner Heppenstall, a number of short stories and plenty of journalism and criticism.

Her three favourite London fictions are Angela Carter's *Wise Children*, *Down and Out in Shoreditch and Hoxton* by Stewart Home and Alex Kovacs' *The Currency of Paper*.

Favourite 'odd' London locations ... let's go for no.w.here in Bethnal Green and LUX in Dalston (as they hold the legacy of the wonderful London Film-Makers' Co-operative).

Courttia Newland is the author of seven works of fiction including his debut, *The Scholar*. His latest, *The Gospel According to Cane*, was published in 2013 and has been optioned by Cowboy Films as a TV serial. All of his works are set in West London where he grew up, specifically Shepherds Bush and Ladbroke Grove. As he now lives in Forest Gate, East London that's more than likely going to change. But obviously not any time soon.

His favourite London books are *Soft* by Rupert Thompson, *East of Acre Lane* by Alex Wheatle and *Dead Air* by Iain Banks.

His favourite London spot was the empty area that had a huge mud mountain in Paddington, written about in *Soft*, now long gone and gentrified.

Koye Oyedeji is south London through and through. Born in Greenwich and raised in Walworth. He has the lumps to show for it. As writer he's contributed to books, newspapers, magazines and journals, and London always has at least a cameo role his work. But anyway, here are the takeaways: One. He's not conflicted about his lifelong support of Arsenal, after all, like him, their roots lie south of the river. Two. Things are changing. He thinks the makers of *Monopoly* ought to raise the property price for the Old Kent Road. Three. He splits his time between Washington DC and, yep, you guessed it …

His favourite London novels are (London, Airstrip One, in) *Nineteen Eighty-Four* by George Orwell, *The Buddha of Suburbia* by Hanif Kureishi and *In The Ditch* by Buchi Emecheta.

His favourite odd London location is the White City Estate where he would spend the summer holidays out of school there with his aunt. There was something magical about being right by what was then the central BBC office and listening to the constant traffic of the A40 Westway at night in bed.

Irenosen Okojie attended a convent school in Plaistow, quit piano lessons in Ilford and had a near death experience in King's

Cross. She'd quite like to participate in an egg and spoon ra[ce?]
with Mae Carol Jemison, Zap Mama, Andrew Dosunmu an[d]
Jim Jarmusch amongst others and then invite them round for
pepper soup at hers afterwards. Her debut novel *Butterfly Fish*
was published by Jacaranda Books. Her short story collection
Speak Gigantular will be out in 2016. She lives in Newham.

Three of her favourite London books are *In The Ditch* by Buchi
Emecheta, *A Concise Chinese English Dictionary For Lovers* by
Xiaolu Guo and *The Ballad of Peckham Rye* by Muriel Spark.

One of her favourite London locations is Highgate Cemetery.

Gareth E. Rees is author of *Marshland: Dreams & Nightmares on
the Edge of London* (Influx Press, 2013). He also runs the website
Unofficial Britain. His work appears in *Mount London: Ascents In
the Vertical City, Acquired for Development By: A Hackney Anthology,
Walking Inside Out: Contemporary British Psychogeography* and
the spoken word album with Jetsam, *A Dream Life of Hackney
Marshes*.

Three of his favourite London fictions are *Christie Malry's
Own Double Entry* by B.S Johnson, *Mother London* by Michael
Moorcock and *Hawksmoor* by Peter Ackroyd.

His favourite odd location is the path by the River Lea outside
The Anchor & Hope pub, High Hill Ferry in Hackney.

o Saro-Wiwa was born in Port Harcourt, Nigeria, and raised England. Her first book, *Looking for Transwonderland: Travels n Nigeria* (Granta, 2012) was named *The Sunday Times* Travel Book of the Year, 2012, and selected as BBC Radio 4's Book of the Week in 2012.

Noo has contributed book reviews, travel, opinion and analysis articles for *The Guardian, The Independent, The Financial Times, The Times Literary Supplement* and *Prospect* magazine, among others. She lives in London.

A favourite London novel is *Saturday* by Ian McEwan

Her favourite London location is Leather Lane in Clerkenwell. It's got the best falafel in London (at King of Falafel), plus an outdoor market where you can get everything from old-edition glossy magazines to clothes to plantain with rice.

Aki Schilz is a writer and editor based in London, where she has lived since she was three months old after a journey across the ocean from Osaka, Japan. She moved from W7 (Hanwell) to E5 (Clapton) in 2014. She is co-founder of the #LossLit Twitter writing project alongside Kit Caless, and co-editor of *LossLit Magazine*. Her poetry and fiction have been published both online (*Mnemoscape, tNY.Press, The Bohemyth, Cheap Pop Lit, Annexe, And Other Poems*) and in print (*Popshot, The Colour of Saying, Kakania, Best Small Fictions 2015*), and she is the winner of the inaugural Visual Verse Prize and the Bare Fiction Prize for

Flash Fiction. Aki works at The Literary Consultancy, which based in Clerkenwell, an area full of glass buildings and med types. She works in a glass building, but is not a media type. She tweets micropoetry, much of which is inspired by the beauty and the brute of England's capital city, at @AkiSchilz.

Her favourite London books are *Londoners*, by Craig Taylor, *A Concise Chinese-English Dictionary for Lovers*, by Xiaolu-Guo and *The Shapes of Dogs' Eyes*, by Harry Gallon

Her favourite London place is halfway up Primrose Hill some time before 6am when the birds are out, or in the shade of the tree at the bottom of the hill sliding down from Gunnersbury Park Museum.

Nikesh Shukla is the author of the critically acclaimed novel *Meatspace*, the Costa-shortlisted novel *Coconut Unlimited* and the award-winning novella *The Time Machine*. He is the editor of *The Good Immigrant*. He wrote the short film *Two Dosas* and the Channel 4 sitcom *Kabadasses*. Nikesh grew up in London. Well, Harrow. But Harrow's in Zone 5, and counts as a London Borough. So it's London, okay?

Three of his favourite London books are *NW* by Zadie Smith, *The Buddha of Suburbia* by Hanif Kureishi and *The Lonely Londoners* by Sam Selvon.

His favourite London place is Diwani Bhel Poori House.

ay Singh was born in Varanasi, India. She had a nomadic ...dhood that established a habit that continued into adulthood. ...e has studied and worked in Pakistan USA, Mexico, South Africa, Chile, Spain and the UK. She has lived longest in London and has so far managed to quiet the itchy feet (albeit barely). She has published three novels, a nonfiction book on single women in India, as well as numerous short stories and essays.

Being a nomad, she can't think of a book entirely set in London, but likes Salman Rushdie's *The Satanic Verses*, William Gibson's *Pattern Recognition* and Georgette Heyer's *The Grand Sophy*.

One of her favourite places in London is the top floor of the Foundling Museum in Bloomsbury.

Stephen Thompson was born in London. He is the author of the novels *Toy Soldiers, Missing Joe, Meet Me Under The Westway*, and *No More Heroes*.

Away from writing novels, Stephen is the editor and publisher of the online literary journal, *The Colverstone Review*, and a lecturer in Creative Writing at the University of Winchester.

Three of his favourite London fictions are *Running Hot* by Dreda Say Mitchell, 'Reports of Certain Events in London' by China Miéville and *To Sir, With Love* by E.R.Braithwaite.

His 'off-piste' London location is Wanstead Flats.

Stephanie Victoire has resided in areas all along the south branch of the Northern Line, between Colliers Wood an Kennington. In 2010 Stephanie graduated with a BA in Creative Writing from London Metropolitan University in Holloway Road. Stephanie is now 31 years old and lives in Wimbledon with her Irish partner, and is currently working on a novel.

A favourite London book is *Atonement* by Ian McEwan.

Her favourite odd London location would be Cannizaro Park next to Wimbledon Common, with over 100 different species of trees, an aviary, a duck pond, 300 year old oak trees, and lots of nooks and crannies to hide away in.

Tim Wells is made of reggae, lager top, pie and mash and Leyton Orient FC. Ich voyn in Stamford Hill.

Three of his favourite London fictions are Arthur Morrison's *The Case of Laker, Absconded*, James Herbert's *The Rats* and Daniel Defoe's *A Journal of the Plague Year*.

His favourite London place is Postman's Park.

Will Wiles was born in India in 1978. He is the author of *Care of Wooden Floors* (2012), which won a Betty Trask Award, and *The Way Inn* (2014). His next novel, *Plume*, is set in London.

His three favourite London books are *Hangover Square* by Patrick Hamilton, *253* by Geoff Ryman and *Towards The End Of The Morning* by Michael Frayn.

...ll's favourite place in London is at the University of East ...don library, watching the planes land at City across the ...ater of the dock.

Eley Williams is a writer based in West Ealing. Crossrail is coming, the trees whisper. Currently lecturing at Royal Holloway, University of London, she also assists at independent publishers Copy Press and is co-editor of fiction at *3:AM* magazine. Some of her short stories have appeared in *The White Review*, *Ambit* and *Prospect* journals. Ho Chí Minh worked, briefly, at the pub where much of her contribution to this book was drafted.

Three of her favourite London fictions are Virginia Woolf's 'Kew Gardens', from *Monday or Tuesday*, Robin Jarvis' *The Deptford Mice* trilogy and the online account of Sinclair — 'the happy wanderer' — and his encounters with the city. Collated by his friend, the writer and composer Timothy Thornton, it is available to read here: @SinclairInRuins

Her favourite odd location in London is the caption beneath The Panyer Boy's bas-relief near 119 Newgate Street.

cknowledgements

The editors would like to thank everyone who supported this project on Kickstarter — you're helping open up new avenues and possibilities for independent publishing. Here's to the future.

Thanks to all the brilliant authors who contributed. Without you we wouldn't have a book and we're proud to be publishing you.

Thanks to Sanya Semakula for the initial edits and taking to Influx like a cormorant to the River Lea. Thanks once again to the big man Chris Smisson for his cover art and design. Thanks to Katherine Stephen, our proofreader. Thanks always to Meghna Gupta and Nina Robertson.

And thanks to London; especially Tottenham Hale, where the idea for this book took root.

This book was made possibe thanks to the support of the following people:

Iain Aitch

Richard Ashcroft

Marco Attard

Chris Baines

Briony Bax

Anne Beech

Adrian Bhargava

Adam Biles

Steve Birt

Oliver Bonnington

Darren Bourget

Tiffany Bowley

Victoria Briggs

Ellie Broughton

Lindsay Brown

Peter Brown

Dana Bubulj

Mike Burn

Tarah Butler

Max Cairnduff

Valerie Caless

Chris Caley

Canning

...iel Carpenter

...ver Chamberlain

...imon Clark

Vince Coccia

Nathan Connolly

Neil A Cook

Derek Cooper

Thom Cuell

Claire Dean

Jamie Delano

David Dinaburg

Andrew Elderkin

Andrew Fenwick

Harry Gallon

Rob Gear

Jonathan Gibbs

Matthew Gilbert

Marcus Gipps

A M Goodwin

Dan Grace

Colin Griffiths

Jim Groome

Robbie Guillory

Thomas Hardy

Karen Hart

Francoise Harvey

Peter Haynes

Frank Hemsley

Turan Holland

Joseph Howley

Simon Hughes

Tom Jeffreys

Håvard Jektnes

Peter Johansson

Sam Jordison

James Kemp

Laura Kenwright

Jonny Keyworth

Burkhard Kloss

Michael Layhe

Alexander Lopera

Rowena Macdonald

Gautam Malkani

Marcin Manek

Greg Marsh

Rohit Mateti

Chris McLaren

Davide Melis

Daniel Miller

Mills

nit Mohindru

uan Monaghan

Rachel Moody

Rachael de Moravia

Kevin Mullen

Joshua Nanke-Mannell

Dominic Naughton

Mike Newman

Tim Nolan

Lara Pawson and Julian Richards

Alex Perryman

Matt Petzny

Oliver Pickles

Diana Pinkett

David Poole

Sean Powley

Richard Pye

Howard Rees

Simon Rolfe

Ingeborg Rosenberg

Catherine Rowley-Williams

Bradley Russo

Ben Salavati

Susanne Salavati

Adam Salt

Matt Salts

Andrew Sanders

Penelope Schenk

Christina Scholz

Leila Segal

Chris Sharp

Richard Sheehan

Murray Steele

Melissa Stevens

Jason Stewart

Dan Taylor

Subhan Uddin

Tom Victor

Cat Vincent

Stephen Walker

Paul Watson

Emma Wayland

Chris Welch

Jayne White

Traci Whitehead

Peter Wiles

Christopher Williams

Alex Wybraniec

Benjamin Young

Neil Young

INFLUX
PRESS

Influx Press is an independent publisher based in London, committed to publishing innovative and challenging fiction, poetry and creative non-fiction from across the UK and beyond. Formed in 2012, we have published titles ranging from award-nominated debuts and site-specific anthologies to squatting memoirs and radical poetry.

www.influxpress.com

@Influxpress